Crazy Maybe

The Crazy Series, Book 1

By

A.D. Justice

Stephanie –
Be your own brand of
Crazy!

Lots of love!
AJustice

Be your own brand of
Crazy!

Lots 2 love!
Sophia

CRAZY MAYBE

DEDICATION

This book is dedicated to Pete *"Choo-Choo"* Justice –
my Daddy.

He passed away during the creation of this book and I
miss him every single day.

I love you, Daddy!

I will always be Daddy's girl!

BOOKS BY A.D. JUSTICE

CRAZY MAYBE PLAYLIST
(In order of appearance)

The songs included in this book add flavor to the storyline. Listen to the words of the songs as you read along.. I hope you enjoy the musical aspect of the story!

1. I'm With You – Avril Lavigne

2. Stupid Girls – P!nk

3. Buttons – Pussycat Dolls

4. Beautiful With You – Halestorm

5. Familiar Taste of Poison – Halestorm

6. Crazy In Love – Beyonce

7. For My Sake – Shinedown

8. Just A Fool – Christina Aguilera & Blake Shelton

9. Umbrella – Rihanna

10. Indestructible – Disturbed

11. Gunpowder and Lead – Miranda Lambert

12. If Today Was Your Last Day - Nickelback

ACKNOWLEDGEMENTS

From the bottom of my heart, I want to say *Thank You* to:

Each and every person who purchased this book! Please rate this book and leave a review on Amazon or Goodreads. I read each and every one of them!

To my husband, thank you for sticking with me through the hours and hours of late nights I sat in front of the computer working on this book.

To my children, thank you for believing in your mom.

To my friends, who have asked repeatedly when the next book will be out and anxiously awaited its arrival.

To the many book bloggers who supported me, guided me, answered my questions and helped get me out in front of the readers.

To my awesome Street Team and Best of the Best Beta Readers who have supported me tirelessly and relentlessly.

I want to say a very special *Thank You* to my dear friend and fellow book junkie, Ana Isabella, for reading and re-reading multiple versions and giving your honest feedback. Your support means so much to me!

CHAPTER ONE

ANDI

I feel his eyes burning into me from all the way across the room. I'm in a gym with more than twenty sweaty men. Some of them are sparring in boxing rings, while others are lifting weights, when I suddenly feel the weight of someone's eyes on me as if it were a hand actually touching me. I let my eyes slowly wander around the lower level of the twenty thousand square foot *Tough Enough* gym and our eyes lock. There's no doubt that he's the one - because he's staring at me and I swear if he were Clark Kent, his eye lasers would already be burning through me right now.

I've never seen him here before and I've been here every day for almost seven years now, so I know he must be looking to join. This is one of the most sought after gyms by up-and-coming fighters because of Mack Weaver, the owner and famed boxing trainer. Mack has a knack for finding the next big name in fighting and every other guy here is waiting for his turn. Mack took me under his wing years ago and I'm the only one who's ever been brave enough to call him Pop. He allows it because he knows he's the only real father I've had since mine died when I was little.

I remember seeing this guy at the club last night. He was actually hard to miss because I could feel his eyes on me then, too. Of course, I was onstage singing karaoke so there were a lot of eyes on me, but his are the only ones I *felt*. He's tall, over six feet, with thick, jet black hair that could make a woman beg to run her fingers through it. His cheekbones and jaw must have been carved from pure granite and his naturally tan skin color makes his blue eyes fierce. And he is the most stunningly gorgeous man I've ever seen.

He must be quite a brawler – in the ring and in the street. I can tell by the way he carries himself and how he's not the least bit intimidated in this room with all the other boxers. He's definitely a heavyweight because he's too big and muscular to be anything else. Watching his ripped, hard muscles flex and contract as he moves is hypnotizing. The mixture of black and colorful tattoos that cover his upper arms amplifies his bad boy looks.

It's pretty obvious why he'd even notice me – I'm the only female in this gym full of muscle-bound boxers. But the look in his eyes is not one of curiosity about what I'm doing here. It's not even blatantly sexual, like some of the guys who rake their eyes up and down my body when they first see me. He looks at me like he's a predator that's about to pounce and devour me whole. I'm not sure yet if that's a good thing. His gaze is intense and I can't figure out exactly what he wants with me.

A lot of the guys hit on me when they were new to the gym. They figure since I'm the only girl here, I must be looking for my next fighter to take home with me. And, since every single one of them think that they are the *only* man God made for a woman's pleasure, they are more than happy to help me out. Never happens though–I work with the fighters and there's no way I'd disrespect myself like that. But I don't get that feeling from him–I don't think he's trying to add another notch to his bedpost.

Crazy Maybe

I know I'm staring at him but I can't seem to stop myself. Neither of us moves our eyes or even smiles, but I feel electricity arcing between us as he moves closer and closer. I'm vaguely aware of the yelling going on around me. It's so frequent and familiar in this gym that I tune it out a lot. When there are two guys beating the crap out of each other in the ring, someone is always yelling. But it suddenly occurs to me that I need to be engaged in this particular fight, so I tear my eyes away from his and try to focus on what's going on in the ring.

I'm not actually a trainer but after being beside Pop at ringside for so long, I've picked up a thing or two. My job right now is to watch the fighters closely and figure out their weaknesses so they can each work on improving their skills. I watch to see when their guard is dropped, if they open themselves up more when they throw a certain punch, and anything else that could make them lose a fight. It's a tough job sometimes when both guys are going at it hard. Or when I'm distracted by a tall, sexy man who is standing directly behind me and has my skin tingling like I've touched an electric fence without even laying a hand on me.

I inhale a deep breath as the bell rings, signaling the end of this round, and I turn around to face him. What I see first when I turn is a finely sculpted, very thick chest staring back at me. I slowly lift my eyes, taking in his tattoos peeking out from under the tank top that's stretched across him. My eyes glaze over at his bulging biceps and traps, before I dare to look into the deep pools of his blue eyes. I could drown in these eyes and die happy. This is so not like me.

"You looking for someone?" Mack's voice calls out to the dashing stranger.

"Yeah - Mack Weaver. Know him?" The dashing stranger answers Mack but doesn't take his eyes off of me.

"I'm Mack. Over here, boy." Mack's rough voice sounds even more intimidating now, deep and commanding. I don't know if it's the lack of eye contact or the blatant way this guy's staring at me that has Pop riled, but I have a feeling it's probably a little of both.

One side of his mouth quirks up slightly, as if he's amused but hiding it from everyone but me, before he turns his eyes to Mack. And in that look, I'm pretty sure he recognizes me from last night, too.

He holds out his hand to shake Mack's, "Lucas Woods. Good to finally meet you. You're highly recommended. I'm here to talk to you about you taking me on, being my trainer."

Mack looks him up and down with his all-too-knowing eyes. Mack can size up a fighter faster than any trainer I've ever seen. He used to be a boxer himself, when he was younger and "had more piss and vinegar than sense," as he always says. Now he just likes working with the guys and seeing how far he can take them. He already has a serious contender lined up for the light heavyweight division and he doesn't usually take on more than one at a time since almost all of his time is devoted to his fighter.

Vaguely aware that Mack and Lucas are continuing their conversation, I can't help but take in all that the view has to offer. I'm consciously trying to keep my breathing under control—that's how much he affects me. His manly cologne mixed with a scent that is purely him is like an assault to my senses and an aphrodisiac I wish I could bottle and sell. As I blatantly check out his tattoos, one unique design on his bicep catches my eye

4

and I realize I've seen him before last night at the club. How could I have not realized this was the same man?

LUKE

When I decided to come to this gym, I had no idea she would be here. But as soon as I stepped inside, she's all I could see. Whatever sense and reason I had just flew out the window as soon as I saw her standing there. Her blond hair is pulled back in a ponytail and the pink horizontal streaks match that skintight tank top she's wearing, showing off her muscular arms and perky breasts. Those toned legs seem to go on forever out of those short Yoga shorts she's wearing, the ones that hug her hips and ass so well that I can see the muscles flexing and contracting underneath when she moves.

She feels me staring a hole into her from behind, I know she does because she turns her head and her eyes meet mine. And just like that, we're connected from across the room. My feet start moving toward her without conscious thought. All I know is after seeing her on stage last night, and the way she looked right into me as she sang, I will have her one way or another. Seeing her here today is a sign, but the way she's looking at me right now is proof.

I don't know what she's doing here with all these damn guys, most of them boxer wanna-bes. Maybe she works here? Or maybe she's dating one of the dickheads sparring in the ring? Either way, I'd gladly take on either or both of them for just one night with her.

5

Crazy Maybe

Though I seriously doubt one night would be enough for me. If the look in her eyes is any indication, I won't have to work too hard for it. I'd bet serious money that she wants me as much as I want her.

I don't see any other women in here but there's no way anyone could miss her. Not just because of her hair, or that sexy right arm with a sleeve of tattoos that stretches up onto her shoulder, but because she is the most beautiful creature ever. She looks the complete opposite today than she did last night at the club.

Today, her face has a serious, *don't-fuck-with-me* look and is scrubbed free of makeup. Last night, her hair was down, long and wavy around her face, her eye makeup had a come-hither look to it, and her clothes were less revealing than what she's wearing now, but were still sexy enough to make me have to keep certain parts of me under the table well after she left the stage. She's gorgeous either way, but all I can think is how much I want to grab her hair – whether it's down or in a ponytail – in my fist and completely own her.

Apparently someone has noticed how I'm looking at her because the booming voice alerts me that I may be standing a little too close to her. But even as I speak to the voice that asked what I'm looking for, I'm having a really hard time tearing my eyes away from her. I give her a small half-smile when I hear the pissed off tone answer me, and I finally turn and introduce myself to *the* Mack Weaver. The man I'm here to talk to about being my trainer and helping me become a professional boxer.

I hold out my hand to shake Mack's, "Lucas Woods. Good to finally meet you. You're highly recommended. I'm here to talk to you about you taking me on, being my trainer."

Crazy Maybe

He looks me over, sizing me up, and with this guy, I know first impressions are very important. I just hope my blatant ogling of this girl doesn't get me immediately tossed out on my head. I stand tall, in my fighting stance, and let him make his decision.

"Any experience in the ring, kid?" Mack asks, piercing me with a somewhat sideways glance, as if he already knows the answer and is waiting for me to confirm his assumptions.

"Not professionally, but I've done pretty well in the unofficial circuit," I answer confidently.

His smirk tells me he knows exactly what I mean. It's kind of like saying a homemaker is a domestic engineer. It's the same fucking thing – only the title makes the job sound more appealing. I know this, he knows it, but I'm sticking with my version of it. I would never show anyone that I'm ashamed of it, ashamed that I haven't made more of myself in all of my 26 years. And I'm not about to start in front of *this* man, either.

After what feels like a damn eternity, but really was probably less than a minute, our staring contest comes to an end when Mack nods. I hope it's an approving nod but either way, I'm not leaving here without accomplishing what I set out to do. I will become a professional fighter. I think he sees the determination and complete resolve in my eyes.

Mack holds his gaze directly on mine, his challenge to me is clearly being set. His normally deep voice seems to boom even more as he says, "All right then. Let's see what you got, kid. Andi, check him out for me – put him through the usual and see if he can hang with the big boys."

I look over and see the girl of my dreams – both when I'm awake and asleep – is still standing beside me and now she's looking at me completely different than just a few minutes ago. Another man is standing beside her, eying me in much the same way Mack was doing as he was sizing me up. He looks like he's an assistant trainer with his sleeveless t-shirt, sweat pants and gym shoes. He's muscular but not buff like the other fighters in here.

I turn to fully face him and start to speak, "So, Andy, I guess-," when my beautiful little vixen suddenly cuts me off.

"Um, Lucas, right?"

I flash her my killer smile, the one that always has the girls falling at my feet. "Just a minute, sweetheart. Let me finish with Andy here and then I'm all yours."

She smiles back at me, but it's not the smile I'm expecting. Her smile makes me think of the cat that has a fool-proof plan to eat the canary...but the canary has no clue the cat is even around. It's a shit-eating grin that frankly would make me a little nervous if I wasn't so aware of all the manly men watching me right now.

I turn back to Andy and finish, "So, Andy, as I was saying, I'm ready when you are."

The guy smiles back at me, "I'm Tom. *She* is Andi," he says as he gestures toward my little vixen, who is still giving me the same shit-eating grin. *Well, isn't that just fucking great?*

CHAPTER TWO

ANDI

I tried to stop him before he embarrassed himself, but when he so arrogantly dismissed me while smiling at me, I decided to let him open his mouth and insert his foot. Until he choked on it. I'm not even trying to contain my smile and satisfaction at this little triumph. I mean really – that smile he gave me? He might as well have patted me on the head while telling me to go back to the kitchen and fix him a sandwich.

He's obviously used to silly girls dropping their panties as soon as he flashes them that smile that he immediately thought it would work on me. That's more than a little insulting since he doesn't know shit about me. A guy like that is more than a turn off to me – I like a man who is confident but not stuck on himself. And he is definitely stuck on himself. I might just have more than a little fun with this one.

"Lucas, right?" I ask again, not hiding the contempt in my voice at having to ask him the same question twice.

"Yes – but you can call me Luke," he replies, but this time with much more humility and without the fall-on-your-knees smile.

He's almost somber, as if his blunder will cost him more than a temporarily bruised ego. It is in this moment that I realize – his dream is in my hands and he knows it. This is actually very humbling for me because I don't take this part of my job here lightly. There's a

9

different fleeting emotion in his eyes that I can't quite place before it's quickly masked, but I know better than to mess with his head right now.

I hold out my hand, palm up, as I say, "Give me your hand." He gives me a skeptical look for a few seconds, as if he's weighing whether or not I'm serious, so I raise my eyebrows and incline my head toward his hands, silently giving him the command again. He raises one hand and I cover it with both of mine.

While holding his hand, my fingers glide over the callouses on his palm and fingers. I feel every ridge and bump. Feeling of each finger individually – my thumb and index finger gently stroke each knuckle. I then move to the back of his hand and feel each knuckle there before moving on to every bone in his hand. I hold his hand and move his wrist in a circular motion, testing mobility and feeling for any tension or resistance.

Before I finish the first hand, I hear his breathing become heavier and faster. I can see the quickening rise and fall of his massive chest as I take my time with his hand. He takes a half step closer to me and now he's towering over me. I can feel his hot breath and his all-male scent envelops me. I'm not short by any means but I'm not super-model tall either. I'm just the average five-foot-five-inch female. He's a couple of inches over six feet tall, with wide shoulders, muscular arms, trim waist and muscular legs. There's not an ounce of fat visible on him anywhere I can see with him wearing his tank top and shorts.

The hands and wrists of a fighter are important – any weaknesses in them could mean the difference between a win and a career-ending loss. The fact that my touch is turning him on is just a plus that I hadn't intended and I really have to focus to keep from enjoying it too much myself. Right now, I'm pretty sure I have ADD because I can't keep my mind where it's supposed to be. That's even more obvious since I didn't even notice William approaching us from the other side of the gym until he was almost touching my arm.

Luke's smooth voice is low but it still startles me when he says, "You have a great voice. I liked watching you on stage last night."

I can feel the warmth spread to my cheeks and I know I'm blushing. For one thing, I jumped a little when he spoke, but the main reason I'm blushing was the way he said it. He knew I was looking at him, singing to him, last night. I didn't have a clue who he was and with the lights pointed at the stage, I couldn't even see him that well. But I saw his eyes well enough and they were glued to mine just like they were earlier today. I considered approaching him after my song was over but I chickened out. I'm not into one-night stands and any girl who leaves a club with a guy knows that's all it will ever really be.

I finally find my voice after the heat in my face starts to fade. I smile at him and respond, "Thanks. It took me a few minutes to realize that you're the guy I saw there last night. Those stage lights sort of blind you, but I recognized your eyes."

William Lancaster is a big guy and has been coming to Mack's gym for several years. He's not really interested in being the next big name in boxing but he does enjoy sparring with the others. His muscles aren't cut and defined like most of the other guys in here, but make no mistake that the man is all muscle. He's thick like a power lifter. I think he has a bit of a crush on me though he's never made a move. It could be more of a protective big brother thing, I'm really not sure. But right now, one thing I am sure of is that he doesn't like Luke.

"Andi," William says with a deceptively calm voice, "why is this guy so close to you?" William is talking to me but his eyes are cutting through Luke like a hot knife through butter. I have to give Luke credit – he doesn't move or show the slightest bit of fear. That's actually pretty impressive because William is no less than daunting.

"It's okay, Will. Pop asked me to check him out and I need to make sure his hands are okay before I put him on the bag or the speed ball." I keep my voice calm and even because William will not hesitate to pounce on him if he hears the slightest tremor in my voice. He would take it as fear when I'm really just hyperaware of the intense feelings Luke stirs deep in my belly...and I mean low and deep.

Luke maintains eye contact with Will, and even though I respect him for it, Will is a little like a wild animal in this sense. Eye contact is a direct challenge and he's surprisingly fast for his size and thickness. I place one hand on Will's arm, causing him to look at me and break the silent argument of which man has the most testosterone. I don't do this to make Will "lose" this contest; I do this to save Luke without embarrassing him.

I give Will a sweet smile, truly meaning it because I know without a doubt he would protect me and I love him for it. "I'm okay, Will. Really. You know I'd tell you if I was uncomfortable."

"If you say so, Andi," Will replies to me warmly before turning his gaze briefly back to Luke and hardening his voice as he continued,   "I still don't like how he's looking at you, though. He'd be...*safe*...if he remembers that."

I still hold one of Luke's hands in mine and I feel him tense, his body preparing for a fight and I quickly squeeze his hand and slightly tug on it. Not enough that Will would notice but enough for Luke to look at me. I barely shook my head from side to side, signaling "no," and allow Will walk away to resume his workout. The fire burning in Luke's eyes is unmistakable and that fury is now aimed at me. Still, he doesn't scare me, even though I don't really know him, I have no doubt that he would never hurt me. Even if Will wasn't just a few feet away.

LUKE

I thought I was totally fucked when I basically shushed her when I was calling the guy "Andy." Turns out Andi is a girl...my little vixen. I did not see that coming at all. Who knew? All I could think of at that moment was how she was about to kick me out and I'd have to answer my family's questions about my dream being flushed down the toilet.

My parents are good people but they don't understand or support my dream at all. My dad thinks I should go into some kind of business, or work for him, and make a fortune like he did. Like my brother and sister both did. My mom is embarrassed by my boxing dream. She thought I should stick to what I originally went to college to be, but that path is lost to me now.

Mom can't tell her friends what I'm really doing because she can't stand the thought of them looking at her with such pity of how I turned out. Surely they would have to wonder what my parents did wrong with me, right? I'm the black sheep and I know this is my last shot to make my dream a reality. If I'm turned away here, there's nothing else for me to do. No other trainer around here can do what Mack and his team does.

She had every right to skewer me right in front of every man in the gym for the way I treated her. But she didn't. She did just the opposite – she let me keep my dignity and acted as though I didn't just treat her like shit. She just earned every bit of respect I can give her and I fully intend on giving her that respect. It may kill me because there's hardly anything I want more right now than to throw her over my shoulder and carry her off to my man-cave to have my way with her.

But right now, she's focusing on my hand and it just feels too damn good to move. I'm thoroughly enjoying this – how the smooth skin of her hands feels as she gently massages the roughness of mine. She checks every square millimeter of my hand for weaknesses. If her hands feel this good on my hands, I can't imagine how good they'll feel when she puts them on my body. That's what I'm fantasizing about right now, ever since she took my hand in hers.

When she first told me to give her my hand, I wasn't sure if I should trust her. She had every reason to humiliate me in some insanely embarrassing way, but the look in her eyes when she motioned for my hand was warm and inviting. Not cold and calculating. I reluctantly gave her my hand and now I'm so damn glad I did. Nothing – and no one - has felt this good in a long time.

I knew it would be her after she sang that song last night. The way she looked at me from the stage, I was sure she was singing it only for me. The words of *I'm With You* still ring in my head and I don't even like Avril

Lavigne's music – chick music. But I hear it in Andi's voice and I wonder if the words have meaning for us. We don't know each other, but as girly as this sounds, it also feels like we do know each other.

I would never admit this shit to anyone – not her, not my friends – they'd all think I've turned into some pussy. But she had to feel it, too. Last night when she sang to me and right now, when she's rubbing my hand with her velvety touch, there's a connection between us.

She just admitted that she saw me there – she said she recognized me by my eyes today. I knew she was singing to me. The words still play over and over in my head. Every word was meant for us but the chorus stays with me. She's taken my hand in hers and I feel her on another level.

I'm so lost in thoughts of her hands, her voice, how she looked at me when she sang those words, and how she looked at me when I walked in the gym today, that I don't even realize there's a giant standing about a half-inch from us. And that giant is *pissed*. He's apparently pissed at me as he questions Andi about why I'm so close to her.

I didn't even realize I had moved in closer to her but now that he has pointed it out, I realize that I am really damn close to her. I know I can't move now without showing weakness. Andi's calm voice speaks to the giant and calls him Will. Will's gaze hasn't moved from me at all even though he continues to speak to Andi. I refuse to look away because I'm not backing down from anyone – not when I have so much on the line.

From my peripheral vision, I see Andi's hand moving to Will's arm and he finally looks away from me. She speaks to him again and I see him relax somewhat. He likes her – no doubt about it. But he wants to protect her more than anything else and right now he sees me as a threat to her. When Will turns to issue an indirect threat to me, I am ready to throw down. No man threatens me and then doesn't back up his words.

I am planning my first move when I feel Andi squeeze my hand and lightly tug on me until I look at her. I can see her barely shake her head, telling me not to carry out my plan of jumping the un-jolly giant standing beside us. I can see pleading in her eyes and she distracts me long enough that Will walks off with the last word in our silent war of determination.

When I realize he not only got away with threatening me, but I didn't even say one word in retaliation, I am beyond furious with her but even more with myself. *Since when do I let some girl distract me this way? This is un-fucking-believable!* I can't help but think that she did that to get back at me for hurting her little feelings earlier. Add *getting played* to how I was just made to look like a chump and pussy and now I'm beyond pissed. I can't even see straight.

Keeping my voice low to avoid causing a huge scene, I basically hiss my words at her. "*What. The. Fuck.* Do you think you're doing? Don't *ever* even try to call me down again." I lean in closer to her face with each word until I'm really in her face. I know I'm a big guy and I expect her to be scared and yell for Will to come save her.

And I'm completely wrong in assuming she'd be scared of me. I watch the fire build in her gray eyes until they become more of a gray-blue as my words and my stance sink in. She closes what little gap I left between us as she hisses her retort to me.

"You have NO. FUCKING. IDEA. Who you were just dealing with. Not only is he far more trained than you are, he has been coming here for YEARS and Mack would never tolerate a new guy fighting with Will.

16

Especially over something as stupid as your fucking pride. I just saved your ass and no one else in here even knew what was going on. You should be kissing my ass right now!"

"How would you know he's 'more trained' than me?" I growl back at her.

"I said FAR more trained," she growls back. *Damn, this girl isn't backing down from me even one inch.*

Then she continues to shred me with her next words, "And I *know* because I've seen you fight before! Professional boxing rules are quite a bit different than your *street boxing rings*, but Will's been trained by the best and he's damn good. From what I saw of your fight with *El Toro*, you wouldn't stand a chance against Will right now."

I glance around the room, checking to see who all had heard our little interaction, but thankfully no one was paying attention. Not even Will. I need a minute to think about my response but I have none.

If she knew I'd fought El Toro, she must have been there. If Mack trusts her to "check me out," then there's no doubt she knows what to look for in a fighter. And add yet another strike to my ego and confidence.

"Can I do my job now?" Her voice is calm again and holds no trace of the anger she just spewed at me. Okay, I started the fight and deserved the anger from her in return, but I'm not admitting that it's my fault right now. She just keeps surprising me and throwing me completely off balance. I simply nod once and she starts her examination of my other hand in the exact manner she did the first one. She gives no indication of any confrontation at all and after a minute or two, her touch has a calming effect on me.

"I didn't mean to be so harsh, Luke. I'm sorry for that. I had planned to tell you that I'd seen you fight

17

before and I know the rules of the street circuit are different than pro boxing, but you have real talent. But I didn't plan to make it sound like a put-down. If this – going pro - is what you really want, I believe you can do it."

She is so genuine – her tone, her words, her demeanor – they all prove she means what she said. She isn't just blowing smoke up my ass. And those words, her apology and her belief in me, is the best thing anyone has ever said to me. In my whole life. And just like that, she showed me again that she deserves every bit of respect I can give her.

Again, all I can do is nod at her, hoping she knows with that one nod that I both accept her apology and appreciate her words. The irony of the situation isn't lost on me though – I'm not that stupid. I'm the big, strong fighter but I can't even find the damn words to apologize to this petite, beautiful woman who keeps throwing me lifelines even though I've done nothing to deserve them. Or her.

I have to question which one of us has the real strength. That's not even true – I can already see she has me beat, hands down, no contest, game over.

I'm with you, Andi. I'm with you.

CHAPTER THREE

ANDI

After the intensity of the morning, Luke and I settle into a more comfortable routine as we make our way around the gym. He is tireless as we work on weight lifting, noting his max-out weight, before moving to the speedball and the punching bag. After that, we move on to his cardio-max with running sprints, mountain climbers and burpees.

By early afternoon, Mack has Luke in the ring sparring with one of the other newer guys. What I said to Luke was true – he has skills and he'll be a good fighter, but he still has a lot to learn before he can get ring time with the more experienced guys. I know he has something to prove but putting him in that situation would do more harm to his confidence than he even realizes. If – or I should say *when* – he lost to someone more experienced, he wouldn't even consider that they'd had years more training than he's had. He would only see failure and defeat.

Only a few people here at the gym know this, but every week day after work, I volunteer at a youth center. I see people every day with the same look Luke has in his eyes – hunger for his dream but no one to believe in his ability to attain it. Skill, stamina and training are important, but so is having someone believe in you. I see the talent in him, just like I see the talent in the underprivileged teenagers I work with, and I want to help him see it, too. See it and believe it.

Crazy Maybe

I'm standing back now, just watching him spar. Mack and Tom have taken over with Luke after my initial assessment and having nothing to do gives me way too much time to think. This, working at the gym with the fighters, isn't my official job. Pop took me under his wing and started teaching me to defend myself when I was sixteen and became legally emancipated from the state. I started hanging out here with him and learned everything I could learn from him. Now I do it just because I like it.

When I see the sparring match is about to end, I approach Mack at the side of the ring. "Hey Pop, think you can get a couple of the guys in here to spar? Might be good for me to explain to Luke what I've been doing ringside."

Mack smiles at me knowingly – he knows my word choice is to let Luke save face with the other guys, at least in his mind. Everyone in here knows me and knows how long I've been with Mack and they have no problem taking input from me. Luke, however, would see it as a weakness since he doesn't know me, or any of the guys here for that matter.

"Good idea, Andi. Come on down here, Luke. That's enough for one day. Let Andi explain her job to you." Mack waits for Luke to remove his headgear and gloves then climb out of the ring before he continues.

"Listen, son," Mack levels Luke with his dead-on gaze, "Andi's been with me for a long time now. I've personally taught her everything she knows about boxing. She's helped every guy in here improve his skills – so don't be shy about asking for her opinion or taking her advice. She wouldn't steer you wrong." A couple of the guys standing nearby confirm Mack's praise of me and I watch as Luke's face and shoulders visibly relax, just a little.

Mack calls for a couple of the lighter weight guys to climb in the ring and I explain to Luke what my role is in these matches. I point out how one of the fighters always cocks his right shoulder back, even just slightly, before he throws a right cross. Even that slight movement would give away his intentions and allow the other guy time to block and counter punch. Something as small as that gives the enemy the edge, and no fighter can afford that.

Then I encourage him to help me watch for other clues. This is part of his training even if he doesn't realize it. It will help him just as much if he pays close attention to his opponent's body mechanics when he's in the ring. It's not all about brute strength – strategy and intellect plays a big role in who gets to the title fight.

I'm impressed but not shocked when Luke identifies a couple of key giveaways on his own. I smile at him as I say, "Good eye. Very good eye. Try to remember to watch for this next time you're in the ring. Every fighter has their own quirk to some degree. It's hard to keep the next planned move a complete element of surprise. The really good ones keep most of their moves under wraps, but sometimes something as simple as which way they shift their eyes will give them away."

Luke nods but has a faraway look in his eyes for a minute. Then he turns and looks at me and I see a newfound understanding in his facial expression. "I think I know why I almost lost my last fight now. Damn, that makes perfect sense."

We watch the guys in the ring for a few more minutes before Luke speaks to me again. He doesn't look at me, but leans over slightly so I know he's talking to me when he says, "I'd appreciate it you'd watch me next time I spar and tell me what you see."

Crazy Maybe

I turn my head and look up at him and, seeing me turn to him, he looks down at me. His expression is genuine – there's no double entendre meaning to his words. "Ok, I'd be glad to, Luke." His return smile is warm and appreciative. So I continue with a semi-teasing tone, "But be warned, if you argue with what I say, I will video you and prove it to you."

His laugh comes from deep in his chest and he is thoroughly amused. "You've got a deal, Andi." With a blatantly flirtatious wink and his beautiful blue eyes sparkle with mischief as he adds, "Any time you want to video me, you just let me know. Especially if you're my co-star."

Damn, the man is sexy. He makes me rethink my self-imposed "no-dating fighters" rule for a minute. But I mentally shake some sense back into my head. I'm sure he's a complete player and I'm not interested in the whole friends with benefits thing. Still, I enjoy spending time with him way too much and I feel drawn to him more than I want to admit, especially to myself.

Being in a gym full of testosterone-laden alpha males, there isn't much I haven't heard before so it's pretty hard to offend me in that aspect. His retort was pretty tame in comparison, so I just laugh and gently shake my head in response. The clock on the wall grabs my attention, though, as I note how late it is and I have things to do before meeting my girlfriends at The Beta Room, our favorite watering hole, nightclub and general hang-out spot.

"Hey Pop, I'm taking off now. Need anything before I leave?" I call to Mack across the room. He turns and smiles at me, "No, darlin', you go ahead and have fun with your girls tonight. Call if you need me."

Suddenly my feet leave the ground and I'm being hoisted up in the air by a pair of big, muscular arms that have encircled me from behind. I let out a squeal of laughter while playfully yelling, "Put me down, you lunatic!" Of course, he doesn't. He turns me upside and keeps walking toward Mack, completely ignoring the choice names I lovingly call him.

I know exactly who it is because this is how he greets me every time he returns from one of his trips. I met him soon after I met Pop and he's the guy who's slated to be the next light-heavyweight champion. He's a phenomenal fighter and an all-around great guy who's been like a brother to me since we first met.

When my head is finally right side up and my feet are back on the ground, I quickly turn and jump in his arms for a big bear hug. "Shane! 'Bout time you came home!" He's been away at a special conditioning camp a friend of Mack's owns in Las Vegas for the past couple of weeks and I've really missed him. He's the one person I can talk to about anything and one of the only two men I trust implicitly.

As my arms go around his neck and my cheek is close to his, I catch a glimpse of Luke's face over Shane's shoulder. He doesn't look happy at all. In fact, he looks downright pissed off and possessive – like he wants to throttle Shane for touching me. I don't know why I suddenly feel a twinge of guilt for being so excited to see Shane but I'm not about to examine that right now. Luke is making his way over to us and I suddenly feel the need to diffuse the situation before it gets out of hand.

LUKE

I love the way Andi's face flushes red with embarrassment when I compliment her or flirt with her. It tells me that I'm getting to her like she does me. She wouldn't respond this way if she didn't feel at least some attraction toward me. She tries to play it off like she isn't affected when I offer to let her co-star in a video with me.

But what really impresses me is how giving she is – even though she just met me and I've even been an ass toward her more than I've been nice today. I'm trying to make up to her for that now. I was out of line and I know it. After Mack and a couple of the other guys openly praised her about how she helps improve our skills, there's no way I would even think of refusing her help.

That's why I asked her to watch my next sparring match and give me some tips. That, and because she's the first person who has genuinely believed in me and my dream. I appreciate her more for that than she will ever know. Being looked down on by the rest of my family because I don't meet their definition of "success" is getting old but I don't get the sense she'd ever make anyone feel that way. It's just not in her nature.

I'm more than a little concerned at how quickly I'm becoming enamored of her. She has a way of just pulling people to her. That's obvious as I watch how the other guys in here interact with her. They're protective of her and they respect her, but they also include her in conversations that would embarrass lesser women. She just takes it in stride and gives just as good as she gets. It's obvious she's earned their trust and a lot of these guys don't seem to give that up easily.

In one day with Mack and Andi, I've learned more about best practices, techniques and strategies than in all my years of street fighting combined. The exercise program she designed for me is pure genius. I'm already pretty damn buff, if I do say so myself, but her regimen just amped up my routine to the max. I can't wait to see what else I learn from this great group of people who just openly took me in today.

Even Will the Giant seems to be warming up to me, but that may be because I've kept more than three inches distance from Andi for the last several hours. But now I'm watching some pretty-boy manhandle her and I don't like it one bit. He wrapped his arms around her from behind as she was saying goodbye to Mack. She didn't even know he'd come up behind her. I looked around at a couple of the other guys and they had an amused smirk on their face but no one looked surprised.

Pretty-boy flipped her upside down and just walked off across the damn gym with her laughing, screaming and calling him every name in the book. When he put her down, she turned on him and I half expected her to lay into him for touching her like that. But imagine my surprise when she flew into his arms instead. His arms wrapped around her waist and crushed her to him and there's no doubt she liked it.

The sight of Andi in Pretty-boy's embrace has me seeing red. I don't even realize my feet are moving fast in their direction, my strides quickly eating up the space between us, the space where Pretty-boy carried her away from me. My eyes never leave them as they continue their embrace and her bright, honest smile aimed at him is like a dagger in my chest. Andi meets my gaze and I see a flicker of something that looks like a mixture of guilt and a brief glint of fear.

Gently, Andi pulls back from his embrace and keeps that sweet smile on her face. His back is to me and he doesn't know I'm coming up behind him. Andi takes a step to the side and extends her hand toward me, "Shane, let me introduce you to someone."

Pretty-boy Shane follows Andi's gaze and outstretched arm as he turns fully to face me. Andi's voice still sounds happy as she introduces us, "Shane, this is Luke Woods. He just started with us today but he has an impressive background of fights. Luke, this is Shane Fowler. Shane is in line to be the next light-heavyweight champion, and for all intents and purposes, he's my brother. Pop pretty much adopted us both when we were teenagers."

Shane extends his hand to shake mine as he smiles, "How ya doing, Luke? Welcome to the family, bro!"

If he noticed how I was charging toward him and Andi, or how red with fury my face must be, he has the good nature of not mentioning it. I extend my hand and shake his, noting a firm grip but nothing in it is threatening.

"Thanks, Shane. I appreciate that. Good to meet you."

My eyes flick to Andi and I see her visibly exhale a really long breath. She must have been holding it while she waited to see what I'd do. Shit, I feel like such a dumbass right now. The guy's like a brother to her and I just made a complete fool of myself over a girl who isn't even mine. *What the fuck is wrong with me?* Maybe I need to go back to the club tonight and find a hot barfly to ease some of my tension before I go off on the wrong person. Like Shane – the guy who's favored to be the next light-heavyweight champion.

I can feel Andi staring at me, and she expects me to look at her, but I just can't make myself do it. I know she deserves better than this from me but I can barely keep myself in control around her. That's pretty obvious from everything's that went down today. The vision of her in another man's arms is still fresh in my mind and I can't seem to shake how much I hated seeing that.

I'm cool with Shane now after she said he's basically her brother, but this jealousy thing is new to me. I don't get jealous over girls. They get jealous over me. They cry, beg, threaten-hell, even fight each other over me. But I've never reacted to any of them like I just did with Andi. And I don't like it at all. I don't like someone else having that kind of control over me so it's best to stop this attraction now before it gets out of hand.

After another half-hour of getting to know Shane and hearing all about the intense conditioning camp he just finished, Andi finally says goodbye to everyone again. She gave up on trying to get my attention a while ago. When she turns to pick up her stuff, I finally look at her again and I feel like such a dick.

From her profile, I can see her confusion etched in her beautiful face and she has a sad look about her that wasn't there at any other point during the day. I silently swear at myself because I know I did that to her.

She saw me coming for Shane and she moved quickly to save me from my own actions again. She's almost to the door when I finally call out to her, "Andi!" But she keeps going like she didn't hear me.

Shane's big hand claps me on the shoulder, "Hey man–why don't you come out with us tonight? Several

Crazy Maybe

of us guys are going to The Beta Room. Andi will be there, too."

"Sure–sounds fun. She go there with her boyfriend?" I incline my chin toward the door Andi just left, indicating I'm asking about her. I'm trying to be as nonchalant as possible, but I know I'm transparent as hell.

"Nah, man, she doesn't have a boyfriend. She'll be there with her girlfriends. If you're looking to hook up with someone for the night, most of her friends are pretty hot." Shane sounds casual but his eyes are hard as steel. The message is loud and clear – *hook up with her friends but don't even think about Andi.*

"You got something going on with Andi, man?" I give my best smile and keep any emotion out of my voice. Just two guys chatting here–nothing to see.

Shane's laugh has no humor in it, "No, Luke, nothing like that. She really is like my sister. We practically grew up together under Mack's guidance. And as her only brother, there's absolutely *nothing* I wouldn't do to protect her. From anyone."

Shane's hard eyes pin me to the wall and he knows it. He knows I'm somewhat interested and he's letting me know we will have no problems as long as I leave Andi alone.

"Plenty of guys try to pick her up every weekend at the club. She goes to have fun with her friends, have a few drinks and laughs, and she loves to sing karaoke. She's great at it, too. But she's not a one-night stand kind of girl and I'm not about to let anyone take advantage of her. She's too good of a person for that. She deserves better."

"What if that's what she wants? A one-night, no strings attached, good fuck?"

28

Shane's scowl increases as the timbre of his voice deepens. "She *doesn't* want that. At all. And anyone who wants that with her will have to get through me first. And I can guarantee you one thing—no man who would treat her like that will ever get through me."

I give him a single nod and say, "You're a good brother, Shane."

And I am a complete shithead.

CHAPTER FOUR

ANDI

I'm sitting in the club with my girlfriends Christina, Tania and Katie, and we're on our third round of drinks. Christina leaves the table for a few minutes and has two rounds of tequila shots for all of us when she returns. I've just finished telling them about my confusing day with Luke and the shitty way it ended when I left the gym. Or I should say, the shitty way he ended our day.

Yeah, I heard him call for me when I was walking out the door, but that's just it. He waited until that exact moment and I know he counted on me either not hearing or not caring that he yelled my name. And he was right. By that time, I wouldn't have turned around for him for anything in the world. So, knowing how pissed off I am at him and how much that is so unlike me to care enough about any man to even get pissed off, my girlfriends have decided I must *secretly* like him.

I vehemently disagreed with them on that assumption. There's no way it's a *secret*. That royally pisses me off, too.

So, here we are with Christina passing out tequila shots to go with the pitcher of Bahama Mamas we've already finished off. The waitress stops by the table and Tania orders another pitcher. It's going to be one of those kinds of summer nights in Hot-Lanta. The kind where I will undoubtedly end up bowing to the great porcelain god and swearing I'll never have another drink.

Christina lifts her shot glass for a group toast, "To the hot men who thoroughly piss us off!" We laugh and shout the toast back to her in unison before tossing them back. In keeping with tradition, we slam our empty shot glasses on the table and Katie refills our glasses with the Bahama Mama mixture.

From the corner of my eye, I see Shane, Will and a couple of other guys from the gym enter the club. And bringing up the rear is Luke. *Just fucking great.* I must have been pretty obvious in my reaction because when I look back at my friends, all six eyes are glued to me.

"Yeah, that's him," I say on a heavy sigh.

"Nice."

"Very nice."

"No wonder you're so hot and bothered."

It's good to have friends you can count on to cheer you up, take your mind off things, and help you make the best decisions. It's really too bad that those are not the kind of friends I have here with me right now.

I look back in the guys' direction and see Shane scanning the room for me. I hold up my hand and wave when his eyes are looking in my general direction. Recognition sets in on his face and he leads the group toward our table. I stand and help Tania pull another table and chairs beside ours to make room for everyone to hang out together. Shane pulls me into a hug and kisses the top of my head in his normal, brotherly fashion.

There's a great DJ tonight and he's playing the best dance songs. One of the best things about this club is the mixture of music they play. There's a mixture of rock, country, pop, hip hop, and R&B. The mixture would be a turnoff for some, but most of the people here love the variety. Fast songs or slow songs – all the best songs on the air – all in one club. It's awesome.

Crazy Maybe

Almost immediately after they sit down, Luke starts openly flirting with Tania right in front of me. My mind knows we have no relationship whatsoever. My mind knows I have no claim to him. And my mind knows that other than a little harmless flirting, he's made no moves on me. But my mind apparently isn't in charge right now because it both hurts and makes me mad. It's like he's doing it on purpose and that's just mean.

So far, the DJ's been playing all fast songs that make you want to move, especially after you've had a couple of drinks and a shot of tequila. Apparently Christina has the same idea because she suddenly yells for us all to do our second shot then hit the dance floor. She also saw how Luke was hitting on Tania and she wanted to get us all away from the table before Tania cussed him out. Or worse, wasted her drink by throwing it in his face.

We all toss back the throat-burning liquid, chase it with more Bahama Mamas, and leave the guys as they order their pitchers of beer. One of Usher's older songs, "*Yeah!*" is playing and the sensual bass is thumping through the huge speakers throughout the room. The large flat screen TV's that are strategically placed throughout the club play the official video and the images occasionally flash to show the people on the dance floor.

I'm feeling a little more than a slight buzz when I hit the dance floor, and with my mounting frustration, I really just want to let loose. My body is moving with the music and I'm dancing with my friends when I feel a hard body move in close behind me. I look over my shoulder to see a handsome guy moving in time with me. When I don't object, he moves closer and puts one of his arms around my waist, pulling my back against his front.

Crazy Maybe

Melted together, we continue to move, sway and grind to the music. Katie points to the TV directly in front of the dance floor and I see myself with the handsome stranger bumping and grinding behind me. I lift my hand up and wrap it around the back of his neck and my fingers gently stroke the hair on his nape as we continue dancing. He wraps his other hand around my waist and turns me to face him. I wrap my arms around his neck as he puts one of his legs between mine so that we're aligned chest to chest and pelvis to pelvis.

The people on the dance floor part like the Red Sea as Shane and Luke barge through on their way toward me. I meet Luke's hard gaze with a challenge in my own eyes before turning back to my dance partner. The song ends and a slow song begins without missing a step. My handsome stranger leans down to whisper in my ear, "Dance with me again?" I nod and tighten my grip around his neck.

I look over my shoulder at Shane, who has stopped a couple of feet away, and shake my head *'no.'* He doesn't like it at all and I know him well enough to know that he's weighing his options. I tilt my head slightly to the side and give him a pointed look, one that says *'don't fuck with me tonight.'* He knows me well enough to know it will not end well if he goes against my wishes right now.

Katie steps up in front of Shane and asks him to dance. He agrees and they stay beside me as we finish the slow song. Christina and Tania have already found other dance partners so Luke returns to our table to sit with the other guys. He's giving me dirty looks but I pretend not to see him. What right does he have to be mad at me for dancing with someone when he was hitting on one of my best friends? Right in front of me!

Crazy Maybe

When the song ends, I step back from my dance partner and thank him before Shane grabs my hand and pulls me off the dance floor. Like I said, I know Shane well enough to know now is not the time to fight him.

"What the hell do you think you're doing, Andi?" Shane angrily demands when we're just outside the dance area.

"I'm having fun with my friends, Shane! What's your problem?" I ground out back at him.

"That guy was all over you and you were just letting him!"

"Don't lecture me about that, Shane! You take home a different girl every damn night!" I would laugh at the shocked look on his face if I weren't so pissed off right now.

Shane stutters for a minute before spitting out, "That's different, Andi, and you know it!"

"Come off it, Shane. It was just a damn dance - I'm still here. I haven't left with anyone. Yet."

Shane's jaw is clenched shut and the muscles on each side are twitching from the force. His nostrils are slightly flaring from his angry breaths and his face is turning blood red. I wonder to myself if he's about to have a stroke from his elevated blood pressure.

Through his clenched teeth, he spouts, "Andi. So help me God. You are not leaving here and going to some strange guy's house."

I smile sweetly at him, knowing that my smile mixed with my next words may actually make the top of his head pop right off. "You're right, Shane. I won't go to some strange guy's house. I'll be sure to take him home with me instead."

I walk off, leaving him there to process my words alone while I make my way back to the fresh pitcher of Bahama Mamas. I refill my empty glass and down a couple more glasses within a few minutes. When I look back up, some half-dressed girl is sitting Luke's lap and rubbing her hands up and down his chest. He leans in and says something in her ear, to which she giggles and furiously nods her head '*yes.*' My imagination just ran away with me on what she so eagerly agreed to.

LUKE

Going out with the guys feels really good. It's been a long time since I've had fun with a group of guys who have the same aspirations I do. They get me, they get why fighting is in my blood, and they don't judge me for it. So tonight, we're going to The Beta Room and having a good time. I try not to let the fact that Andi is there influence how I act. I don't want to think about her and I don't want the guys to know I'm having a hard time keeping her off my mind.

As soon as we walk in the club, I spot her. Shane is still looking for her, but like a homing beacon I've already zeroed in on her. Though I pretend I haven't. She just did a tequila shot with her girlfriends and I'm trying to reel my tongue back in my mouth after seeing what she's wearing tonight. Every other male with a pulse is doing the same thing. She doesn't even realize how many guys are staring at her right now.

She looks good enough to eat in that black dress. It hugs all her curves a little too well—and holy hell, there's no back on it. It ties behind her neck, leaving her shoulders and back completely exposed all the way to barely above her ass. The material is stretched tight across her ass and thighs and moves with her like a second skin. Damn, this is going to be a long night.

She gets Shane's attention and he leads us to their table where Andi and another girl are setting up a table and chairs for us to sit beside them. I purposely choose the opposite side of the table and at the other end. I don't think I can stand to sit beside her and not touch her. I watch her take another shot before she heads off to the dance floor with her friends.

The waitress comes over to take our drink order and we ask for a couple of pitchers of beer. We're talking and looking around the club when I see Shane completely freeze then bolt to his feet. I follow his gaze to see some guy dancing with Andi and he has his whole body plastered to hers. I jump to my feet, knocking my chair over and fall in beside Shane as he plows through the crowd to get to her. She sees us and gives me a dirty look while she molds further into this guy's arms.

Even though I know I really deserve the dirty look, I can't stand seeing him all over her like this. Yeah, it was shitty of me to flirt with her friend like that right in front of her. I realized it was a mistake the minute the words were out of my mouth. Her friend is sexy and Shane had already made it clear that Andi is off-limits for a one-night stand. But this feeling I get around Andi doesn't feel like a one-night stand. I don't know what it is, though, and I'm admittedly hesitant to put a name to it.

I saw the look on Andi's face and I know I need to call a truce, make amends for it. No matter what, we need to at least be friends. But at the rate we're going, we won't be able to stand each other by morning. Watching her press closer and closer to this dickhead on the dance floor during the slow song doesn't help my resolve to only be friends with her. At all.

Shane finally drags her off the dance floor and I see them fighting but I have no idea what they're saying. She looks mad as hell though. From the purely murderous look on Shane's face right now, I don't think I want to know whatever it was she said before she walked away from him. While I'm watching Andi, I feel something land in my lap and I snap my head around.

There's a drunk, half-dressed girl sitting in my lap and giving me an open invitation to take her home. She's obviously already out of it and is rubbing her hands on my chest. The music is so loud I have to lean in to her ear for her to hear me when I ask, "It's hard to walk with those beer goggles on, isn't it?" She laughs and exaggeratedly nods her head at me.

I smile and politely help her stand back up but she doesn't leave. She's just waiting patiently beside me. I glance down at Andi and I see a similar look on her face—hurt, confusion, and then what looks like pure hatred. *This has gone far enough.* I stand to move around the drunken girl and Shane is standing in front of me.

"We need to talk," Shane says with such finality all I can do is nod and follow him to an area behind the bar where the speakers aren't so loud.

He doesn't give me a chance to ask what's up before he starts.

"Look, man. When I said I'd protect Andi, I meant it, but I wasn't trying to warn you off her if you're really interested in her. Like for more than just a piece of ass."

I'm not even sure how to respond because I don't know what I want from her. I just met her and I can't promise it'll last more than one night.

Crazy Maybe

Shane continues, "I heard before I even got to the gym that you and Andi seemed to be into each other. If that's true, I have to tell you—you are royally fucking this up. Ignoring her, flirting with her friend, then with that other girl. Andi's planning on taking some stranger home with her tonight. She's never done that, Luke. Make your mind up about her but don't screw her over."

The thought of her going home with some other guy tears me up because I know I want her. I'm just not really a relationship kind of guy. As much as I don't want to say it, the words just tumble out before I can catch them. "She's grown, man. If that's what she wants, I say she should go for it."

Shane gives me a disappointed look and, while shaking his head in disbelief, says, "Your loss, man. Your loss."

He walks back to the table and then leads one of Andi's friends to the dance floor. I scan the area but I don't see Andi anywhere and my heart pounds. At this very moment, I know without a shadow of a doubt that she's already left with someone else. Her one-night stand.

The anger hits me hard and I decide that's exactly what I need, too. A night of meaningless sex with a meaningless person whose name and face I will forget by this time tomorrow night. As I round the bar, the girl who was mauling me just a few minutes before steps into my line of sight and I make my way to her. I grab her hand and pull her to the dance floor without asking.

The DJ is playing another slow song so I pull nameless-girl in close to me. She wraps her arms around my neck and I let my fingers slide down her sides, feeling the side of her breasts and her stomach. When my fingers reach the hem of her shirt, I slide my hands underneath it, stroking the skin on her stomach and around to her back.

She angles her head up and before I know it, she's pushing her tongue in my mouth for a very aggressive kiss. She lets out a little moan and I know she's more than ready to go. I grab her hand, ready to pull her to the door, when I take a step and realize Andi is standing in front of me.

From the look on her face, I know she saw the whole thing. Her mouth is slightly open, as if she just sucked in a shocked breath and is still holding it, and her face is pale. The anger hasn't even hit her yet — only the shock. I see movement over Andi's shoulder and I slightly shift my eyes to see Shane watching me, nameless-girl and Andi. I'm suddenly keenly aware that Andi didn't leave with anyone–she was probably just in the fucking bathroom and I overreacted again.

Andi squares her shoulders, steels her spine and collects her wits quickly. Her emotions are stamped down and a hard mask is pulled over her beautiful face. My only coherent thought is, *"What the fuck have I just done?"*

I drop nameless-girl's hand and ignore her protests as I slowly walk away from her, following in the direction that Andi just went. She's back at the table with the other girls. When I sit, I realize nameless-girl has followed me and is now in my lap since there aren't any open chairs at our table. Andi looks over and sees this girl in my lap and our eyes meet. She looks hurt at first...then really, really mad. She gets up and heads toward the dance floor but keeps going past it.

Suddenly, Andi's on stage, standing in front of the microphone. The DJ is queuing up the music for her. When it starts, I immediately recognize the song. She puts on a good show, but there's no doubt to whom this song is dedicated. The song is *Stupid Girls*, by Pink. She blatantly sings the bridge, the part about how vain they are, directly to me and the stupid girl sitting in my lap.

I watch in awe as Andi drops to her knees on the stage, her back arched so her chest is sticking out, and her profile is to the audience. She looks so damn sexy. She's at the part where Pink speaks seductively during the song. When Andi starts this part, she flips her hair back in an overly exaggerated way.

Then she runs her hands up her stomach to just under her breasts and pushes them up toward her chin as she looks over her shoulder at me. *Damn – that little move just put me at half-mast!* She nimbly jumps back to her feet and finishes the song. The DJ is blatantly impressed with her talent, as is the rest of the club because the catcalls and whistles abound.

The DJ calls out to the audience, "What do you guys say—do we want Andi to do one more song for us?" The drunk and disorderly crowd goes wild and the DJ looks at Andi, "You heard 'em, girl, now sing it for us," and he starts the music to *Buttons*, by the Pussycat Dolls.

Perfect, for the next several minutes, I have to sit here and watch her moving her body in every suggestive and tempting way imaginable as other guys' hands try to touch her. She is definitely putting on a good show.

A bouncer has to grab one guy who tries to climb onstage with her after she sings one especially enticing part of the song that basically says she can't get the guy to help her take her clothes off. Andi's running her hands up and down her torso in the most seductive show performed outside a strip club. Every fucker in here is revved up—all for her.

Crazy Maybe

Andi finally leaves the stage and I see several motherfuckers lined up waiting to get her attention as she maneuvers around people on the dance floor. She doesn't stop for any of them but she gives them her warm smile as she keeps walking, including the guy she was dancing with earlier. I've pushed nameless-girl out of my lap and not so nicely got rid of her. She's already found someone else's lap to sit in. Fine with me-maybe I can find a way to convince Andi that I'm not a complete dickhead.

Over the next hour, I watch Andi order one shot after another, dance with the girls and a few guys who try to cut in on them. She keeps on until she's barely able to stand on her own. Even drunk, she ignores me when I try to talk to her. I think she's trying to get to the point where she'd let some random guy take her home. Even completely shit-faced drunk, I still don't think she has it in her to go through with it. And that gives me much more satisfaction than it should.

CHAPTER FIVE

ANDI

The little pinpricks of sunlight streaming through my closed blinds are causing me serious pain. If I could remove my head and put it in a vice, I think I would feel much better, because I swear the damn thing is about to split in two. I think I must have passed out before I had to experience the spinning rooms or the puking that always follows the spinning.

I'm not really sure though because I can't remember getting home.

Or getting undressed and into my bed.

Or to whom the hair sticking out of the covers belongs.

Oh shit, what have I done?

I need to get to my bathroom, take some ibuprofen and drink some water. I should've done it before going to bed last night. But with how I feel this morning, I'm pretty positive I didn't. I don't even know who is in my bed with me but I can feel that I'm not wearing any clothes. This is so not good. I look around on the bed and on the floor beside me until I find a shirt.

A man's shirt. A nameless, faceless man that I don't remember bringing home, or getting naked with, or getting in the bed with. And he's still here. This won't be awkward at all.

I snatch it up and quickly pull it over my head before I ease out of bed. I'm doing my version of the walk of shame to my own damn bathroom. I am pathetic. I close the bathroom door and lock it behind me before digging the Advil out of the cabinet. I take a long, hot shower, letting the water spray all over me and wash away whatever happened last night. I feel more human, not quite full human yet but at least *more* human, after my shower.

After I brush my teeth, comb my wet hair and wrap a towel around it, I put on my robe and take a deep breath before stepping back into my bedroom.

And I freeze dead in my tracks.

Luke is sitting up in my bed, leaned up against my headboard, with a stupid, shit-eating grin on his face. *Of all people, why the hell did I have to bring him home with me?*

"Good morning, sunshine," he has the audacity to smile at me and sound chipper. "How are you feeling?"

"Better, after a shower." Even to my ears, my voice is flat and void of all emotions. It's the only way I'm keeping them in check. My head is precariously sitting on top of my shoulders right now and I'm desperately trying to not disrupt that balance.

His smile increases and his voice takes on a low, sexy rumble when he answers, "Good. I was afraid you'd feel pretty rough. Does that mean you're up for a late-morning repeat of last night?" He pulls the covers back on my side of the bed and pats the mattress, inviting me to get back into my bed.

Not one to back down, I can't help but take this moment to burst his ginormous ego-bubble.

"I was actually hoping you could help me with that, Luke," I say as I move to sit exactly where his hand was, forcing him to quickly move it out of my way.

His smile quickly fades, but he isn't giving up yet. His brows are furrowed and his eyes are crinkled at the corners. "Help you with what, exactly?"

Crazy Maybe

"I'm afraid I don't remember anything about last night. How we got here. Where my clothes went. How we got in the bed together..." I intentionally left it here, knowing he would take full advantage of my alcohol-induced amnesia.

"Oh, yeah, baby, I can definitely try to help refresh your memory." He slowly starts leaning toward me and I know he expects me to jump back away from him. *Sorry to disappoint you, buddy.*

"Well, what's strange is—I'm not sore. *At all.* So if we had sex, as you're implying, I guess that means you have a *really tiny* penis and I didn't enjoy it much at all. If that's the case, then no, I'm not up for a repeat of last night. One disappointment is enough for me. Thanks for the offer, though. I admire how you don't give up. Can I call you a cab to get home or do you have your car here?"

I keep a straight face while waiting for him to digest everything I said. It takes about ten seconds before I see the red creeping up his neck until it takes over his entire face, ears, and head. The low, mean growl comes first, and then his thundering roar comes soon after. If my head felt just a little better, I would be more amused. But it really isn't bad entertainment considering my current hangover state.

This time when he really does make a lunge for me across the bed, I jump up and scoot across the room farther away from him.

"Something you'd like to say, Luke?" I innocently ask.

"Say? Oh no—I have nothing to *say*, Andi. But I definitely have something to *show* you," he challenges.

I sigh dramatically, "Luke, seriously, we don't have to go through this again. Your secret's safe with me. I promise."

Crazy Maybe

And now I know how fast the big guy really is—because he is out of my bed and has me pinned against the wall before I can even scream. Not that I would have screamed because my head isn't quite ready for that yet.

He grabs my wrists and pushes my arms up over my head, pinning them to wall. The gleam in his eye is wild and dangerous...and sexy. He grinds his hips into me, pushing his impressive erection between my legs as he growls into my ear, "Baby, *if* I'd made you mine last night, you would definitely remember it and you would most definitely still *feel* it this morning."

A shudder runs down my spine and goose bumps pebble across my skin at his words, his insinuation, and his possessiveness. Right now, I am definitely not thinking about my throbbing head since I have other body parts that are throbbing in a very different way. I'm actually glad he has me pinned to the wall with his weight, otherwise my knees would have already buckled and I'd be a quivering mess in the floor. And I freaking love it!

Excuse me while I interrupt these thoughts to get back to the angry man in front of me.

He's still in challenging mode, daring me to dispute his alpha-male, Neanderthal-ways, empowering words. I answer him with my full-blown, mega-watt smile that neither laughs nor mocks him but lets him know I've just totally played him. His eyes narrow as he studies me for a few seconds before realization and understanding crosses his face.

"You play a dangerous game, little girl," he snarls, but with much less venom than just a minute ago.

"You started this game, little boy," I gently chide, raising my chin in defiance.

He shakes his head and I feel more than hear the rumble of his light chuckle as it ripples through his chest. A chest that I have to say is pretty impressive, now that I'm getting a look at it while he's standing in front of me wearing only his boxer briefs. *Nice, very, very nice.*

He widens his stance so that we were more even in height and puts his forehead against mine. He is staring into my eyes and when he speaks, the sincerity in his voice is clear. "I'm sorry, Andi—for what a jerk I've been. Can you forgive me? Give me a chance to make it up to you?"

LUKE

I'm holding my breath, waiting for her to answer me. This girl has turned me upside down and inside out so many times in less than one day and I know I want to at least give this an honest try. Last night, when I thought she'd gone home with another guy, I was out of my fucking mind with jealousy. Then when she saw me with the drunk, nameless-girl I wanted to crawl in a hole and never come out. For whatever reason, I know that hurt her.

Which is crazy, right? I mean we just met and I shouldn't have even been concerned with what she thought or about hurting her with a one-night stand. But it does matter, I am concerned, and I don't want to do anything to hurt her. So whatever this is between us, however far it goes, and wherever it takes us, I've decided to see it through to the end. The only thing I know for sure is that today is not the end.

So now I'm just waiting for her to confirm it. I'm still looking in her eyes and silently willing her to take a chance on me. Again. She lets out a small sigh and simply says, "Okay." But her tone is genuine and heartfelt, just like she is. I can't stop the rush of feelings that suddenly engulf me.

I brush my lips against hers once, then twice, and on the third time, she responds and kisses me back. I still have her pinned against the wall and she feels so soft and sweet under me. I release her hands and she immediately wraps them around me, rubbing her hands slowly up and down my back. My hands move up and I pull the towel off her head then thread my fingers through her still wet hair. I tilt her head slightly to the side and slide my tongue across the middle of her lips, urging her to open up and let me in.

When she does, I can't contain my growl of approval and our kiss becomes urgent and demanding. Her tongue is velvety soft and she drives me into a fucking frenzy with the way she caresses and sucks on my tongue. Her hands are on my chest now and her fingers are lightly tracing the striations of my muscles, heating me to my core with no more than her touch on my skin.

I've kissed countless women in my life, but in this moment, this is the first real kiss I've ever experienced. This is the first kiss, the only kiss that has ever branded me and rocked my entire world. I am really getting worked up now and I know I need to back off. I want to spend time with her, getting to know her, and give whatever this is between us a fighting chance. Reluctantly, I slow the pace until I can naturally pull away from her.

Crazy Maybe

We're both panting like we've just finished a marathon and we're forehead to forehead. After taking a minute to catch my breath, I finally feel like I can speak. I step back so I can see her full reaction to my words.

"Andi, whatever this is between us, I want us to take it slow."

She gives me a skeptical look, like she thinks I'm feeding her a line. She pushes herself off the wall to stand up straight and nods.

"Fine, if you want to go slow, then we'll go slowly. But I need to know what you mean by '*whatever this is between us.*'"

I run my fingers through my hair in frustration. I don't know how to put in words what I'm feeling. "I don't know what it is. I'm not a relationship kind of guy. Or at least I haven't been. But I know I want you and I want to see where this goes."

My answer does not please her. This is evident from the fire in her eyes that is darting out at me. But she controls it impressively.

"All right, Luke. We'll see where it goes. But just know that until you can say something other than you '*want me,*' we'll remain just friends. And not friends with benefits. We'll get to know each other as friends first."

What the hell am I supposed to say to that? I just backed my own damn self into a corner that she knows I can't get out of. I huff, loudly, run my fingers through my hair again, and finally agree to her terms.

"Whatever you say, Andi."

"Do you have any plans for today, Luke?"

"Nope. What do you have in mind?"

"I'll dry my hair and we can go get some breakfast. Then we'll decide what to do from there."

I nod and watch her walk back to her bathroom. I brought a clean change of clothes with me last night just in case I didn't make it home from the club. I grab them out of my truck and shower in the guest bedroom while Andi is still getting dressed. Thirty minutes later, she's ready to go and dressed casual in a tank top, shorts and sandals. She has very little makeup on and her hair is pulled back again, and her beauty absolutely takes my breath away.

I didn't get a chance to really look around last night after getting Andi home and carrying her into her house. Not that she remembers, but she passed out before we even got her out of the club. Her friends undressed her and put her in the bed. I stayed with her because I was really worried about leaving her alone in that state.

I was threatened within an inch of my life by everyone in the group if I did anything to her – especially by Shane. After a lot of promising, they finally left and I slept with one eye open in case she woke up and needed me. Good thing for Andi, she slept the worst of it off and woke up feeling very little effects from her binge.

I can't take my eyes off her as we walk out of her house, which is actually a large, expensive home in a nice area on the outskirts of northeast Atlanta. The sun is bright and she quickly puts her sunglasses on to shield her eyes. We head to her car and she notices my truck parked in her driveway and her lips suddenly form a thin line. I know she wants to ask me about how she got home and got naked, but she decides against it and unlocks her car.

"I usually park in the garage, but there are some boxes in my parking spot. I got home late yesterday and didn't have time to move them. But the other side is open if you want to move your truck inside. I can get the other door opener."

She's always so considerate. I just can't get over that she's the ultimate beauty and personality package.

I shake my head no, "It's fine. I don't mind leaving it parked outside if you don't mind."

She smiles, "Okay, let's go eat then."

She picks a small sidewalk café that's about ten minutes from her house. I grew up in this general area and my parents still live here but I've never eaten at this place. She chooses a table outside, even though it is early springtime in the South, which normally means it's hot as hell and 120% humidity. But it is a beautiful day and there's a slight breeze that makes it bearable. We order our food and the waitress leaves our drinks with us.

We're talking, laughing, and just generally getting to know each other and it's great. I've never felt more relaxed with a girl like I do with her. I just finished telling her a pretty funny story from high school about me and she's wiping tears of laughter from her eyes when I feel someone stop beside us. I look up into the eyes of my mother and father, and they are eying Andi suspiciously.

I already know what they see when they look at her. The pink horizontal stripes in her hair, the tattoo-sleeve on her arm and shoulder, her casual dress, and the fact that we're having breakfast together. They think she's one of my sleazy, one-night stands and I'm instantly defensive. My father lightly clears his throat to draw our full attention to him.

Andi looks at my parents with a genuine smile and they both looking at her with their fake smiles that never quite reaches their eyes. Andi may not know this, but I sure as hell do. Andi looks at me and raises her eyebrows, as if to say, "*Well?*"

"Hi, Mom. Dad. Small world, huh?"

Mom laughs a little nervously but neither of them answers. They just look back and forth between Andi and me.

"Mom, Dad, this is Andi Morgan. Andi, these are my parents, Linda and Sam Woods."

Andi extends her hand to my mom first, then my dad, and tells them both she is glad to meet them. Their reply is simply, "Likewise." Mom starts telling me about Gran's birthday party at my parent's house next month. When she takes a breath and leaves an opening for someone else to speak, Andi offers them each a seat and asks if they want to eat with us.

I didn't think they would accept her invitation. The way they look at her, like she is beneath them with their snobbery, makes my blood boil. But when they accept and actually thank her, I noticed a bit of thawing in their normally cold demeanor. By the end of breakfast, Andi has them both eating out of her hand. They are both ready to adopt her and take her home with them. Before my mom leaves, she makes Andi promise to come to Gran's birthday party with me.

I look at Andi without trying to mask my amazement and fascination with her. She really has no idea how wonderful she is, because she asks me simply, "What? Why are you looking at me like that?"

"You are amazing, Andi. Seriously. How did you do that?"

"Do what, Luke?"

"They love you! They don't like anyone—not even me!"

Crazy Maybe

"Are you crazy? They love you! You hung the moon and stars in their eyes. You'd have to be blind to not see that."

I just shake my head at her. I must be blind because I don't see what she sees.

CHAPTER SIX

LUKE

It's the day of Gran's birthday party. The last month has been hectic and crazy and wonderful. I've spent every day with Andi, either training at the gym, chilling at her house or at my apartment, or just going out somewhere to spend time together. Oh yeah, and somehow she talked me into being part of her karaoke skit at the club tomorrow night, so we've been practicing that for the past two weeks, too. Thank God she didn't ask me to sing.

We're still in the "friends" stage because she's still giving me time to define what "this" is between us. She is stubborn as hell and won't be the one to give it a name. She's making me face it and she won't budge an inch until I do. I can't even count how many times I've tried to kiss her and she will turn her face so my kiss lands on her cheek. Then she smiles like it's no big deal. She's making me fucking crazy! And I wouldn't trade one minute of my time with her for all the one-night stands in the world.

She's excited about meeting all of my family even though I've tried to tell her they aren't all that much to get excited over. She's never spoken of her family, outside Mack and Shane, but they're not her blood relatives. I've tried to casually bring the conversation around to her family but she's a master at dodge and avoid. She's somehow distracted me every time, so I

53

get that she's not ready to talk about it. That's cool–we have plenty of time.

We're in my truck, heading to my parent's house and she's fidgeting in the seat beside me. She won't let me kiss her but she will let me hold her hand, so I have it firmly grasped in mine. I would never admit this to any living soul, but I'm so tied up in knots over her that I'll gladly take the handholding. At least I get to touch her that way. I feel like a damn elementary school boy who's thrilled to hold a girl's hand for the first time. It's just what she does to me. And what I do to myself by delaying telling her I want a committed relationship with her.

"You're not getting nervous, are you?" I playfully ask her.

"Maybe a little," she laughs, "but I'll be fine."

"My parents already want to adopt you and disown me. My whole family will love you. Just watch out for my brother. He'll try to steal you from me." And I mean this literally. Brandon will fall in love with her, too.

Did I just infer that I'm in love with her?

What the hell?

"You can never have too many friends, Luke," she declares without a hint of sarcasm. I start to worry that she really only sees me as a friend.

"I better not catch you alone with him, Andi." I use my stern voice, the one that says I'm not even fucking kidding. Not that it has ever worked on this woman.

She says, "Fine, Luke," and I feel my racing heart start to slow down until she finishes her sentence, "I won't let you catch me."

I snap my head to look at her, ready to fight tooth and nail for my place in her life, and I see the gleam of absolute mocking in the twinkling of her eyes. She is enjoying this so much. She will probably flirt with

54

Brandon just to get to me. I should've kept my fucking mouth shut because she will *so* use this little tidbit against me. *Wench.*

We arrive at my parent's house a few minutes early but it looks like the whole gang is already here. Andi looks absolutely perfect in her form-fitting black capris, her sky-blue flowing shirt that would be baggy if not for the white scarf/belt thing she has tied around her tiny waist. Her little toenails are painted the same color as her shirt and are peeking out of her black sandals. My God, she is more than I've ever imagined a woman could be.

My sister, Alicia, is younger than me but she married early and has two rug-rats that I love with all my heart. Being Uncle Luke has been pretty cool. My nephew Jacob is five, my niece Callie is three, and they are both so much fun. They both know my truck and as soon as Andi and I step out of it, the front door opens and they come flying out to meet us. I hug them both and lift them up in the air, playing our usual game of airplanes while Andi watches and laughs along with us.

I introduce Jacob and Callie to Andi, who kneels down to be eye to eye when them, and she proceeds to charm the kids just like she did my parents. Before we make it across the front lawn, both kids are attached to her like little leeches. Alicia meets us at the door, and within minutes, she and Andi act like they are long lost sisters. I roll my eyes to myself at the thought of what my brother will do when he meets her.

And here we go...Brandon just arrived and is making his rounds. I know it the second his eyes find Andi because his big mouth stops moving. Brandon is two years older than me and we actually look a lot alike. We've frequently competed for the same thing, including girls. But there's no way I'm letting him put the moves on this one. *No. Fucking. Way.* I try to head him off at the pass but he just pats my shoulder as his "hello" as he makes a beeline for my girl, who's now sitting with my sister and Gran.

"And who is this beautiful lady? Alicia, you said you didn't have any friends you could set me up with that I'd be interested in. I can promise you, I'm interested in this one." Brandon is really laying it on thick.

"Brandon! We can't take you anywhere!" Alicia is laughing, knowing what a flirt Brandon naturally is. "This is Andi, and she's *Luke's* date."

Gran is watching me with those knowing, all-seeing eyes of hers and an obvious smirk on her face. She knows damn well that Andi is more than a friend to me even if I haven't said it to anyone.

"Oh, Luke and I aren't dating. We're just friends." Andi declares to Alicia, but the whole room full of people stops buzzing and every eye is boring into me, telling me that I'm fucking crazy. Every eye, except Brandon's eyes, which are still glued to Andi. I'm pretty sure I just growled out loud at her revelation.

"You have no idea how happy I am to hear that, Andi," Brandon is moving to sit beside Andi on the loveseat, even though my sister already occupies the other seat. Brandon will just sit on her if she doesn't move fast enough. My brother is openly ignoring me and eating Andi up with his eyes.

I cut through the room full of people who are still looking at me as if I've suddenly sprouted a few extra heads. I take Andi by the hand before Alicia has time to get out of Brandon's way, thus preventing Brandon from fully getting to my girl. I pull Andi up to stand beside me and wrap my arm around her waist–being intentionally and blatantly possessive, especially in front of Brandon.

Crazy Maybe

"Not a snowball's chance in hell, Brandon. Go find your own girl."

My brother knows me all too well. His smug smile tells me he knows he's pushing my buttons as he says, "I think it would be more appropriate if *you* go find *your* own girl. You and Andi are just friends, after all."

I'm not doing this in front of everyone.

"Andi, let me introduce you to the rest of my family and show you around the house," and with that I lead her away from my brother, who is now openly laughing behind me. I feel somewhat better when Andi settles her hand in mine and gives it a slight squeeze.

ANDI

I absolutely love Luke's family—every one of them. They have all taken me in with open arms and made me feel like one of them. It's been so long since I've had a family, my emotions threaten to get away from me and I have to find something to take my mind off it before I start crying and make a fool out of myself. For all of their problems, and every family has problems, not one of them can really understand what it would mean to lose everything and be totally alone in this world.

I understand it all too well. And that makes being here with Luke's parents, siblings, grandparents, aunts, uncles, and cousins all the more bittersweet. I've talked at length with every single person here, even with his brother Brandon, who is actually just a big softie even though he gives Luke hell. I think everyone asked me,

57

in one way or another, exactly what Luke was doing at the gym.

When I explained the boxing career, what it takes to make a boxer, how much determination and grit a man has to have to even step in the ring, I could see them look at Luke in a completely different manner.

After explaining it to Luke's dad, Sam, I think he was actually fighting back tears and he looked so damn proud of Luke. It makes me wonder if they've had words about it before but Luke wasn't able to express his feelings or fully explain what all is involved. In any case, I think Sam, and everyone else here, understands now.

Luke didn't like it when I talked to Brandon, but I made sure Luke was beside me and he was included in the conversation. Though I teased Luke about not getting caught with his brother, I would never actually betray him like that, even if "this" weren't going on between us. Whatever "this" is. For all of Brandon's flirting, I don't think he would actually betray Luke like that either, but I'm not sure Luke is convinced of that.

Sam grilled out an enormous amount of chicken, burgers, and hotdogs. Luke's mom, Linda, made everything else and we all ate until we were overstuffed. After we finished the main course, Linda brought out the birthday cake for Gran. She insisted I call her Gran because she's now adopted me as her granddaughter. Gran's presents started piling up on the table in front of her and she was beaming with pride.

Once her presents were opened and everyone had their piece of cake, I stole away from the table to get her gift from me out of my purse inside the house. Luke had told me a lot about Gran over the past month we've been hanging out together, but I wasn't comfortable giving her present to her in front of everyone else.

Crazy Maybe

I brought the small box to the back yard table where Gran was going back through all her presents and sat down beside her. "Gran, I don't have a lot of experience with this kind of thing. If you don't like it, it's okay–we can go exchange it for whatever you want. But after Luke described you to me, I thought you might like this."

Gran's eyes lit up when I put the box in her wrinkled hands and I felt Luke watching me from across the yard. Somehow I can always feel his eyes on me. He slowly made his way over to where Gran and I sat, curiosity getting the best of him. I suppress a laugh but Gran's knowing eyes dance with mischief. "That boy is in love with you, Andi."

Dodge and deflect activated, "Open your present, Gran!"

She pats my hand, knowingly, and slowly removes the wrapping paper from the black velvet box, giving Luke time to get to us before she opens the lid. She gasps when she sees the necklace inside and tears spring to her eyes. The necklace is really simple, but I found it at a vintage shop and it is beautiful. The charm is an owl made of silver and the body is set with small stones–a mixture of sapphires, emeralds and rubies.

"Do you not like it, Gran? It's okay if you don't, really. I will take you to exchange it for whatever you want." *Oh my gosh* – I've just made Gran cry at her own birthday party! I couldn't feel any worse if I tried.

Gran straightens her back and looks at me with a stern eye, "Don't even joke about that, child! I absolutely love it! It reminds me of the one my mother used to wear. It looks exactly like her old one." Gran then grabs me in her arms and kisses me square on the mouth, like I was one of her kids and had always been.

Now I have tears in my eyes and I'm hugging her fiercely, like I'm almost afraid to let her go.

But I do let go and when I pull back from her, I look up at Luke and I can't read the look on his face. Before I can say anything, Gran nudges me and asks me to put the necklace on her. She then proceeds to prance around the yard, making everyone look at her necklace. I can't help but smile as I watch her. She's just so cute and funny. Luke moves behind me, wraps his arms around my waist, and pulls me close to him. He leans down so he's right at my ear and he speaks softly, so only I can hear him.

"You are *the most* amazing person I've ever met, Andi," and he kisses me on the cheek. Brandon watches us from a few yards away and I can't help but wonder if this is just for show, to warn Brandon away from me.

But *this*–how he's holding me, the tone of his voice, the sultry way he whispered only to me, and even the kiss on my cheek–*this* all feels like so much more than friends. But he won't say it and I won't say it until he does.

I want it–I want him. I want the more-than-friends stage with him but I won't push him for it so that he'll just blame me for it later. If he doesn't come to that conclusion on his own, we won't ever move past the friend stage, no matter how much it hurts me. I don't ever let the hurt show, though. I'm sure he knows I'd love to have more but I won't pressure him for it.

I will gladly take our time together as friends where I get to know the real Luke. There is no one else I want to date. Not that I dated much before he came along, anyway. But if he starts dating someone else, I will back off and let that be the end of any hope I have of us being more. Until then, I'll take all the time he will give me and love every minute of it. Especially like this, when we're with his family and having so much fun.

I hear Luke talking to some people a few feet away and he's talking about me. "Andi is a phenomenal singer. You should hear her! She can sing most anything and she plays the guitar and the piano."

They all turn and look at me with interest. My eyes dart nervously from one person to another. Surely they don't expect me to sing here, at Gran's party.

"Andi," Luke's smooth voice calls out, "sing us a song, sweetheart." The people around him smile and chime in their agreement.

"Umm, I don't know about that. I don't have any music and I haven't practiced anything...and this is Gran's party. That would be rude of me." I'm hedging and they all know it.

"I would love to hear you sing for me on my birthday, Andi," Gran's beside me again, smiling as she takes my arm in hers. "Sam and Linda have an acoustic guitar you can play and sing for me. Gather around, everyone!" Gran calls over her shoulder to everyone and they all gather around us as Alicia hands me the guitar with a smile. *Great...no pressure...*

I don't think they would like most of the songs I sing at the club, so I pick a slow song by Halestorm that I've loved since the first time I heard it. I can play it all on the acoustic guitar and keep it tame for Luke's family. Luke walks up with two bar stools and takes a seat beside me. "This song is called *Beautiful With You*," I say then start strumming the guitar strings.

This song is meaningful to me for several different reasons. Guys frequently hit on me so I know I'm at least attractive. But I've never felt beautiful. I'm sure it has everything to do with my childhood issues. But I'm feeling more beautiful after spending so much time with

Crazy Maybe

Luke, and I don't mean just in physical appearance. I mean beautiful inside, where it matters the most.

The lyrics to this song speak to so many things I've been through—being beautiful to someone else despite your mistakes and flaws. Someone who understands you and knows the scars you carry inside and out, but only loves you more because of them. That's how Luke makes me feel, and while I can't dedicate it to him in front of everyone, this song was written for him from my heart. Even if Lzzy did sing it first.

I purposely keep my eyes from locking on Luke's while I am singing. It's already so obvious that I'm crazy about him so I don't need to add to it. But I feel him intently watching and I can see him in my peripheral vision. Brandon moves directly in front of me during the song. I half expect Luke to move his barstool to block Brandon's view but Luke doesn't seem to notice anyone or anything besides me.

Everyone claps enthusiastically and Gran rushes me, elbowing both Luke and Brandon out of the way, to give me the first hug. One of the cousins bumps Luke with his elbow and Brandon sweeps in while Luke's distracted. I laugh and hug Brandon until Luke realizes what's happened and pushes Brandon aside. Luke wraps his arms around me for a hug, whispers in my ear, "You *are* beautiful," and kisses me on the cheek. I can feel my face heat up as I reply "Thank you," because I don't know what else to say.

Later, we say goodbye to Gran and Gramps, the aunts, uncles, and cousins, until all that's left is Luke's immediate family. I walk to the back yard to start gathering the leftover dishes and start cleaning up. I'd never leave Luke's mom to do all this alone, especially after she was the one who made so much of the food for us. After a few trips back and forth with loaded arms, I deliver the last load to the kitchen and walk back out to gather the garbage.

The outdoor string lantern lights are lit, casting a soft glow across the yard and the lights are twinkling off the water in the pool. It would be romantic if I had a boyfriend to share it with, but I only have a guy who is a friend, and who is still in the house. I stop for a minute just to take in the whole backyard landscaping, getting ideas for my own yard, when I feel a pair of strong arms wrap around me from behind.

"Penny for your thoughts?" Luke murmurs in my ear.

Dodge and deflect activated again. He hasn't said it yet and he's not going to trick me into saying it first. "I've had a great time tonight with your whole family. Thank you for bringing me, Luke."

"My whole family is in love with you, Andi. I've had to fight them off the whole time just so I can keep you for myself."

His words are so sweet and I could read between the lines if I really wanted to, but I'm sticking to listening to his actual words and his actions. Until he says it and shows it, we are only friends and I will hold him to meaning exactly what he says. No double meanings accepted.

"Your family is great, Luke. And they are all so proud of you and what you're doing."

With that, he turns me to face him before he speaks again. "The only reason they're so proud of me now is because of you, Andi. Because of what you told them about boxing and what you told them about me. They see me through your eyes now. You have no idea how much that means to me. How much I appreciate you standing up for me like you did today."

I'm so overcome with emotion that I can't speak. I knew he needed someone to believe in him, but I saw firsthand today how he's been alone in his dream. Much like I've been alone in my life. I reach up and gently stroke his jaw with my hand and he leans his cheek into my hand. His eyes hold mine and even though I want–I desperately want–to read his feelings through his eyes, it could very well be only gratitude. I won't put my heart on the line for a simple case of gratitude, no matter how hard I'm biting my tongue right now to not say the words first.

Brandon saves me from biting my tongue in two when he joins us outside. "Sure looks like more than 'just friends' to me, Luke. You sure you don't have something to tell us?" The light teasing is evident in his voice, so it's clear he's not trying to start a fight. He must know plenty about Luke's commitment phobia.

Luke's spine straightens at Brandon's words and his muscles tense up. He's still looking at me but the adoration I saw just a few seconds ago has been masked. I am so disappointed right now, I can't even hide it, so I lower my hand and look away from Luke. He still hasn't answered Brandon's question, and I don't think he plans to at this point.

"I guess I should finish picking up for your mom," I hear the disappointment in my voice despite my best effort to keep it out. I can't help but feel like that's the same as putting pressure on him–like in a passive aggressive way. That's not my intention at all, so I busy myself with garbage bags and picking up used paper plates, plastic forks and spoons, and paper towels. I make efficient work of it and step around the side of the house to put the garbage bag in the can.

When I come back around, Luke and Brandon are locked in a heated discussion, both struggling to keep

Crazy Maybe

their voices low and only between them. But I hear Luke loud and clear when he says, "I've told you we're only friends. Andi told you we're only friends. That's all we'll ever be, so let it go, Brandon. She's not your concern."

And just like that, my heart is broken. I step back into the shadows of the house so they don't know I heard Luke. The time we spend together, the snuggling, the kisses, and the words he's said to me—they're only gestures for a friend. Even though I've told myself over and over not to read into it, I guess my heart never really listened. Apparently, I was more invested in him that I even told myself, because hearing those words come from him just ripped my heart out of my chest.

Taking a deep breath, I stroll around the corner of the house again to find them in the same challenging position. I intentionally look down, picking imaginary lint off my clothes, as I called out to Luke, "I'm worn out, Luke. Are you about ready to take me home?"

Their demeanor instantly relaxes and Luke responds, "What if I don't want to let you go?"

Brandon smirks and looks at him incredulously, but I pretend to not notice it.

His words are yet another stab to my heart, since I know he doesn't mean it, and this situation is yet another test of my acting skills. "Oh, I think you'll survive without me, Luke."

Luke cocks his head to the side and narrows his eyes at me suspiciously. Apparently my voice wasn't as convincing as I tried for, but after the emotional family day, I'm doing well to not be a blubbering mess of tears and snot. This is the best he gets right now.

"I need to say goodbye to your parents and Alicia. But first, it was great to meet you, Brandon. Don't be a

Crazy Maybe

stranger," and I hug his neck before walking in to find the rest of the family. After saying 'thank you' and sharing hugs all around, Luke and I leave and he drives me home with little conversation.

He knows something is wrong but he doesn't just come out and ask, so I'm not forced to dodge and deflect. His lack of curiosity is a dead giveaway that he knows what's wrong but doesn't want to talk about it.

Before he put the truck in park, I open the door to get out. Standing in the open door, I ask – rather meekly for me, "You still going to be part of my show tomorrow night?"

"Of course, Andi. Why wouldn't I be?"

"Just making sure. I'll see you tomorrow."

He waits until I am safely inside before leaving, but I don't turn and wave goodbye to him this time. It's all I can do to get to my door without breaking down. Once I am sure he was gone, I slide down the door to the floor and cry until I have no tears left. I eventually drag myself to my bathroom, get ready for bed, and take a cold washcloth with me, hoping it would help keep the swelling down in my eyes.

CHAPTER SEVEN

LUKE

I'm thinking back over the night on my way home after I drop Andi off at her house. Brandon's words keep coming back to haunt me. He started his shit with, "Sure looks like more than 'just friends' to me, Luke. You sure you don't have something to tell us?"

Brandon is such an ass. He's said that shit in front of Andi on purpose. He knows something more is up between us but it's like it was his mission to get me to admit it tonight. He watched Andi all night. I know he did because I alternated between watching her and watching him watch her.

It's not that I don't trust Andi. I just can't hardly take my eyes off her because she takes my breath away. I can't believe how well she fits in with my family. They are all completely taken with her.

And when she sang that song for the family, I was completely mesmerized. I knew she could play since she's strummed a couple of songs for me during the time we've been spending together. But hearing her sing that song was different.

She uses songs to speak for her sometimes. I know that was a song she knows by heart but I could tell from her very demeanor that she felt insecure. Not just about her looks, but it seems she's uncertain about her very worth. She doesn't show her vulnerable side to anyone easily, but I doubt anyone here even recognized the signs but me. The more I learn about her, the more complex she becomes to me, and the more irreplaceable she becomes, too.

Gran is a sly little minx, but she caught me off guard earlier by saying what a good couple she thought Andi and Brandon would make. Then laughed maniacally when she saw the look on my face.

I had no idea Andi got that necklace for Gran but she couldn't have picked a better gift. She remembered everything I've said about Gran and somehow knew exactly what to get her. Seeing how much Gran was affected really gets to me in a good way.

I had to tell Andi how much I appreciate her but I didn't want it to be a big display for everyone to hear, especially Brandon. So I nuzzled close into her ear and whispered to her how amazing I think she is. When she melted into my arms, I had to fight to keep from performing a *totally inappropriate* display of affection in my parents' backyard.

She just feels so good in my arms that I don't know how I can ever let her go. And that very thought scares the shit out of me, so I eventually let her go and walked off to talk to my cousins. Of course, they asked me about Andi and what's going on with us. Damn, every single man there was more than willing to take her off my hands and they openly told me.

Bastards.

My dad and my uncle approached me after I'd finished threatening my cousins' lives if they so much as looked at Andi wrong. Brandon had been lurking and listening to my conversations, in between watching Andi and doing everything he could to get into her conversations. I turned to talk to my dad and uncle but still kept Andi in my sights–and Brandon.

"Luke, your Uncle Alex and I have been talking to Andi," my dad's tone of voice was genial, instantly telling me how much he enjoyed that conversation, "and she told us all about what you're doing at the gym. How hard your training is. How dedicated you are to it. I just want you to know, son, how proud I am of you for sticking with it. I believe in you, Luke, and I want you to know I understand, now, why you want this."

I was literally speechless.

My Uncle Alex picked up the conversation, "Yeah, Luke. Andi explained what it's like to step into the ring and what it takes to even get ready to do something like that. I'm damn impressed with you, Luke. I can't wait to see you make it big," Uncle Alex's sincerity was palpable. Being Uncle Alex, he couldn't help but add, "I'll be sure to tell everyone I taught you everything you know."

I laughed at that and looked between the two brothers and I still didn't really know what to say. "Thanks, both of you. I appreciate your support. It really means a lot to me. I'll even let you get away with taking the credit, Uncle Alex," I added with a wink. They carried a plate of food to the table and each clapped my shoulder in another show of support as they passed by.

More people came up to me at different times during the party to congratulate me on my boxing career, telling me how impressed they are, and giving me encouragement. Every one of them had talked to Andi, and with every conversation Andi had apparently been singing my praises. No one has ever done that for me before and at this point, I've lost count of how many times this girl has saved my ass in one way or another. And that only adds to my belief that I do not deserve her. At all.

Still, she deserved to know what she's done so when I found her alone in the backyard, I intended only to walk up to her and thank her. But somehow my arms automatically went around her waist and I pulled her firmly against me and melted into her. She looked so small and alone, just staring off into the yard, so I asked what she was thinking.

I don't think her answer was at all what she was thinking but I let it go. When she told me how proud my family is of me, I finally remembered the original reason why I walked out her to her. I turned her around in my arms and told her that it was only because of her and what she'd said to them. The way she was looking at me had me completely tongue-tied. She wanted to say something, I was sure of it, but she kept it in. I was trying, however unsuccessfully, to tell her how important she is to me when Brandon had to fucking interrupt with his question.

I know Andi felt me tense up when Brandon said it looked like we were more than friends. And I saw the disappointed look on her face when I didn't confirm it. Of course we looked like more than friends but it's none of his damn business. The thing is, I know I should have just said it. I should've just told Brandon, and Andi, that I'm already crazy about her and I want us to be more than just friends, but I didn't. Andi pulled away and started cleaning up from the party while Brandon and I faced off again.

When Andi went around the house, Brandon's anger flared at me, "*She's. Not. Megan!* You have to stop blaming yourself for that. It wasn't your fault. Everyone can see that but you! Andi is great and she's obviously crazy about you." The more Brandon talked, the madder he got. He stuck his finger in my face when he continued, "You're pushing her away, man. When you lose her, you will be sorry."

I hissed back at him, insisting we're just friends and we'll never be more than that. Brandon immediately called bullshit on me and when I didn't answer, his demeanor completely changed. He stared me straight in the eye and said, "All right, brother. I believe you. So, if you're just friends, you won't care when I call her and ask her out. Right? Mind putting in a good word for me?"

The motherfucker wasn't even kidding. He's not just goading me—he really wants to try to take Andi away from me. Right at that moment, Andi came back around the house and called out to me, asking if I was ready to take her home. I said the first thing that came to my mind after Brandon's unbelievable request.

"What if I don't want to let you go?"

I saw Brandon's smirk but ignored him. *Dick.* Thankfully Andi didn't seem to notice it but her answer, and more specifically her tone, was unusually cold when she said I'd survive without her. *Where the hell did that come from?* I know the disgusted look Brandon gave me all too well—he really wanted to punch me in the face.

Andi then hugged Brandon goodbye and his eyes met mine when he took her in his arms. The challenging look in his eyes said, "*If you don't make her yours, I will damn sure make her mine.*"

Over my dead fucking body, brother.

Andi went inside to say goodbye to the rest of my family and I followed after her to keep her close to me, keep her away from Brandon, and to keep from getting into a brawl with my brother.

Andi was quiet on the way back to her house and I know why. I know she was thinking about what Brandon asked, what he insinuated, and how I didn't confirm it to him. I let her down and I don't know how to fix it now. I should've said it at the house, in front of the whole damn family, and told her how wonderful and amazing she is. But I just drove on in silence until we got to her house. I was about to ask if I could come in when she suddenly jumped out of my truck.

Then she stunned me by asking if I was still going to be in her karaoke skit tomorrow night. Of course I'm still going to be there for her. We've practiced almost nightly over the past two weeks and she needs me to be in it for it to work the way she planned it. Why would she think I would back out on her the night before?

She closed the door and walked off to her front door before I could say another word. And like a damn mute idiot, I just sat in my truck and watched her walk away. Brandon's words suddenly came back to haunt me. *When you lose her, you will be sorry.* I feel like I'm already losing her and I just fucking found her. The closing of her front door felt like a bad omen–like she was shutting me out.

Now I'm alone and can't get her off my mind. I can't just sit here and do nothing when I feel her slipping away from me, so I pick up my phone and text her.

Still awake, beautiful?

My phone pings after a few minutes. I didn't think she was going to answer at first.

A: Yes

Are you ok?

A: Yes

Enough of the yes or no questions since she's obviously not elaborating with her answers.

I wish you were here with me.

And I wait again for the ping.

A: You have plenty of friends to keep you company.

I don't want a friend.

A: What do you want then?

You.

ANDI

You? *You?* What the hell does that mean? Yeah, I know he *wants* me but that's just not the same and I can't do this anymore tonight. I turn off my phone, put my cold, wet washcloth over my eyes, and wait for sleep to take over. I finally fall asleep but it's a fitful sleep and I dream about him all damn night. At six o'clock the next morning, I'm wide-awake so I get up and face the day.

Around eight o'clock, I decide to go for a run and work off some of this frustration. For every time I think of him or about how much his words hurt, I punish myself by running harder. So, my run today has been pretty brutal because I can't seem to stop the thoughts. I know he's at the gym right now working out and sparring but I couldn't bring myself to go. After two hours of running, I'm completely spent from pushing myself on so little sleep last night. I do a cool-down jog back to my house, taking my time and enjoying the country view.

When I turn onto my street, my house comes into view and I'm both relieved and disappointed that his truck isn't parked in my driveway. To get my mind off my own problems, I decide to spend the rest of the day at the youth center before going to the club tonight. The karaoke contest officially starts tonight. I've planned an elaborate set, so I'll have to get there early to set up.

When I walk in my bedroom, I see my cell phone on my nightstand and realize I never turned it back on this morning. I power it up and when it's fully loaded, I see I have several text messages waiting for me. Sighing, I tap the icon and see they're all from Luke.

But I don't deserve you.

I wish I could say how I feel.

You still awake?

Sweet dreams, beautiful.

None of these make me feel any better. Or tell me where we stand now. He had no trouble telling Brandon we were only friends and would never be anything more. That makes it hard for me to believe he couldn't say we're more than friends, if he really thought we are. I have turned this over and over in my mind until I'm dizzy. I shower, get dressed and head down to the youth center. Helping the kids always makes me feel better.

I spend several hours today working with the inner-city youth. The center offers many different services these kids wouldn't normally have access to, like tutors for school, coaches for different sports, creative arts, music, computers, and anything else we can get instructors to come in and teach. Most of the kids love it and come here every day that it's open.

Shane and Will come down a couple of times a month to coach some of the older boys on boxing. We have a strict policy on who is allowed in this program, though. When the center first opened, a couple of boys signed up for boxing lessons only to go back and show their gang members and use it against other kids. We learned quickly to be very selective of this program's participants. The only ones allowed in now are the ones who want to make it their career one day, who have never been in trouble, and have no gang ties. So far, our stricter policies are working well.

Crazy Maybe

I close up the center and start the forty-five minute drive home. I haven't received any texts or phone calls from Luke today and I can't help but feel disappointed. Even though I know Mack has kept him busy all day.

I don't want tonight at the club to be awkward, so I decide to send him a text when I get home. He did send me several last night that I never answered and I kind of feel guilty about that. Even if we were only friends, I still wouldn't ignore him like that.

When I pull in my garage, I send him a quick text that doesn't have any hidden meaning.

Been busy today – bet you have too. See you soon.

A couple of hours later, I arrive at the club to set up the stage for my song. Luckily, no one else has quite an elaborate setting, so I have the back part of the stage to myself. The curtains will hide my set up until it's my turn. I've set it up to look like a bedroom.

The area is basically rectangular, so the bed is arranged catty-corner in the back left corner. On the wall opposite the bed, there's a small table with roses, a bottle of wine and a wine glass with a small amount of wine in it. Luke will be dressed in all black and is playing the part of the death, which is seducing me as I sing. The lyrics of the song fit the set up perfectly, and with Luke's amazing body, it'll also be insanely erotic.

Right now, I'm wearing a simple, navy blue tank swing dress that flows easily over my curves. It stops just above mid-thigh, and adding my nude, strappy heels makes my legs look fabulous. But this isn't what I'm wearing during my show. For that, I borrowed a button down shirt from Shane, and that's all I'll wear, besides my black lace bra and matching silk panties. I'm going for the full bedroom look, so I wanted to wear a man's shirt like I just put it on after getting out of bed.

Crazy Maybe

I finish making sure everything is set up the way I want it, close the black curtains, and turn to find Luke watching me intently from one of the tables. His arms are folded across his broad chest and he's wearing all black just as I asked him to do. His black Under Armour shirt is skintight and I can see all his chest and arm muscles bulging under the material. His black jeans fit him perfectly, and his long, muscular legs are drool worthy. He's also wearing black boots that make him look even more badass than the scowl he's giving me right now.

It's still early so there's hardly anyone here that doesn't work here. The crowd won't be here for another couple of hours. I keep my eyes trained on Luke's as I make my way down the steps and walk toward him. His eyes rake over me from my head to my feet, then again from bottom to top, and I see a flash of desire that's quickly pushed down and replaced with more than a little hostility. I decide to approach him in my usual manner and not let him get to me.

"Hey there," I say warmly. "How was your day?"

He narrows his eyes and keeps his arms firmly crossed across his body, as if he's completely blocking me out. His response is short and curt; his tone holds a hint of challenge and suspicion.

"Fine. Yours?"

"It was good. Busy, but I got a lot done today so it was worth the time." I smile at him as I'm talking, trying to be as casual as possible. He seems a little more tense than usual and I am really not up for a huge blow up after crying myself to sleep last night.

"Oh? What did you do today? Who were you with?"

There's no doubt that he's suspicious and obviously thinks I was off with another guy. Though why that would bother him since we're *just friends* is beyond me.

I take a deep breath and consider how to explain the youth center to him without opening up a lot of questions I'm not ready to answer yet. I decide to go with the simplest answer that is also truthful, even if it doesn't explain everything.

"I don't think I've mentioned that I volunteer at a youth center for inner-city kids in downtown Atlanta. The boxes that were in my garage were donations for the center, so I took them down this morning, spent the day organizing and working with some of the kids that showed up."

He looks surprised and relieved at the same time. "A youth center? Really?" This time his tone of curiosity isn't also accusing.

"Yeah, I've done it for a long time now. A few guys from the gym volunteer there, too. They come in every couple of weeks or so," I shrug my shoulders and say, "It's as good for us as it is the kids."

He doesn't say anything else but the look he's giving me now is completely different than just a few seconds ago. He amazes me with how he can go from cold to hot and everything in between so quickly.

He inclines his head and eyes toward my dress and asks, "Is that what you're wearing for your song tonight?"

"Umm, no, I have a change of clothes in the dressing room in the back. Want to go grab some dinner with me? I can show you around backstage when we get back." I'm kicking myself for asking him that. I was going to state that I was going to eat but ended up asking him if he wanted to go instead. Just great.

CHAPTER EIGHT

ANDI

This restaurant was such a bad idea. The dark, intimate atmosphere is so not what I need with my *friend* right now. That's what he is–he confirmed it for me last night. I had to ask if he would still be part of my act tonight. Part of me really hoped he'd say no and make up some excuse. It's hard to see him and not want more from him. Part of me was really glad when he said yes because it's hard to not see him at all. I'm so screwed.

Our damn waitress isn't making things easier for me, either. She can't take her eyes off him and I swear she's trying to slip him her number every time she walks by our table. Her last attempt, during our salad and while she was refilling our drinks, really pushed me over the edge. Besides just being damn brazen, it was just plain rude. I'm sitting right here beside him at a restaurant that is not meant for friends or siblings. I mean seriously, she knows we're here together. Even if we're not *together*.

On her last attempt, I snatched the note from her hand and thanked her sweetly before saying, "How sweet. Bless your heart." Which, in this case, is Southern speak for *'you are a complete dumbass.'* She got the hint and quickly left our table. I scowled after her and crinkle the note in my fist before I realized what I was doing. I wanted to hold her stupid little note over the lit candle that's sitting in the middle of our table and watch it burn to ashes.

Luke is not even trying to hide his smile at my blatant act of jealousy. "Something wrong, Andi?" His cavalier attitude makes me want to tear into him but I know I must refrain from fits of jealousy, rage, and general insanity in public.

"Sorry about that. That was just rude of her to keep doing that in front of me. Here you go," and I hand him the little slip of paper that has her name and number on it, along with a crookedly drawn heart. *How ridiculous.* He looks at the note in my hand then back to my eyes, obviously confused at my actions.

Luke quizzes me, "Why would you *want* me to have her number?"

It seems I've unintentionally showed my hand. I'm not good with these damn games and I really just want to be honest with him. I take a shaky breath and look down at the white linen tablecloth, apparently longer than I realize because his warm hand covers my hand, the hand that still holds the waitress's phone number. I look up and see concern in his eyes and remind myself it's only friendly concern.

"Because you told Brandon we would never be more than friends. So if you're interested in her, I won't stand in your way." I can't even begin to describe how much that hurt to say it out loud to him. But I'd rather get it all out now and get it over with than go another day like the last twenty-four hours have been.

"Let me guess. Brandon called and asked you out so you're ready to kick me to the curb, right? Fine. That's just *fucking fine.*" Luke is really pissed now and I have no idea what he's even talking about.

I reply just as forcefully, "What the hell are you talking about? Brandon didn't call me and I wouldn't go out with him even if he did ask me."

This gets his attention and adds to his confusion, "You wouldn't go out with him?"

Now I'm confused. "No, I wouldn't. No offense to him - he's a great guy and all..." *but that would just be too weird since I've fallen for his brother.*

He's still unsure as he asks, "Then why did you say that?"

"Because I heard you say those very words to Brandon last night. Outside, at your parents' house. I was cleaning up and I heard you when I came around the side of the house. You were pretty loud, so I know I didn't misunderstand you."

I had no intentions of blurting this out to him—ever. I'm really at my wits end with trying to decipher his male code to find out if he wants more from me than friends or not. For most of the night, I really thought he was ready to take a chance. But I felt like a complete fool when I heard what he said to Brandon. If he only wants to be friends, I will be a friend to him. But I can't keep up this kind of relationship with him any longer.

And handing him that damn waitress's number? That just plain hurt. So I know without a doubt that I couldn't stand hearing about his dates like I do with Shane. Shane and I talk openly about his dates and there's not one bit of jealousy or hurt feelings. I laugh at Shane's exploits—he always has an interesting story to tell about his latest conquest. Knowing that Luke would want that with someone else, but not with me, would be unbearable.

So, I'm sitting here uncomfortably waiting for Luke's response. He has to know he can't deny saying it. I recited his words back to him basically verbatim. I really fell for him too fast, so I can't blame him for not feeling the same way about me. I can't be mad—I have no right to be, I *know* that. I just don't *feel* that.

When he doesn't respond for what feels like an eternity, I feel the need to fill in the uncomfortable silence.

"Look, we can be just friends. You told me you're not a relationship kind of guy and that hasn't changed. It's okay. After tonight's performance is over, we won't have to spend so much time together."

The more I talk, the more it hurts, but someone has to say something. All this time together hasn't changed his mind and I refuse to be his friend with benefits. Not judging anyone else—that's just not for me. I obviously get too attached, too easily, and too fast. Otherwise, I could have wild monkey sex every night. This is my curse, though.

LUKE

Well, fuck me.

First, she ignores my texts from last night. Then she goes all day without calling, texting or coming to the gym. I've been worried about her all day and couldn't wait to see her. I didn't get a wink of sleep last night for thinking about her and how she acted when she got out of my truck. Then after I sent her all those texts last night and she didn't respond when I told her I wanted her, I was sure I had crossed the line and she didn't want me after all.

Crazy Maybe

Then I find her at the club, dressed to the damn nines and looking sexy as hell. She didn't even hear me come in, but if she'd been meeting some other guy I was damn sure going to put a stop to it. The past few weeks of hanging out with her have been great and I wasn't about to let some other fucker step in and mess up my good thing.

But when she tried to give me the waitress's note just now, my first thought was she was trying to get rid of me. Everything added up to that until she repeated the words I said to Brandon. My blood was fucking boiling, thinking my brother had called her or made a move on her. I would beat his fucking ass and I wouldn't care what my family thought about it.

Then she said she heard me say it, and right now I'm sure being sucker-punched in the gut couldn't hurt worse than this feeling. I can't even blame Brandon for this. This is all my fault. All my doing, because I wouldn't be a man and say what I really wanted.

How do I come out of this without looking like a weak-ass punk? I sigh heavily and think to myself, "*You don't. You deserve what you get.*"

I take her hands in mine and look deeply into her eyes, keeping my gaze glued to hers to hopefully show my sincerity. I'm eternally grateful for how this restaurant is designed. Rather than having the table separate us, the seats are designed for couples to sit intimately beside each other, sharing food and spending quality time together. She's so close that the sweet scent of her perfume invades my senses every time she moves.

"Andi, first of all, I'm sorry I ever said that to Brandon. It's not how I really feel at all. Brandon and I have a difficult...history. Also, I didn't want to say anything to him before I'd even talked to you about it. I really hate that you heard that."

She looks at me with blatant skepticism and I don't blame her. I've given her so many mixed signals and if I'm completely honest, I don't even know that I can do this. But what I do know is I don't want to go another day like today-without seeing her, hearing from her and thinking I'd lost her. My concentration wasn't for shit today, and if it hadn't been for Shane, I probably would've left the gym to go find her.

I stroke my knuckles across her cheek and feel a twinge of electricity move through me. I open my hand and place my palm on her cheek then push my fingers into her hair while my thumb lightly strokes along her neck. She closes her eyes for a moment and leans into my touch and I'm captured again by how beautiful she is.

"You're so beautiful, Andi. You literally take my breath away when I look at you," I whisper to her. "Please just...forget I said that to Brandon. He was trying to rile me up and I just wanted to block him."

I watch as she swallows hard but her eyes are still averted from mine. She nods and turns away from me. She reaches for her glass and I notice the trembling in her hand.

"Talk to me, Andi."

She takes a minute but she finally answers. "I've never been one to hold in my feelings, Luke. I've always believed it was best to just put them out there...to be up front so there's no confusion. But I've went completely against that with you because I...well, I wanted you to come to your decision on your own. Without any pressure from me. But I can't do this anymore."

My heart just stopped beating.

I'm sure I'll keel over in the floor any second now. When she finally looks at me, the pain in her eyes is so evident that I almost wish I would just fall over.

"I can't pretend that I only want you as a friend. I meant when I said I don't do one-night stands or friends with benefits though. If you think you want anything more than friends with me, you have to be sure because I can't do this back and forth anymore. Decide what *you* really want, Luke, and do it soon...or I'll make the decision for you and it'll be final."

Well, shit. Did she just really give me an ultimatum?

"If you only want a friend, that's fine. I will be friends with you but nothing else. No flirting. No touching. No more mixed messages. *Just friends*. And I'll move on. Just...decide."

I nod and before I can say anything in response, the flirty waitress returns, much more subdued this time since Andi embarrassed her, and places our dinners in front of us. We somehow make it through the meal with idle conversation and go back to the club together. Several of our friends are already there and we make our way through the crowd to join them at our usual table. Just as we sit down, I look up and saw Brandon moving through the crowd toward us.

Isn't this night just getting better and better? Yeah, because he wasn't even looking at me. He is making a beeline for Andi. *Ah, hell no!* Andi sees him and stands to hug him and I can't withhold my sarcasm.

"Well, look what the cat dragged in."

Andi, sweet as ever, keeps her eyes on Brandon and says, "Have a seat!" So, of course, the bastard sits in the empty chair beside Andi, forcing me to lean up and look around her to see him.

Crazy Maybe

"What are you doing here, Brandon?" I demand rudely.

"Alicia mentioned Andi was singing tonight and we wanted to hear her," Brandon answers coolly, not even bothering to take his eyes off Andi while he answers me.

"*We?* Who is *we?*" I ask sardonically before I see Alicia and her husband, Greg, making their way to our table. Shane and Will grab a couple of chairs for them and I make introductions all around the table.

I make the stupid mistake of removing my hand from the back of Andi's chair and Brandon's arm quickly takes up the empty space. I take Andi's hand in mine and ask, "Dance with me?" She nods and I shoot Brandon a warning look as I stand up.

A slow song comes on when we get to the dance floor and I pull her in tight against me, brushing a kiss on her cheek. I feel a small shudder run through her as her body molds into mine. We start moving with the music and I tighten my arms around her just a little more.

"Andi," I murmur in her ear then pull back so she will look me in the eye. She looks up at me from under her long lashes, with a hint of shyness about her that sends a sudden protective impulse through me.

Before I can say anything else, someone comes up and taps Andi on the shoulder, "You're up in ten minutes."

Andi nods at the rude moment-stealer and looks back at me. "You ready for this?"

I nod at her and look around the club as she takes my hand to lead me backstage. *Holy hell – there are a lot of people here tonight!*

CHAPTER NINE

ANDI

I'm not over-analyzing why Brandon is here. Or why Luke seems so pissed about why Brandon's here. I'm not even going to think about what Luke was about to say when Mitch came up to tell me my song is coming up soon. I'm just going to get in character, sing my song, and have fun with a bunch of great people tonight.

I will not think about how seductive this song is or how my body will react to singing it to Luke in front of the entire club.

I will not think about it.

I will not.

Shit, that's all I can think about.

I lead Luke backstage and show him to the dressing rooms since we didn't have time to do it after dinner. He doesn't really need the dressing room since he's already wearing his "costume." Well, except for the Lone Ranger-type mask that he'll be wearing. I may have forgot to mention that to him before because he's not looking real happy as I hand it to him.

"Please? It'll work, trust me," I console him as innocently as possible. He huffs and puffs a little but finally concedes.

His consent earns him a kiss on the cheek. "If I'd known you were going to do that, I would've turned my head and made you plant it square on my mouth," he seductively chides me.

I playfully tell him to behave before adding, "Give me just a minute to change and we'll get set up on the stage." He nods and waits outside the dressing room door for me. I may have also forgot to mention to him that I'll only be wearing a man's button down shirt onstage.

Yeah, I definitely forgot to mention this little fact. When I open the door and casually say, "Come on, Luke," he quickly grabs my arm and twirls me around to face him.

"Where the hell are the rest of your clothes?" He is literally growling the words at me. I mean, I've read about how men "growl" out a response, but I'm almost positive he's about to turn into some kind of man-beast right in front of me.

"This is it–this is my costume." My eyes are big and innocent, like I have no idea what he's referring to. His eyes narrow to mere slits in his face, which by the way, has turned into a lovely shade of scarlet-red due to the high volume of blood rushing for the top of his head.

"The hell you say! You are not going out there like this!"

"Yes, I am. This fits the scene, Luke." I stay calm, knowing that yelling right now will only delay us getting the stage even more.

"Whose. Shirt. Is. That?" Each word is pointed, sharp and holds deeper meaning that he will even say out loud.

"Shane's." This answer visibly relaxes him for a split second.

"WHY THE HELL IS IT UNBUTTONED?" He's just now realized this little fact.

"It's not unbuttoned," I start but his stance becomes increasingly menacing, "all the way. The last two are buttoned."

Crazy Maybe

He is about to go nuclear when Mitch saves me as he calls out, "Andi, you need to be onstage now."

"Okay!" I happily rush toward the back entrance to the stage and call over my shoulder, "Luke, put your mask on and get in position."

Luke has no choice but to follow me now and he knows he has to be quiet because the previous performer isn't quite finished yet. I take my place at the table with the wine and roses while Luke crouches down to hide behind the bed. When the curtains open and the music for my song starts, I'm transformed into another world and I forget all about Luke being pissed off about my lack of clothing.

The microphone is fit snugly over my ear so I can use both hands freely and move about the stage. I'm singing *Familiar Taste of Poison*, by Halestorm tonight. Love is the familiar poison. The wine is a metaphor for love. Her lover urges her to consume all of it, until she is completely consumed with him, but apparently he doesn't need her as much as she needs him.

The music starts off slow and ominous, but seductive and alluring at the same time. My voice is soft as the song starts. After the first couple of lines, I pick up the wine glass and empty wine bottle and move to the front of the stage. Luke stands up from behind the bed, wearing all black and holding a long-handled sickle in one hand. I sing the next few lines of the first verse and begin the chorus.

As I sing, I sit on the floor of the stage and lay the empty wine bottle down beside me. I then take a small capsule filled with a white powder, break it open, and pour it into the wineglass as I finish the last line of the chorus. The music continues while I drink the wine with the imaginary poison in it.

Crazy Maybe

I put the glass down and stand back up, leaving the empty bottle and glass lying on the stage floor well in front of me and out of the way. Luke, playing the part of death, lays the sickle down, steps out from behind the bed, and stealthily moves to the front of the stage, until he's standing just behind me.

I look over my shoulder at Luke as I sing the first line of the next verse.

He's behind me but my movements mimic his, as if I'm his puppet on his string while he's seducing me until he completely owns me. He's so close to me, his front to my back, as death continues to seduce me, and I sing the rest of the verse.

My voice becomes a little louder and more forceful as I repeat the chorus. After the first line of the chorus, Luke's arm snakes around my waist. Because my shirt is unbuttoned, his hand slides inside the shirt and is warm against my skin. He pushes himself closer into me from behind and tightens his grip around my front.

At the end of the chorus, Luke moves around to my side and I turn to fully face him, our profiles to the audience. The crescendo of the music and my voice hit the high point of the song. The pull I feel to him is intense. We didn't rehearse it this way, but I can't help but be drawn into him. My arm reaches out to him, encircles his neck, and our faces are mere inches apart as I sing the next verse to him, oblivious to the throngs of people watching.

My hands are on his face and our eyes are locked in place on each other, never wavering. I feel his muscular arms move down my back until they rest just under my ass. Suddenly, he lifts me up and my legs wrap around his waist. I'm still singing to him but we must look like we're making love on stage. And I don't even care because I am so lost in this man right now.

Crazy Maybe

As I sing the last repeat of the chorus, he begins walking back to the far side of the bed, so he can lay me down on it but not block the audience's view of the show as I continue singing to him.

My legs are straight and my arms are folded over my chest, as if I'm now dead, and Luke leans in and deeply kisses me, sliding his tongue in my mouth and gently caresses mine. Just as the music starts to fade away, he stands erect and holds the sickle again, as if death itself is now standing over my lifeless body.

The curtains close and the crowd erupts in thunderous applause. I open my eyes and Luke helps me stand up off the makeshift bed as he takes his mask off. The curtains open again and we take our bow at the front of the stage.

I'm the first one to turn around and head backstage. My feet quickly carry me toward he dressing room. My body is still humming with electricity from Luke's touch and his kiss. I can't even think straight but I can feel him behind me, close on my heels. I march into the dressing room but I can't turn around just yet. I hear him come in behind me and slam the door shut.

Before I can blink, I'm spun around and pushed up against the door. Luke lifts me and my legs instinctively wrap around his waist. He leans in and greedily takes my mouth with his. The kiss is furious and feverish, like neither of us can get enough. His obvious erection is grinding into me and every thrust is excruciatingly delicious through the flimsy silk panties I'm wearing under this shirt. The shirt that is now being pushed off my shoulders as Luke's mouth moves down my neck and onto my collarbones.

LUKE

If anyone had told me that karaoke could be considered foreplay, I would've said they were full of shit and obviously not doing it right. That is, before tonight, while I was onstage with Andi and had to use every bit of my restraint to not make her totally and completely mine in front of the whole damn club. Especially when she climbed up my body and wrapped her legs around me.

We did not rehearse that scene like that, but when she moved into me while singing that song, it just felt so natural. Of course, while we rehearsed our parts, she wasn't actually singing the song. We just played the original song over and over. But *holy hell*, Andi singing it while staring into my eyes made me seriously afraid I was going to embarrass myself onstage.

I really didn't like her wearing just that button down shirt and her sexy bra and panties onstage. But I have to admit that it really did fit the scene she created. And I really appreciated it when my hand slid under the shirt and across her silky smooth skin. Speaking of silky smooth, I about lost my shit when I slid my hands under her ass to lift her up to straddle me. But she's never wearing anything like that on stage again. EVER.

Now I'm following her to the dressing room and she's moving through the people milling about back stage like a fucking freight train. I don't know if she's trying to get away from me or trying to get alone with me, but I'm not giving her one damn second to push me

Crazy Maybe

away. Enough's enough. We are good together and we're going to give this attraction a chance.

I close and lock the door behind me and grab her up before she can overthink it. She's so responsive to me that I'm not sure who initiated the kiss but it's awesome. I have her pinned against the door and her legs are around my waist again. She feels so damn good, like she's made for me, and I haven't even got inside her yet. It's all I can do to break the kiss and move down her neck to other interesting areas.

I push the shirt off her shoulders easily – Shane's a big guy so this shirt swallows her whole. I lick, kiss, and bite down her neck to her collarbones. I'm amazed at how sexy they are. I push the shirt down more until her arms are free and the shirt pools around her hips. I pull back to look at her flushed face, lips swollen from our kiss, her breasts moving in time with her heavy breaths, and I'm again floored at how beautiful and sexy she is.

I take one of the taut buds of her nipples in my mouth through the lacy bra she's wearing and lightly tug on it with my teeth. She moans approvingly and her hand tightens into a fist in my hair, slightly pulling on it and driving me into a frenzy. I'm about to tear the bra off her body when the door behind us suddenly vibrates from someone pounding on it.

"Hurry up in there, Andi!" The voice on the other side of the door calls.

Andi drops her head to my shoulder in frustration before answering, "Ok, Sandy, be right out."

"We *will* finish this later tonight, Andi." I am leaving no room for argument. This is killing me to let her go but I do enjoy watching her put her dress and high heels back on.

Once she finishes dressing, I wrap my arms around her and add, "Andi, I don't want a one-night stand or a

92

friend with benefits. I want to be with you and only you. I want to give us a chance."

Her answer sends shivers down my spine. "I'm with you, Luke. I'm with you."

The other girl comes rushing in the room as soon as Andi opens the door and we make our way back to our friends. Alicia gushes at Andi over her performance and everyone congratulates us on the show but I give all the credit to Andi. "This was all Andi's creativity. I just did what she told me to."

Brandon's knowing eyes picked up on a change in me with Andi. "You two sure are good friends, Luke." I see Andi tense at his dig and know she is thinking about my words from last night.

"Yeah, I couldn't ask for a better friend than Andi," and her head quickly jerks in my direction as she looks up at me in disbelief, "and I couldn't ask for a better girlfriend, either." I smile at her and watch as her face visibly softens and her gorgeous smile fills her face.

Brandon can't hide his blatant look of satisfaction at my declaration. I admit that I have to consider that my brother is a better man than I've given him credit for in the past. I sit down beside him and he leans over toward me, "Best decision you've ever made, little brother." I nod thoughtfully, knowing deep down, he is completely right.

We're hanging around the club until they announce which contestants will move on to the next round. Of course, Andi is one of them because she was phenomenal on stage. Her next round is two weeks from tonight.

Knowing there is nothing else holding us here, I am not ashamed to admit that I ushered my *girlfriend* out of the club because I have more exciting plans for us tonight. And none of them involve an audience. I follow

Crazy Maybe

her back to her house and I absolutely cannot wait to be the one to undress her this time. She pulls into her garage and opens the other door so I can park my truck inside. As the door slides back down, I steal up behind her where she's about to unlock the door.

I slide my arms around her waist from behind and kiss the side of her neck. She's struggling to get the key in the door and I'm enjoying the affect I have on her, so I run my fingers up her sides when she suddenly shrieks and tries to jump away from me. Only she's between the door and me with nowhere to go. Seems I've found a ticklish spot on her so I do it again. And again.

Now she's laughing so hard she can barely hold her keys. She wiggles in my arms until she is able to turn and face me. She holds up her hands in mock surrender and laughingly warns me to stop or we'll never get in the house. The look of pure happiness and playfulness takes me by surprise. Suddenly I can't get inside the house fast enough. I smile and take the keys from her hand and step into her, again pinning her between door and me.

The passionate kiss that suddenly erupts is unbelievably hot and all consuming. I am suddenly so rock hard its painful and only Andi can make it feel better. Without breaking contact, I somehow manage to unlock the door and carry her to her bedroom. We fall to the bed together, never breaking apart, and even though the dress she's wearing tonight barely covers her ass, it suddenly feels like she has way too many clothes on.

I feel the unwavering and unyielding need to help her with this predicament.

94

CHAPTER TEN

ANDI

My college science professor denied that the human body could spontaneously combust. I beg to differ, Dr. So-and-So. At this very moment, I'm positive you are full of shit because my body feels like it will burst out in flames any second now. Especially when he does *that right there*–oh my god! Thank you, sir. I will definitely take another.

My hands move down his wide shoulders, firm back, and to his narrow waist where I find the hem of his shirt. I start pulling it up to take it off of him when he suddenly reaches one hand back, grabs the shirt, and whips it over his head in under one second flat. His bare skin feels incredible under my hands. I can feel every move of his muscles, every cord and ripple in his back and shoulders.

"It's time for you to slip into something more comfortable, Andi," he whispers seductively in my ear and I just melt even more. He rolls to my side and I stand up beside the bed. I splay my hands out across my chest and slowly move them down the front of my dress, swaying seductively until I reach the hem. Then I slowly pull it up and over my head, revealing the matching black bra and panties he'd seen earlier.

As my arms pull the dress over the top of my head, Luke suddenly springs from the bed and holds my hands behind my head. He steps back and looks at me appreciatively and longingly. I take in his devastatingly handsome face, his chiseled chest, and his washboard abs. He is beautiful all over but he's still way over-dressed with those black jeans on. I try to pull my hand out of his grasp to help him with those pesky jeans but he holds tighter and shakes his head 'no.'

"This is just about where we got to when we were so rudely interrupted earlier," his deep voice rumbles, before his mouth finds my nipple again. I moan in pleasure, as Luke moves one hand into my hair and grasps it firmly. He increases his pressure, tugging on one nipple with his teeth, and then he moves his attention to the other one.

All the flirting, teasing and touching leading up to tonight has made it impossible for me to wait one more minute. "Luke, *please...*"

"Please, what, baby? Tell me what you want."

"I can't wait any longer. Please, Luke."

He lets go of my hands and my dress falls to the floor. My hands are now free and immediately find the button on his pants. Within a couple of seconds, he sheds his pants. His body is pure perfection and I suddenly want to run my tongue over every inch of him. I reach out to touch his stomach, running my fingers along the ripples of his six-pack and down the V that runs down each side and disappears under the waistband of his boxer briefs.

His blue eyes darken with lust and anticipation. I dip one finger just under his waistband and lightly scrape my nail along the sensitive skin. I lightly brush the head of his impressive manhood and feel it jerk in response at the same time he inhales a sharp breath with a hiss. Moving both hands around his waist, I flatten my palms against his back, fingers pointed downward, and slowly inch them into his briefs and scrape my fingernails against the cheeks of his ass.

Crazy Maybe

He growls in pleasure then quickly sheds his briefs, standing before me completely naked with all his glorious muscles showing. His hands go around my back and deftly unhook my bra, letting it cascade down my arms until it drops to the floor. His big hands raise and take both of my breasts in his hands, caressing and kneading them at first. Then he starts rubbing his thumb across my sensitive nipples, causing me to arch my back and move closer into him.

My hands mold around his sides and then move down to grasp his long, thick shaft that is standing erect, at full attention right in front of me. I grasp him with both hands, cupping his sensitive balls with one hand while stroking his impressive length with the other. Luke pulls me in to him and kisses me thoroughly, melting me again and making my legs weak.

His fingers trail down my stomach until he reaches the very core of me. His hand strokes me lightly through the silky material first, finding that it is already drenched with my want and need. His fingers move the flimsy material aside and stroke my wet core that is waiting just inside. His all-male groan of approval sends shivers through me.

"My God, Andi, you're killing me."

Before I can answer, his thick finger plunges inside me and I loudly gasp in pleasure. I'm already so close and he's barely even touched me. When his thumb circles my nub while his finger keeps moving in and out of me, I have to grip his shoulders and hold on. He feels my orgasm building, clenching his finger inside me and my breathing and moans getting louder.

He urges me on, softly muttering in my ear, "That's it, baby. Let me hear you." Then his thumb presses a little harder on my nub as he inserts a second finger inside me. I can't hold back my scream of pleasure as

97

the waves of my climax claims my entire body. He's watching me with pure hunger in his eyes and complete longing to finish what he's started. I'm so ready for him, but there's something I need to do first. So when he loosens his grip where he's helped hold me upright, I willingly drop to my knees in front of him and take him in my mouth.

LUKE

I'm going to fucking explode just watching her. That was the most incredible sight I've ever seen and now I just want to see the look of pure satisfaction on her face over and over again. I want to be the one–the only one–who gives her that look. I love how much she wants me. She's so wet right now and I can't wait to take her, finish making her mine. I just released my hold on her so I can move her to the bed, but she has completely taken me by surprise. But in a completely different way.

She just dropped to her knees and wrapped her beautiful, plump lips around me. I swear I've died and gone to heaven. Her mouth feels so damn good–wet, soft, and velvety. Her tongue is circling round and round and it feels incredible. She is almost taking the full length of me in her mouth until I hit the back of her throat over and over again. My hips reflexively move in time with her and I'm completely lost in her until I suddenly realize I don't want this kind of happy ending right now.

Crazy Maybe

I inwardly groan, my body is revolting against my mind's decision to stop her obvious talents. But my hands obey my mind's command and still her, "Baby, you are amazing, but I want nothing more right now than to be inside you."

I pull her to her feet and cover her mouth with mine, my tongue darting in her mouth and dancing with hers as I walk her backwards to the bed. When her knees hit the bed, I gently push her shoulders down so that she's sitting, then I nudge her until she's flat on her back and her lower legs are still hanging off the side.

I pick up her feet one at a time and put them on my shoulders. She raises her head to look at me as I lower my mouth to her nub. I dart my tongue out, circle her nub, and her hips buck against my mouth. She likes it. I smile and go back to work on her, but this time I suck it into my mouth and let my teeth lightly graze across it.

She's breathless as she says again, "Luke, *please*, baby...."

"What, sweetheart? Tell me what you want. Anything, baby."

"You. I want you *inside* me. *NOW!*"

I lift her and move her fully onto the bed and position myself above her. I'm positioned at her wet entrance and I'm about to push into her when the wetness registers and I realize I'm not wearing a condom.

"Shit."

"What's wrong, Luke? What are you waiting for?"

"I don't have a condom with me, baby."

She lets out a loud groan and every masculine cell in my body loves that she wants me so badly.

"I'm clean, Luke. I haven't been with anyone in...a few years...but I get tested along with everyone else at the gym. And I had birth control implanted in my arm."

Crazy Maybe

I'm so relieved to hear this from her. I haven't wanted to ask about her past boyfriends, but I'm glad it's been a long time since she's been with someone.

"I'm clean, too, baby. It's been a while for me but I've never had sex without a condom–ever. You'll be my first. But I still get tested frequently."

She nods in agreement and I hold her face in my hands, keeping her eyes on mine. I wanted to plunge into her hard and fast until I remember she said it's been a few years since she's been with anyone. I definitely don't want to hurt her. My thumbs lightly stroke along her cheekbones as I slowly enter her, giving her body time to adjust to my considerable size. She fits me like a tight, wet, velvet glove and I know if I moved at this very moment, this would all be over way too soon.

Apparently the wait is too long for my sexy little vixen because she pleads, "Luke, please, *move*." I'm trying to think of anything except how amazing she feels under me, with me inside her, hearing her ragged breaths, and her voice asking me for more. FUCK, this isn't helping! I somehow conjure a mental picture of Gran and it seems to help.

I begin moving slowly until I'm sure I've regained complete control of my soldiers who were threatening to go AWOL. Soon, Andi's ecstasy is pushing me on until she's fully taking me and I'm pushing into her with abandon.

When I can no longer hold back, I reach between our bodies and find her sensitive, swollen nub. I start rubbing it in circles, sending shock waves through her body and through her inner sex walls. They clench me in a viselike grip and I grunt, "Now, baby. Drench me." As if on command, she's coming and I feel her ripples flexing around me and she screams in bliss. I quickly

100

Crazy Maybe

follow her, unable to hold back one more second, and empty myself into her.

I collapse on top of her and quickly realize I must be crushing her petite body under me. I roll over and take her with me so that she's lying completely on top of me. I'm still inside her–I can't bring myself to pull out yet. I feel her smile against my chest and I kiss the top of her head and I stroke her back. I feel her breaths become even and realize she's fallen asleep on top of me.

It is in this moment that I decide I can never let her go. I don't know when or how it happened, but I know without a doubt I am thoroughly and completely in love with this incredible woman. The realization both scares and electrifies me so much I can't relax enough to sleep more than a couple of hours at a time. I wake her up twice more during the night to make slow, sensuous love to her. Each time she's just as receptive to me as she was the first time.

When she wakes Sunday morning, I'm already awake and watching her sleep. She looks so happy and satisfied and I can't help but feel a swell of pride at knowing I've given her at least some of that. She smiles at me when she sees I'm staring and my heart skips a beat.

"Good morning," she says through her sleepy smile.

"Good morning, baby," I answer, stroking her cheek and down her neck.

"Were you watching me sleep?"

"I was. Can't take my eyes off you." This earns me another smile, but that's not why I said it. I literally mean I can't take my eyes off of her–she has mesmerized me.

"So, today is our standard family get together day and my parents want you to come. Want to go with me?" I ask tentatively, knowing how the last visit went.

"I'd love to come with you."

And there's no denying the double meaning in her response and I definitely don't have the heart to deny her. So I pounce on her once again in the bed. Then again in the shower.

CHAPTER ELEVEN

ANDI

I'm really having a hard time focusing on the catalog of outdoor furniture Linda is showing me. I can't stop thinking about last night and this morning with Luke...mainly because I'm delightfully sore from our bedroom acrobatics. I mentally chastise myself and force myself to pay attention. She's showing me the set she wants for the garden area around the pool. It sounds so simple, but I've never had a mother who asked for my opinion before. She makes me feel like a part of the family.

Linda finally settles on one the one she wants just as Sam walks in the room. "Honey, I've decided."

"Wonderful. On what?" His bored, semi-listening tone indicates he's heard this phrase a few hundred times from her.

"The patio set I'm going to get."

This gets his attention. "Hmm...let's see," he says as he walks over to the kitchen table. Linda shows him the page and Sam whistles low and serious as he looks at the price. "It'll have to wait, babe."

Linda nods her head and says, "I was hoping to get it on sale at the end of the season if there are any sets left over."

Linda and I cook while Luke and Brandon are outside helping Sam with some heavy work in the yard. Linda is very witty and her dry, sarcastic humor is hilarious to me. We spend the majority of our time

Crazy Maybe

together laughing at her stories of Luke and Brandon growing up, all the trouble they got into, and how they were with Alicia.

I could listen to her talk about their family life for hours. She's teaching me how to cook some of Luke's favorite dishes. I furiously blink back the tears when she puts her arm around my shoulders and squeezes me to her for no apparent reason.

Sam, Luke, and Brandon all come piling in the kitchen–sweaty, dirty and hungry–from putting down concrete pavers for Linda's extended patio. Linda sends them to clean up before we set the table. Once we're all gathered back in the kitchen, we take our seats at the table. The conversation eventually turns to stories of Luke and Brandon growing up, which leads to questions about my childhood.

Questions and answers Luke and I haven't even discussed yet. I feel bad about talking about it now, in front of everyone, but I don't really feel like I have a choice.

"Andi, do your parents live nearby?" Sam asks in between bites of food. I see Luke's fork freeze in mid-air as he looks at his dad then at me.

"Dad, I don't know if-"

I touch his arm and say, "Its fine, Luke." Then I turn my gaze to Sam and answer him, "They used to live in the area, but they died when I was six." I try to keep my tone casual and light, as if this is a question I answer every day. The truth is I never really talk about them because that leads to more questions.

"I'm so sorry, Andi. We had no idea," Linda doesn't look at me with pity and sympathy, which is the worst. She looks at me with understanding in her eyes.

Sam continues, "What happened? If you don't mind me asking."

Crazy Maybe

Linda gives him a disapproving look before turning to me, "If you don't want to talk about this, we won't push."

"No, really, I'm okay. That's if Luke doesn't mind– we haven't really gotten around to all this yet," I say, looking around the table at the people who I'm beginning to think of as family before turning to Luke. His face softens at my statement directed toward him and nods.

I continue, "They were killed in a car wreck. I wasn't with them but I'm told they died instantly."

"Who did you live with?" Luke asks, and I notice he isn't eating anymore.

I clear my throat to try to expel the emotion building up. Here we go. "My mom's cousin Jean and her husband took me in for a little while. But when Jean found out she couldn't get to my inheritance, she didn't want me anymore, so she gave me up to the state."

"Foster homes," Brandon states, obviously disgusted, "She *willingly* put you into the foster care system. Your own blood kin." His indignation on my behalf is blatant toward Jean. I can't look up at them even though I feel all eyes on me, willing me to look at them and finish my story.

"Yes, I stayed in foster care until I was sixteen and I contacted my parents' attorney. He had been a friend of theirs for years before they died and he remembered me. He helped me gain legal emancipation from the state. I met Mack soon after."

"Did you move in with Mack?" Linda asks, hesitantly.

I shake my head and laugh a little, "No. Mack is a career bachelor and I was a teenage girl. He was afraid of how it would look–for both of us."

105

Crazy Maybe

"How did you meet Mack?" Luke asks. Now he's holding my hand under the table.

I look into Luke's caring eyes and I know what I say next will be hard for him to hear. I start to speak but can't find my voice for a few seconds. "Wow, this is harder than I thought it would be." He squeezes my hand and patiently waits.

"I had been staying in a seedy area of town until I got access to my trust fund and could move to an apartment. So, I was walking back to the motel and," I take a deep breath and watch Luke's jaw muscles harden, "a group of guys came out of nowhere, calling out to me, taunting me. They pretty much surrounded me. Mack was leaving a nearby apartment and the guys knew Mack and knew better than to mess with him. He took me to his friend's place that night and the next day I moved into my apartment. Mack insisted I come to the gym with him every day so he could teach me to defend myself."

Luke swallows hard, taking it all in and considering what to ask next. I know how hard it is to find that balance between curiosity and rudeness, so I try to help fill in some of the blanks.

"I finished high school early at an alternative school and went to college. I had the normal college life. I lived in the dorms my freshman year, made a lot of friends, had fun, and studied hard. That's where I met Christina, Tania and Katie," I stated, looking at Luke. "During college, I realized I wanted to help kids who don't have anyone to believe in them. That's when I started working at the youth center, trying to make a difference for even one."

"That is very impressive, Andi," Sam says sincerely.

"What was your major?" Brandon asks as he fills his plate with a giant piece of chocolate cake.

"Law," I answer quickly, hoping they let it go.

"You went to law school?"

"Have you taken the bar?"

"You're a lawyer?"

"What kind of law?"

They're all fire questions at me simultaneously and I look around the table to each person, unable to hide my nervousness. I know I don't look like the typical lawyer, with the pink chunks in my blond hair and my tattoo sleeve. Not to mention, there's always questions about how I afforded the cost of law school.

"Um, yes, I went to law school, took and passed the bar, so I'm a licensed attorney now. I'm not practicing full time right now, but I do pro bono work with the firm I interned under every now and then. Mostly juvenile justice–sticking with helping the kids."

The term *'stunned silence'* comes to mind right about now. Everyone is staring at me and I have no clue what they're thinking.

LUKE

"Well, dear, I'm beyond impressed with you. This may be extremely rude, and you don't have to answer. But if you're not working, how can you afford to live?"

"Mom!" I half-yell at her. Yes, that is extremely fucking rude to ask and none of her damn business. But it's also the question that's on my mind even if I don't want to admit it.

Andi squeezes my hand and speaks before I can say anything else, "My inheritance. My parents were very successful and their lawyer worked it out for me to have early access to my trust fund. It's been more than enough for me to live on."

Andi and I really should've had this discussion before now. I'm sitting here with my family and just learning all this about her at the same time they are. I saw the hesitancy in her eyes when the questions started. I know part of it is because she realizes she didn't tell me first. I can tell she's holding back. She's not telling the full story, but she'll tell me when she's ready.

We move outside and enjoy the cooling temperatures by the pool. Andi and I sit together on a chaise lounge chair. She's in between my legs, lying back on my chest, and I wrap my arms around her. She lays her arms on top of mine and squeezes, like she can't get me close enough to her. Brandon takes the chair beside us and the three of us are having a friendly conversation. I know Brandon secretly wishes he'd met Andi first and I can't blame him for that. I'm all too glad to have her in my arms so I can't begrudge him a little jealousy over my girlfriend.

My dad brings us each an ice-cold beer from the cooler and I let go of Andi to take mine. A few drops of cold water from the bottle drop on her tattooed arm and my fingertip automatically goes to it, rubbing it in her smooth skin. I take a minute to study her sleeve, taking time to look at the individual tattoos that make it up, and let my finger trace the lines. I think they're both beautiful and sexy as hell on her.

"Not that I don't love it, but what made you decide to get a sleeve?" I ask, noticing that Brandon is also interested in both my question and her arm. Since we've already invaded her privacy as a family tonight, I doubt she'll mind talking about her ink.

Crazy Maybe

She sits up and turns sideways, facing Brandon, but still in my lap. She looks over her shoulder at me, takes my hand and places it on her shoulder. I look at her curiously and she guides my hand down her arm. It doesn't hit me at first but when I realize what she's telling me, my entire body becomes rigid. Except my hand–it decides it needs to feel her arm again to make sure my mind didn't misread what my hand just felt.

It didn't. There are several scars on her shoulder and all the way down her arm to her wrist, where my hand now rests. In my peripheral vision, I can see Brandon watching us intently but he doesn't interrupt. Andi's looking at me in anticipation as if she's afraid of my reaction.

"Luke," she says quietly and her eyes are pleading with me, "I need you to promise me something."

"Name it, baby."

"There are…things…about my childhood I've never told *anyone*. When I tell you, I need you to believe me. Do you trust me enough to promise me that?" Her tone is calm and loving, like she normally is, but there's real fear in her eyes. Fear I've never seen in her before and that bothers me. She's so strong and has obviously faced so much. It worries me what would be left for her to actually fear now. There's nothing I wouldn't do to take that fear away from her.

"I will believe you. I promise, Andi," I say the words so she'll have doubt of my resolve. I mean it with everything that I am.

She nods and turns back to lie in my arms. I don't expect her to say anything, and I've honestly already forgotten my question, but her voice is strong and without emotion as she speaks.

Crazy Maybe

"I got the tattoos to cover up the scars on my arm. I decided when people stare, they could at least have something more interesting to look at."

I squeeze my arms around her tighter, a silent promise that I'm here with her, because I don't know what to say. She doesn't say anything else about it and I don't press. She said *"when"* she tells me and that she hasn't told anyone else. I understand her—when she's ready, she will tell me and only me. She doesn't want anyone else around when we talk about it. My mind is already considering whom it is I will have to kill for hurting her.

The words from the song she sang the night of Gran's party come back to me and I realize the importance of them to her. I now understand why she looked and sounded so vulnerable that night—to me, at least. Everyone else saw the confident Andi, the singer-slash-performer. I saw the words of the song in her, even if I didn't fully understand what it meant to her then. She showed me her scars and she knows I'm still here with her, regardless of them, or maybe even because of them.

Mom and Dad join us around the pool and I notice Dad is especially quiet tonight. I don't know what's wrong with him. He seemed fine when we got here but now he's more distracted and somewhat irritable. He barely joins in our conversations and a couple of times he has no idea what we were even talking about. I know his business has taken a hit lately and I wonder if that's what's on his mind. I have more than a twinge of guilt because I know I've added to his past financial problems.

He's owned his own real estate development company for years and the economy has taken a hard toll. I make a mental note to talk to him later and find out what's going on. When Andi and I leave, Brandon is first in line to hug her goodbye. If I didn't trust her so much, I would have to kill my brother. But I definitely know something is wrong with my dad when he seems hesitant to hug Andi goodbye. She doesn't seem to notice since he does eventually wrap his arms around her.

CHAPTER TWELVE

ANDI

Between the gym, the youth center, and spending time with Luke, the past month has flown by. Luke and I have alternated staying at his apartment and my house but we've hardly been apart at night. School has started back so there are more kids at the youth center in the late afternoons. I've been spending more time there with the kids because so many parents aren't home–whether they're working or just absent from their kids' lives altogether.

There are a couple of girls in particular that I'm afraid could be in danger of dropping out of school or getting involved with the wrong crowd. I don't want to fail them. I feel like we've come so far. I've been working on a scholarship plan for them to get them out of the area and into one of the smaller universities. I talk to them daily about the advantages they would have if they will just apply themselves. I've almost won them over.

Shane and Will came to the center last week and I was surprised to see Luke walk in with them. Surprised and thrilled. While Shane and Will worked with the guys on boxing, Luke took several of the boys outside and taught them how to work in the yard. They spent the day doing manual labor to make the yard look great. I couldn't give the boys, and Luke, enough praise for all they did. Several of the boys even said they enjoyed learning to landscape and making "their place" look nice. I think Luke has sparked a whole new type of interest for the youth center.

It's Friday afternoon and for the first time in what feels like forever, Luke and I have separate plans tonight. I'm going out with my girlfriends—Christina, Tania and Katie—and Luke is going out with Shane, Will and Brandon. I can't help but smile at how jealous and possessive Luke is of me. I mean, does he not own a mirror? The man is gorgeous, he's built like the most desired male model, and he's just all around great. The girls are always after him and he's worried about some guy hitting on me. It's comical, really.

We haven't said those three little words yet, though I think he feels it. I know I do. I almost told him a couple of weeks ago after my last karaoke performance. I sang Beyonce's *Crazy In Love* and made no attempt to hide that I was singing the lyrics just for him. He didn't take his eyes off me the whole time. I left the stage and straddled him in his lap to sing the last verse, just for him.

So, yeah, tonight will be fun with my girls but I also can't wait to get back home and see Luke. We planned on meeting back at my house no matter how late it is. Yeah, we've both got it bad. But I do want to tell him I love him—even if he doesn't say it back. I just feel the need to tell him right now. I don't want to regret not saying it when I feel it so strongly.

Luke calls just as I get home from the youth center.

"Hey baby, what are you doing?" I answer.

"Sitting here missing you," the low, sexy timbre of his voice sends chills through me even through the phone.

"I miss you, too. Wish I could see you. Where are y'all going tonight?" I purr back to him.

"Shane mentioned wanting to see a band playing here this weekend," he says.

I laugh, "Hmmm...I wonder if that's the same band we're going to see tonight."

His sexy laugh rumbles through his chest, "I hope so. Then there's no reason why I can't sit with my girl on the guys' night out."

I want to say the words so badly, but I don't want the first time I tell him to be over the phone. "I hope so, too. I would love to dance with my handsome man tonight. Maybe our friends know us well enough by now to not try to keep us apart."

We talk for a few more minutes before I have to get ready or I'll be late meeting the girls for dinner. We reluctantly hang up, but only after I promise to text him where I'm at and let him know I'm fine. He's so protective and possessive. I only act like I don't love it. I secretly do love that he cares enough to be protective over me.

I call a cab to meet the girls. No way am I driving tonight. I walk in the restaurant and find Katie waiting at our table. She and I order appetizers while we wait for Christina and Tania.

"So, Katie, something going on with you and Shane?" I ask, catching her completely off guard, as I planned.

She chokes on a cheese stick and takes a drink of water before answering.

"Why would you ask that?"

Oh, isn't she trying to be coy with me?

"You know, people only say that when they're stalling and to get out of answering the direct question. That really doesn't work on me. I'm a lawyer, remember?" I say wryly.

Crazy Maybe

Her face turns red and we both know she's caught. "I don't really know what's going on yet. We'll see."

That's as much of an admission as I'm going to get right now so I'll take it. And keep an eye on them. And embarrass them until my questions are answered. That's just what friends are for.

Christina and Tania arrive, fashionably late, and we talk and laugh over dinner. I fill them in on my karaoke status. I made it through another round of cuts and have another week to practice my next song since there's a band playing at the club this weekend. They ask if the guys are going to be there tonight, too. From their excessive questioning, it appears that I'm not the only one who's interested in the guys' whereabouts this evening. Interesting.

We settle the bill, meaning I insist on treating my girls, and we make our way to our usual hangout. The guys are already there and have saved our seats. Funny how we split up and take up the vacant seats. I'm with Luke, of course, but I watch with amusement as Tania sits with Brandon. Then Christina sits with Will. And, finally, Katie sits with Shane. But it's the look on each of their faces that tell the real story. There's something good going on with my little family here.

The band isn't playing yet so the music isn't too loud, but gives enough background noise for a little privacy in conversations. I feel Luke's hand on my face and I eagerly turn to face him. He kisses me like he hasn't seen me in a month, even though he left my house when I did this morning.

"I want to tell you something, Luke. Don't freak out on me, okay?" I ask, never taking my eyes off his and silently willing him to be okay with my declaration.

"Okay," he says slowly, drawing the word out and obviously ready to freak out on me.

Crazy Maybe

I take a deep breath and cup his cheek in my hand, "I love you. I just wanted to tell you."

His hand suddenly goes to the nape of my neck and he pulls me close to him, his lips barely hovering above mine. He sounds breathless when he says, "I love you, Andi. *So fucking much.*" Then he kisses me so sweetly and completely, I am literally melting into a boneless pile of freaking-hot lava right here in my seat.

"If I hadn't promised the guys I would stay and listen to this band, we would be going home right now," his deep voice reverberates from my ear to the very core of me between my legs. I should have brought a change of underwear because mine are soaked right now.

There's no reason I should suffer alone. So I decide to tell him. I lean in so close to him that I'm basically sitting in his lap. I wrap my hand around his neck and pull close to his ear, letting my tongue slip out and trace his lobe. His hand tightens slightly around where it was resting on my thigh.

"You know, baby, just the sound of your voice thrills me so much, my panties are fucking soaked right now."

The fire in his eyes tells me I'm playing a dangerous game with him. A wonderful, sexy, intriguing, dangerous game. His hand is so tight on my thigh I wouldn't be surprised if I had bruises in the shape of his fingers, but it doesn't hurt. It feels good and it's actually making me want him even more. I kiss his lips and lightly run my tongue along the part in his lips. He opens and takes my invitation with vigor. I have the distinct feeling I won't be able to stand up for however long it takes my panties to dry.

With the darkness of the club and the cover of the oversized tables, no one can see his hand as it slowly glides farther up my thigh, then under my dress, until he reaches my soaked panties. When he feels the wetness, he moans in my mouth but continues his exploration. He parts my legs a little more and then his fingers push the flimsy material of my panties to one side. He lightly strokes the wet folds between my thighs, spreading my juices and soaking his own finger in the act, before he pushes it into me and I gasp.

He pulls his head back slightly to watch me as his hand keeps up its ministrations. His thumb finds my nub and applies circular pressure while his finger moves agonizingly slowly in and out. He's still trying to avoid calling attention to us but I know that determined look in his eye. He's returning the favor of my torturing him a few minutes ago. He's going to make me come right here in the club, at the table with all our friends, and he knows I can't stop him without everyone else knowing.

He turns toward me slightly so that his back partly shields me from the rest of the group as his finger and thumb continues to have their way with me. His mouth is on my neck, giving me open mouth kisses and pushing farther into pure bliss, as a second finger joins the party going on between my legs. But the rumble of his deep voice that nearly pushes me over the edge as he hums against my ear, "Tell me who this belongs to, Andi. Say it."

I have no idea how he expects me to speak right now. I'm fairly certain I'm not even breathing. With an extra oomph, his fingers send a bolt of lightning through me and my fingers clench around his arm, holding on for dear life. "Say it, Andi," he demands.

"Yours, Luke. Only yours," I answer breathlessly, still clutching his arm.

"If it's mine, I want to feel it come for me. *Now.*" If I had the capacity for thought, speech and breathing right now, I would show and tell him how much I freaking love this show of alpha-male dominance. But since I can do none of the above at the moment, the only thing I can do is just as he commands. He covers my mouth in yet another sensuous and knee-buckling kiss just as I'm about to scream, thankfully muffling the sound to a whimper that's ignored by everyone else.

I'm still coming down from my Luke-induced high when I see him lick his fingers. *That is so fucking hot.* Without a word or making a scene, Luke stands, grabs my hand and pulls me up with him. We head to the dance floor and I take it for granted that we're about to actually dance. But my man has another idea for me...a better idea, actually.

He leads me through the throngs of people on the dance floor until I realize we're heading to the back of the stage. At the other end of the long corridor that spans the entire width of the club is a bathroom that's for performers only. Since there's no karaoke tonight, it would only be used the band who is currently getting set up onstage. He locks the door behind us and I wrap my arms around his neck, going in for another kiss.

He cups my face in his hands, kissing me so thoroughly, before tearing his mouth away and running his hands down each side of my body. Once he reaches the bottom of my dress, he pulls it up until it's around my waist. Then he grips one side of my panties and jerks them, ripping them completely off me. I'm noticeably shocked at this—turned on, but still shocked—and he smirks as he puts them in his pocket. His hands now on my hips, he quickly turns me around and bends me over the sink as he readies himself behind me. The mirror is low enough that I can see him and he can definitely see me.

"I can't wait until we get home. I have to be inside you," he grunts. In one second, I feel the head of his impressive erection at my entrance, and with a quick thrust, he's buried deep in me and I'm biting on the back of my hand to keep from screaming in sheer pleasure. His thrusts are hard and deep and I'm quickly close to coming again. He's hitting the right spot every time, stretching me to take him fully in me. I know I'll be sore again but I don't care–he feels too good.

He knows–he can feel it and he urges me on. "Now, baby," and again my body complies, as if it's completely under his spell. He feels my inner sex walls squeeze him, vibrating and quivering around his thick shaft as he plunges into me, his releases a guttural moan and unloads into me. He leans over and lightly bites me on the back, like he's a tiger who's just claimed his mate. And he can claim me as many times as he wants to.

CHAPTER THIRTEEN

LUKE

I'm standing in the backyard at my parent's house and my bottom jaw is resting on the ground in front of me. Brandon takes the opportunity to provoke me.

"You're going to catch flies in that hole of yours if you don't shut your mouth," Brandon says dryly.

Whatever. I close my mouth but still look disbelievingly at Andi. She's adorable, standing there looking a little shy and unsure of herself. My mom is gushing at her, hugging her close over and over again. I think Mom may break her soon because she hugs her tighter and tighter with each embrace. Not that Andi's complaining about that, but my little vixen is a little embarrassed at all the attention she's generated for herself.

"Andi, I just can't believe you did this! I just can't get over it!" Mom has said that at least ten times since we got here a few minutes ago. Yeah, we get it Mom, you're shocked.

"It's nothing—really. I just wanted to do something for you and this is the only thing I knew you wanted," Andi tries to explain, hoping my mom will just drop it already.

No such luck. Mom is gushing and running around the back yard to touch everything at least once.

Dad called Brandon, Greg, and me over to their house early this morning because not only has Andi ordered the patio furniture my mom wanted from the

Crazy Maybe

catalog, but she's ordered the whole back yard scene that Mom wanted to create.

Everything's here – the hot tub with a waterfall that creates the illusion that the hot tub is spilling over into the pool, the outdoor kitchen area with appliances, the matching furniture that goes all around the backyard, and all the brick pavers needed for the walkways and retaining walls. She also arranged for several workers to be here to help get everything set up.

Andi smiles at me sheepishly, "It's nice, isn't it?"

I smile and start toward her but Brandon beats me to it. He wraps his arm around her shoulders and presses the side of his head against the side of hers. "It's beautiful, Andi. Just like you. Mom and Dad love it, sweetheart."

I push him away and give him the *don't-fucking-touch-my-girlfriend* look, which he completely ignores. I put my arm around her and pull her close to me, "How many times can I say it? You are *amazing*, Andi."

Her beautiful smile lights up her face as she says, "Luke, you did such a great job at the youth center with the landscaping and directing the boys. Think you can take over here and make sure it gets done the way your parents want?"

I start to answer but my dad answers for me, "That's a great idea, Andi. Linda, why don't you and the boys here," gesturing to me, Brandon and Greg, "divide it up. I have some work I need to finish inside."

Mom is more than happy to push us to various parts of the yard to start working on her dream yard. Andi announces she'll get drinks and snacks together and my father follows her into the house. Mom is absolutely thrilled with everything. Even though she keeps saying over and over that she can't accept all this from Andi, she hasn't slowed down in giving orders of

121

exactly how she wants every single piece installed or where it should be placed.

The thing is, I know Andi will never miss the money that she's spent for my mom's little slice of heaven here. Everything is top of the line and spare-no-expense kind of nice, but Andi doesn't even consider the money when she buys something for someone else. She only considers that person. I've never even seen her look at a price tag. If it's something she knows one of us needs or wants, she gives it without question.

I felt like a total asshole, but after I started training with Mack, she bought me all new boxing gear. I don't mean the cheap, knock-off stuff. I mean top of the line, best name brand, everything I could ever possibly think of needing—gloves, headgear, mouth guards, speed bag, shorts, tanks, boxing shoes, and running shoes.

Most things went into a huge gym bag she bought and it was all just in my apartment one day. She never said a word about it and she was literally offended when I tried to pay her back. I've found other ways of thanking her and doing little things for her. But I've realized she genuinely likes to help others—just like she does at the youth center.

So her generosity today doesn't really shock me. I just had no idea she ordered all this and I'm a little confused as to why she didn't tell me. But then I think I may know why. She doesn't do this for praise or attention. She wouldn't have wanted me to make a big deal of it or tell my mom and ruin her surprise. Andi really amazes me with how loving and giving she is after all she's been through. Where most people would become cold and couldn't care less about others, Andi's childhood problems made her want to be a better person.

Crazy Maybe

My dad has been distant again today. I haven't had a chance to talk to him man to man to ask what's wrong. Right now, there's no way I could get any information out of my mom because she's too excited over her yard project. And if I walk away from the "crew" she assigned me, I know I will be in a lot of trouble. Mom is scary when she's mad, even to a grown man, and I don't want to be the one to catch the brunt of all that is Mom's fury.

Just ask the poor guys who are in her "crew" right now. They're looking longingly at my crew and Brandon's crew, wondering how they drew the short straws in this game of chance. My guys are chuckling to themselves as they listen to Mom chastise her crew for putting the pavers down wrong side up. She won't listen when they try to explain that there is no wrong side up with pavers. She's determined to have the perfect patio, down to the very last concrete block.

After two hours, I realize I am really thirsty and wonder where Andi is with those drinks she was making us. I look around but I don't see her anywhere outside and no one else has a drink. I am instantly glad because for a second there I thought she forgot about me. But now I'm worried because this isn't like her at all. She loves doing things for others and I know she wouldn't have left us to do all the work anyway. I make my way to Brandon and with each step that foreboding feeling gets worse.

"Hey, have you seen Andi lately?" I ask Brandon.

He thinks for a second before replying, "No, I haven't actually. That is strange," he says absently as he looks around the yard. "Hey—where's Mom?"

Now that he said that, I realize I haven't heard Mom fighting with her crew for a while. "Maybe they're both in the kitchen making us something to eat." I say the words but even I don't believe them.

Brandon obviously doesn't either because he gives me the look that says *yeah, right.* "You think Mom would leave all this to go inside and cook for us? Ah, no, I don't think so."

We tell our crews to take a break and we both head for the back door. When I step inside the kitchen, I know something is very wrong in the house of the Woods. There are empty cups sitting on a tray–the ones I'm sure Andi said she's make us a couple of hours ago. There's no food being prepared. There's no one in the kitchen. Brandon and I look around and then back at each other. Then I hear muted voices coming from the formal dining room.

I slowly push open the swinging door to the dining room and hear Andi sniffling. *She's crying?* I can see my dad sitting at the head of the table but I can't see Andi. I move through the doorway and Brandon and I both freeze in our tracks at the sight in front of me. *What. The. Hell?*

Dad has a manila folder on the table in front of him with Andi's name written in black marker on the front. He's looking at her like she's some sort of insect to be stepped on and scraped off his shoe. Mom is sitting to the right of Dad and she has tears streaming down her face, but she's completely silent. Andi is at the other end of the table that is directly opposite Dad, with tears streaming down her face and holding what appear to be photos in her hand.

"You could've just told me you needed it. I would've just given it to you." Andi's voice is barely above a whisper but I hear so much pain in it that I feel my own heart break. She is staring at the pictures as she says it, but I know she's talking to my dad. Even

124

Crazy Maybe

though I have no idea what this is about. She continues whispering, "Sam, you don't know what this could do to you. Please don't do this."

"What the hell is going on in here?" I bellow. I feel like I could take someone's head off right now.

Dad stands and his words just about knock me to floor, "Luke, did you know Andi was committed to a mental institution for trying to kill one of her foster parents? She's unstable, son. You can't trust her and it's best if you stay away from her. For your own good."

"No! That's not true. Luke, you have to believe me," she pleads with me, crying and looking terrified. I look back and forth between my father and my lover, not knowing what to do. My loyalty to each of them is being tested right now and I have no idea why.

Dad walks over and rips the photos from her hands and thrusts them through the air at me. "Here, see for yourself." I take them from him and stare in disbelief at the pictures of a very young Andi in a mental hospital wearing a hospital gown and fighting with orderlies and nurses. Dad gives me the court documents to read.

> *Fifteen year-old female attacked her foster parents, attempting to murder the foster father and harming the foster mother in the process. The court recommends defendant be reprimanded to juvenile detention center until she reaches the age of twenty-one; however, after compelling testimony from the foster parents, the court agrees to reprimand Andi Morgan to the juvenile mental facility, to be released no earlier than her sixteenth birthday.*

Crazy Maybe

"Luke, *please*. It's not what you think. It's not what it looks like—honestly! Please let me explain," she's begging me, I hear it in her voice and see it in her eyes.

How can this be? How can I not know the person I've fallen in love with? How could my little vixen betray me into thinking she's someone she's not? So many things are running through my mind and I keep coming back to the same thing. *She's been playing me. She's been lying to me all this time.* And I'm getting really pissed off about it.

"Not what I think? There are pictures here, Andi! I'm looking at the damn court documents! How could you keep something like this from me? You were in a fucking mental hospital! You tried to kill a man!" My voice is harsh and accusing. My eyes cut her to shreds. I'm pacing the room like a caged lion and I'm ready to start breaking shit.

"Luke. You *promised* me. Remember? You promised to believe me. *Me.* I need you to keep that promise to me right now—right this very second. Please, Luke. Please," tears are running unchecked down her cheeks, soaking her face and her neck. She's not even wiping them away now.

She's reaching out her tattooed arm to me touch me, to seal the bond between us and remind me what I'd just recently promised her. Her eyes are burning through me with so much pain and fear. Her voice tells me she's terrified. She's trying to keep it reined in but at the same time silently reminding me about those scars on her arm. Her outstretched hand is apprehensive to touch me, afraid I will shun her touch. And I do.

I step back from her like she's infected with the plague and hold up the photos and the court paper. "Is this what you meant when you said I'm supposed to

126

believe you? I'm supposed to take your word that *this* isn't real," I shake the photos in her face, "but *your words* are real? Is that what I'm supposed to do?"

Her answer is simple, and to the point, and is like a dagger in my heart. "If you really love me, then yes. Do you think I'd do any less for you?"

"How am I supposed to believe that you haven't been just trying to fool me all this time? That you're not just pretending to be someone you're not?"

"Luke, listen to Andi. I don't care what that fucking paper says, *you know her,* man," Brandon interjects, and spears my dad with a menacing glare. Brandon taking up for my girl, when I'm obviously not, pisses me off worse and I take it out on Andi.

"No. I don't fucking know her at all," I yell at Brandon while pointing at Andi. "This whole *relationship* was built on lies. How can I love someone who lies to me? I've been betrayed before and I won't fucking fall for it again." The venom I spit at her visibly wounds her and though I wouldn't have thought it possible, her tears increase.

"You don't mean that, Luke. You know that's not true, I would never betray you," she sounds defeated. Broken. Infinitely sad. But she doesn't look away from me. Her eyes are still begging me. Her bottom lip is quivering and she's close to sobbing now. The tightness in my chest threatens to take my breath away.

"Did she even bother to tell you about her birthday coming up soon?" Dad asks accusingly.

I shake my head no. "What about her birthday? What's the big deal about not telling me?"

"Her birthday is a big deal, son. She inherits the rest of her father's *billions* then. Doesn't it seem strange that she hasn't told you anything about it?" Dad asks sardonically.

"Luke, man. *Don't. Do. This.* You will be sorry. I promise you that," Brandon warns me. He spears my father with his cutting eyes, "This is insane."

I turn my anger on Brandon then spew, "You know as well as anyone that I've had my fill of lying, conniving women, *Brandon*."

I shake my head in disgust and storm out of the room, throwing the photos in the air behind me. Brandon shouts obscenities at the back of my head but I keep walking and ignore him. I hear Andi's sobs of pain but that doesn't stop me either.

I keep going until somehow I arrive at my apartment and only now does it occur to me that I left Andi behind at my parents' house. I left her without a second thought as to her welfare, how she'll get home, or how badly I've just hurt her. At this moment, all I am focused on is how the owner of my heart could have kept something this big from me.

How the fuck could she have betrayed me like this?

CHAPTER FOURTEEN

LUKE

For the last four hours, I've been in my apartment pacing and steaming mad. I still can't fucking believe she would do this to me. I really thought she was different. I thought she was the most genuine and giving person I've ever met. Turns out she's just really good at hiding the shit she doesn't want others to see. I fucking fell for her act hook, line and sinker and I feel like a complete fucking moron for it.

I fling open the door at the sound of incessant pounding and find Brandon standing there, looking like he's ready to take my head off. Just what I fucking need right now.

"I'm not in the fucking mood, man," I try to shut the door in his face and he shoves into the door with his shoulder, knocking me out of the way and he barges in anyway.

"I don't give a fuck what mood *you're* in," he yells in my face. Then he roars loudly as he runs his hands through his hair in frustration. "You shouldn't have left her like that! You should've listened to her and stood by her. You owed her *at least* that much!"

"She lied to me! What the hell–am I supposed to just forget that?" I yell back.

"About what? What *exactly* did she lie to you about? You knew there was something she didn't tell you. I heard her–she said she's never told anyone, Luke. But she wanted to tell *you* and you promised to

129

believe her. She at least deserved to be heard!" Brandon bellowed.

"What did you expect me to do? Choose her side over Dad's?" I scowl back at Brandon even as I faintly hear that nagging voice in the back of my mind. The one that tells me–*although usually too damn late*–when I've royally fucked up.

"If *this* is how you support someone you supposedly love, you don't deserve her, Luke." His voice is suddenly calm and it's more alarming than when he's yelling. He's reaching the end of his patience with me. I just shake my head and try to end the conversation with silence.

My tactic doesn't work. Brandon knows what's on my mind without me even saying it.

"Luke, she's nothing like Megan. Look, you never would listen to me about Megan. She had been hitting on me for a while but I didn't think much about it until she openly propositioned me. She didn't care which one of us she was with. She was just trying to play both of us. When she kissed me, I pushed her away, I swear. She was a slut, she didn't care, and she's definitely not the standard you should measure any other woman against.

"I know you thought you loved her, man. But, you never looked at Megan like you do Andi. You never cared enough about Megan to even fight with her. The only part of you that was hurt over Megan was your pride and you know it. I didn't betray you–Megan did. What happened with Dad's business wasn't your fault any more than it was mine. And you know Megan's not worth even mentioning again–much less thinking about."

When I don't say anything, Brandon continues, "Not once has Andi ever been even slightly interested in me.

130

Even when you said you were just friends and I was openly flirting with her. I love you, man, if she *ever* looked at me the way she does you, I would take her away from you in a heartbeat.

"You didn't see how it hurt her when you left like that. You weren't the one who *literally* picked her up off the floor. My shirt was soaked from her tears–for *you!* You may never find someone who loves you like that again. You're lucky to have found it once. You should think about that."

Then he walks out to leave me alone with my pain and anger.

ANDI

Oh my God, he just left me. He just walked out and didn't even care that I was stuck there with no way to get back home. He abandoned me at his parents' house–the very people who are blatantly betraying me. I remember falling to my knees and I remember Brandon cussing like a sailor at Luke. Their mom was still sitting at the table and she was crying. Their dad was looking between Luke's back, Brandon's face, and me, crumpled in the floor.

When we heard Luke's truck tires squeal out of the driveway, Brandon picked me up and carried me out to his truck. After putting my seatbelt on me, he drove me home and helped me inside. He stayed with me and we talked for a long while.

He was so nice and supportive. He told me to give Luke time to calm down. He said Luke just overreacted and once he realized it, he would be back and begging for forgiveness.

I'm not so sure about that. This may be just the excuse he needs to get out of our relationship.

Brandon just left and now I'm all alone again. I've gotten so used to having Luke here with me. The silence just punctuates how lonely my life was before him. I'm going to allow myself to wallow in self-pity tonight. I will scream, cry, eat fattening foods, and grieve tonight. And come tomorrow, I will move on. Because that's what I do.

I have to be strong.

LUKE

For the last five days, I've been replaying everything that's happened with Andi up until this point in our relationship over and over again in my mind. I've examined every word, every gesture and every minute we've shared. Brandon's last words to me have been like a fucking recording set on replay and there's no escape from them. It suddenly hits me and I realize how badly I have fucked up. What I have lost and what I will probably never have again.

I know without a shadow of a doubt that I don't deserve her at all.

I've done nothing worthwhile in my life to deserve someone as wonderful as she is. Even my fucking brother believed her–believed *in* her–when I didn't. He was there for her when I wasn't and she fucking needed me. I simply turned my back and left her alone when she needed me more than ever.

Crazy Maybe

At that moment–*that very moment* when she needed me to believe her and I didn't, I broke my promise. I broke her heart. I broke the very love of my life–I broke *her*.

My guilt and humiliation over Megan has tainted my view of relationships overall. I'm seeing that now. Brandon has tried to tell me for the last few years but I didn't want to hear it. Or face it. I've convinced myself that it's much easier to run from my demons rather than face them. But sitting here alone, wallowing in my self-loathing, there's nothing easier about it. There's nothing easy about discovering I've probably lost the one true lover and friend that I've ever known.

I know she's been at the gym because some of the other guys have talked about how differently she's been acting. They haven't come out and asked me yet but I know they eventually will. She's apparently avoiding me, avoiding going to the gym at the time she knows I'm likely to be there. I volunteered at the center again today and she wasn't there either. I wonder if she knew I was there and just stayed away. I've tried to call her but she ignores my calls. I've went by her house but she won't answer the door, if she's even home.

CHAPTER FIFTEEN

ANDI

I had practiced a different song for the weeks leading up to the last night Luke and I were at the club together. The night the band played and the last full night we were a couple and I was truly happy. For the past week, I've been practicing a different song—one that really speaks to my frame of mind right now. I don't know if Luke will be at the club tonight, but in a way I hope he is because I picked this song with him in mind.

I've avoided seeing Luke at the gym but I've still been going. I'm not letting him run me off from something that means so much to me. Shane has asked what's wrong with me lately because I haven't been acting the same. But he didn't ask anything about Luke, so I doubt he knows anything yet.

Luke has called a few times but I couldn't answer. After what happened at his parents' house, I don't know what he's calling to say. To accuse me of more terrible things? To finish his malicious rant? To apologize and actually hear what I have to say? To ask for his favorite t-shirt back that I stole from him?

I can't take the risk—no matter what it is he wants. I can't hear his voice and not have my heart ripped out of my chest again. So I ignored his calls. I hid when he showed up at my house. I saw his truck but I couldn't even look out the window and actually see him—I was afraid I'd go running to him, begging him like I did when he walked out and left me behind at his parents' house.

Crazy Maybe

I'm afraid I will make a complete fool out of myself for someone who never loved me like I loved him.

Love him, I mean. Still. I wonder if it will ever go away, though I know I'm not the first or the last to feel this way.

So I focus on the anger instead. The betrayal of being left there, on my knees sobbing my eyes out, while he callously walked away. Not the least bit interested in hearing what I had to say. Not caring that he'd so easily broken a promise he had just made—one that meant the world to me because I knew it would mean the difference between losing him and keeping him. I just never imagined his dad would be the one who so heartlessly threw me under the bus.

I'm at the club with Christina, Tania and Katie. They're trying to cheer me up but nothing is working. No use in even trying drinks or shots tonight—nothing can infiltrate this huge bubble of anger that has enveloped me. I'm glad in a way because I can use it on stage tonight. Especially since Luke just walked in with the guys and they're headed this way. I look at my girls and we silently, solemnly swear we will not move to sit with them.

Shane and Will give each other confused looks before looking at me. I think Luke is about to walk up behind me so I quickly get up and leave the table. It's about time for my song anyway so like a big chicken, I go hide in the ladies' bathroom until it's my turn.

I make my way onstage and avoid running into Luke on the way. I'm regretting showing him around backstage now because I'm looking around every corner to make sure he's not there first. I have nowhere safe to hide.

Mitch has the spotlights set to a deep red hue and the black curtains are closed behind me. The fog

135

machine is set on low so the mist is barely creeping across the stage. With the fans set on low, my long, thick hair is slightly drifting on the breeze. The combination of the stage effects with my black leather pants, four-inch black stilettos, and a black, backless tank gives it all a fierce look. Exactly the way I'm feeling right now.

There's no elaborate scene to play out tonight. No man's lap to sit in while I sing words of eternal love. No, tonight is all about his broken promise and my new promise. The music starts off instantly fast paced and...fierce...and I feel like every lyric sings directly to him. But it's really the second verse and every word after that spells it out. The song is *For My Sake*, by Shinedown. It's absolutely brilliant and bold. It's also fitting that the song ends fairly abruptly–just like we did.

I keep my eyes on his during the whole song. While I never point at him, I leave absolutely no doubt that this song is only for him. My voice, my movements, and everything else about me is hard, angry and inflexible. I make sure to leave no room for any misinterpretation.

I especially feel that from the second verse to the end of the song really speaks to what I'm feeling right now. I'm blatantly daring him to show me he's not really like every other guy out there who broke his promise, but knowing that he is only reaffirms my decision to be completely done with him.

I know we're making a scene with all of our drama and I want it to stop. But at this moment, I just need him to feel my pain and hear from me that I am putting us behind me for my sanity. At the end of the verse and the chorus that follows, there's no doubt he now knows exactly what's on my mind.

Crazy Maybe

Luke doesn't move during my whole performance. He doesn't move his eyes. He doesn't speak to anyone, not even the waitress who's so blatantly trying to get his attention. A couple of drunk girls approach him but he doesn't acknowledge them. It's too dark to see what his eyes are trying to tell me but I don't even want to know. I've avoided him for a reason. The song is exactly right when it says what he lost was me. For my own sanity, I can't look back.

I acknowledge the applause from the crowd but honestly I don't even care about the contest at this point. If I make it another round or not does not matter to me in the least. I may not even be in the area by the next round. I plan to call and schedule an appointment with the realtor to put my house on the market tomorrow. If it doesn't sell soon, I'm seriously considering just giving it away just so I can get the hell out of Dodge.

I'm barely cognizant of exiting the stage because I'm so wrapped up in my thoughts. I'm considering just walking out the door and leaving now instead of returning to our table. Suddenly I'm hoisted into the air but I just saw Shane still sitting at the table so I know it's not him this time. I don't know who the hell has grabbed me but he's about to get a mouth full of my fist, especially in my current state of pissed off mind. When I catch a glimpse of him over my shoulder, I'm doubly determined to draw blood.

He pulls my ear to his mouth and has the damn nerve to ask, "Did you miss me, baby?" Then he sets me down and smiles at me like I'm a long lost friend. *Ah, hell no!*

I don't return the smile. In fact, if looks could kill, he would be already buried at this point. "Miss you? Have you been gone?" I respond dryly and turn to walk away

137

Crazy Maybe

from the second biggest mistake I've made in the dating arena. I spot Shane barreling through the people to get to us and he's obviously pissed. Will is fast on his heels.

"Brad," Shane's voice is low and threatening, "Don't. Fucking. Touch. Her. Again." He narrows his eyes and punctuates each word to emphasize his meaning.

Will moves up beside Shane and it is a very ominous sight to see a mad Will. His voice belies his eyes and his words, "No, Shane, its fine. By all means, let him put one finger on her. One. More. Fucking. Time." Will's last words are clearly a dare and Brad quickly backs up. Maybe he's not quite as stupid as he looks.

Brad holds his hands up in front of him and answers jovially, "No harm intended, fellas. I just wanted to say hello."

"You've said it. That's the only word you get with her, motherfucker. If I see you near her again, I will pound your face in the ground. You feel me?" Shane grabs my hand and protectively pulls me to his side. I go willingly because I don't want to be anywhere near Brad and I don't want Shane and Will to get in trouble for killing him. He's just not worth the trouble of the going all the way home to get my shovel, dig the hole, and hide the body.

Shane and I turn as one to walk back to the table and suddenly he's pulling me to the side, away from everyone. It's now that I see Luke stood up but never left the table. I guess he was getting ready to have Shane and Will's back in case a fight broke out.

Shane demands, "What the hell is going on with you and Luke?" He actually looks mad at *me*. *What the hell?*

Crazy Maybe

"Absolutely nothing," my voice is flat and I'm doing my best to give him a bored look.

"What does that mean, exactly?" Shane demands.

"It means that there is *absolutely nothing* going on between Luke and me. Exactly nothing. Exactly *absolutely nothing*."

I'm glaring at Shane now and I'm purposely being a smartass. I really shouldn't be, considering how glad I was to see Shane when Brad grabbed me. And how Shane just saved my ass.

"Look, I'm sorry, okay? Things aren't working out with us and I don't want you in the middle," I explain, nicer this time. Shane nods in understanding and lets the subject drop.

I push through the crowd to tell Mitch to put my girls' drinks on my tab and tell them goodbye. I can't stay here and be this close to Luke. I just can't handle it because I simultaneously want to tell him to go to hell and beg him to listen to me. Just hear me out, for crying out loud, I'm not a monster like he treated me. But I can't do either and I just have to get away as far away from him as I can right now.

As I turn to leave, I see Brandon is sitting beside Luke and for some reason, I feel betrayed all over again. They're brothers, I know, but I spent a long time talking to Brandon after Luke left me alone that day. Brandon picked me up off the floor–literally, I fell to the floor on my knees from the pain of watching Luke so callously walk away from me. Brandon helped me. He put me in his truck and drove me home. And he isn't even the one who supposedly loved me.

I didn't tell Brandon what happened–with his parents or with the mental hospital–but I think he did believe me when I said it wasn't what it looked like. I try to tell myself that he hasn't turned on me just because he's sitting with Luke right now. My mind knows it but my heart won't listen. He must know what I'm thinking because he gets up and steps into my only path out of this section of tables.

"Andi," his voice is smooth and calm, "you should talk to him." He inclines his head toward Luke but keeps his eyes on me. He's probably thinking if he turns his head, I will dart around him and be gone. And he would be right.

"*No.*" I narrow my eyes at him, square my shoulders and set my jaw, daring him to continue this foolish conversation.

"Hey, I'm on your side. I've told him what an idiot he is," Brandon says with such sincerity that I don't doubt him at all.

I have no doubt Brandon has done just that. "That doesn't change anything, though. Does it?"

He tilts his head to the side and studies me for a minute. "No, I guess it doesn't," he says gloomily.

I give him one curt nod and a half-smile and keep walking. Once I'm around him, I turn and say with all sincerity, "Brandon, thank you...for believing me. It means more than you could possibly know." He nods in gratitude.

Before I even get to my car, the tears are flowing uncontrollably and I just want to get away from here. I'm reaching for the door handle when I hear a man's soft call just behind me, "Andi." It's just barely above a whisper and his warm breath floats across the top of my head.

I turn and stare into his eyes for a half a second before the warning bells in my head go off. I'm in the parking lot alone with him. Again.

Crazy Maybe

"Brad. Get away from me." My voice holds more warning than I feel inside right now. I can't show him any weakness.

"You know you don't want that, Andi."

"I know I want you as far away from me as possible, Brad."

He grabs my hand and starts pulling me toward the other end of the parking lot. I immediately struggle against him but since he's a big guy, and used to be a boxer at the club before Mack banned him, I don't stand much of a chance against him. But I refuse to go down without a fight and he will at least have some marks on him compliments of yours truly.

In no time, he's pulled me to his car and is trying to stuff me in it when a pair of big hands grab me and another pair of big hands grab him. I'm thrown over someone's shoulder and carried back to my car. I can't make out much in the dark parking lot, hanging upside down and facing a nice and familiar jean-clad ass. But I think I see someone who may or may not resemble Shane wailing on Brad, who is definitely crying like a girl.

There seems to be a theme with the men around me picking me up and carrying me around like they own me. When this particular man puts me down, I'm suddenly at a loss for words—except for one word. *Luke*.

I mumble a *thank you* and he looks as uneasy as I feel. I finally find my voice and give him an appropriate response for what he just did.

"Thank you, Luke. If you hadn't come along when you did...Well, I don't want to even think about that. But I appreciate what you did...stepping in and helping me."

My gratefulness is sincere but I could barely maintain eye contact when I talked to him. It just hurts to look at him and not be able to touch him. Well, except for when I was hanging over his shoulder and ogling his fine ass.

"How could I *not* help you, Andi?" I hear the pain in his voice and the insinuation that I thought he wouldn't help me.

I give him my ultimate *DUH* look but I don't feel the need to elaborate. He knows exactly why I would think that. My only consolation in this whole fiasco tonight is that hopefully he thinks my tear-stained cheeks are from my altercation with Brad.

"I should go." I turn and walk away when I hear him call my name.

CHAPTER SIXTEEN

LUKE

"Andi."

I don't even know what to say. I just don't want her to leave. She stops in her tracks but doesn't look at me. Yeah, I heard the words of the song she sang to me tonight. She didn't sit in my lap this time but I know it was directed at me. I deserve every bit of her anger. I let her down when she needed me the most. She was right about one thing that night–she wouldn't betray me.

"What do you want, Luke?" She's trying to hold back tears. I know they're tears because of me, even though the song she obviously sang for me says she's moving on. I see her shoulders shake slightly and I know she's really trying to not break down right out here.

"Are you hurt? Do you need someone to drive you home?"

After a couple of seconds, she answers with a watery voice, "I'm fine."

She walks off, quickening her pace so my words can't stop her again. I stand frozen like a damn statue watching her drive away from me. I turn to see if Shane has killed the loser, Brad, and see Brandon glaring at me.

"What?" I ask defensively.

"Are you fucking kidding me? You just asked her if she needs someone to drive her home–*after some guy just fucking assaulted her in the parking lot!* How many fucking times have you been hit in the head?" Brandon stalks off toward his car, shaking his head at me in disgust. I jump in my truck and speed off after Andi. Brandon's right—of course she's not okay.

Shane told me a little about this douchebag Brad. When I saw him lift her up off the floor, I wanted to wipe the floor with him. After Shane told me why he hates douche-Brad so much, I wished I had done it. Andi went on a couple of dates with him but wouldn't sleep with him. Shane said Andi knew almost right away that he was trouble. When she turned douche-Brad down, he tried to drag her off, just like he did tonight. No doubt to rape her but something else must be off in the guy's head. He thinks if he just has time alone with her then she'll change her mind.

I would've loved to been the one to give him a beat down. But when I saw him dragging her off and she was fighting with everything she had, I automatically went to her. I want to protect her and love her. It just felt natural to get her first when I knew Shane wouldn't let douche-Brad get away.

I reach her house and see her bedroom light is on so I know she made it home. I scrape my hands over my face, force myself out of the truck, and walk up to ring her doorbell. I don't really expect her to open the door.

I know she'll look out the window, see my truck and tell me to fuck off. But I wait anyway. She doesn't answer after a couple of doorbell rings and I sit down on the porch floor with my back to the door. I lean my head back and turn to look at the doorknob.

"Andi, baby," I say to the door, "I'm so sorry. I'm such a jerk and I fucked this up so badly. I should've listened to you. I should've heard you out. I never should've left you there. I should've driven you home

144

tonight. So many fucking times I should've told you so many things. I want to be the one who always protects you. I love you—with all of my heart and soul, I love you. I miss you, Andi...I miss you so fucking much I can't breathe."

I sit here on the floor of her porch for I don't know how long, hoping she heard me. Hoping she'll open the door and let me in. But the door doesn't open and there's no sound behind it, so I begrudgingly leave. I'm going back to my apartment alone again and it's on the drive there that it hits me hard that I've lost her for good. This isn't me being pissed or being stupid again. This is me realizing the rest of my life will be spent without her.

After enduring two nights of no sleep, I stumble into the living room and turn on the TV for the Monday morning news. I flip through the stations until a familiar face catches my eye. The local news channel is showing a picture of Andi. It's an older picture but it's still her. I can't move as my brain strains to comprehend what the reporter is saying.

"Andrea Morgan, daughter of the legendary Maxwell Morgan, will officially assume control her family's various properties and, of course, their mass media conglomerate with assets estimated to be in the billions, tonight for her 25th birthday. An elaborate, A-list, invitation-only gala has been planned for at the Hyatt Regency Atlanta Ballroom. If you were lucky enough to be on the invite list, you will definitely be in for a treat tomorrow night. If you're like the majority of us who were *not* on that list, you can count on us to bring it to you live."

That's my Andi the reporter is talking about. This is one thing my dad was right about. Andi's birthday is a big deal and she never mentioned the first thing to me about it. But Brandon's words keep coming back to haunt me—*you know her.* I didn't trust in her when that's really the only thing she ever asked of me. I let her down when she desperately needed me. I won't make that mistake again. So no matter what the circumstances *look* like, I will trust her.

The ringing of my cell phone jars me out of my haze. It's my dad. Groaning to myself, I answer. He doesn't even say hello.

"Did you see the news just now?" He barks out at me.

"Yes, I saw it."

"Now do you see what I was talking about?"

"I see that she's inheriting her family's business on her 25th birthday. Isn't that pretty standard for something of this magnitude?"

"I guess so," he mumbles, losing some of his bravado.

"But what I don't see is where she's done anything against me, Dad." I know my tone is accusing and disrespectful, but I can't figure out why my dad flipped out over this. "Something else you know that I don't?"

"Son, it's complicated," his confidence is all but gone now.

I sit up on the edge of the couch, ready to pounce on what he means exactly. "What. Is. Complicated," I ground out. I have a very bad feeling about this.

Suddenly I hear my mom's voice on the line. "Luke, maybe you should come over so we can talk."

Crazy Maybe

I don't remember driving to my parents' house but suddenly I'm barging through the door, calling for them. "Mom! Dad! Where are you?"

My mom meets me on the way to the kitchen and I immediately notice her eyes are bloodshot, red-rimmed, and puffy. She motions for me to follow her outside where Dad is waiting at the patio table. The one Andi bought them.

"What the hell is going on, Dad?" I'm not in the mood for any fucking games.

Dad sighs heavily and looks deeply into this coffee cup, as if the answer is swimming there, before answering. "Andi's father, Maxwell, and I were once business partners. We had a real estate development agreement and he'd bought a key piece of property just before he died. Max had put up all the money for that property to help me out, so my name obviously wasn't on the deed.

"When he died, the property was tied up in probate and I haven't been able touch it. I've lost money on this deal for years. We own the property around it but the development couldn't be done without the one parcel he had bought.

"I realized who Andi was when she told us about her parents' death and how she was put in foster care. So," his voice cracked and he stopped talking for a minute.

"I had a private investigator look into her background. He found the court documents of when she was sent to the mental hospital. Then he visited the hospital and got the pictures of her when she was there. When you walked in during our conversation, I had just told Andi that if she didn't give me that property, I would leak those pictures to the press and

147

the board would block her from taking over her family's business."

He won't even look up at me. The shame of what he's done has taken a significant toll on him. But that doesn't stop the intense anger and outrage at what he's done to Andi. And to me.

I emphasize each word in a menacing whisper while my eyes blaze with fury directed solely at him. "You used and hurt the only person who has ever believed in me without question. Then you twisted everything to turn me against her."

I'm not asking questions. I'm making statements but he still acknowledges what he's done.

"Yes, Luke." A tear drops from his eye but he won't meet my hard stare.

And my response echo's through the yard. "*Why*?"

"My business is going under! We will lose *everything*. The property is an old, dilapidated building and it means nothing to her. She will have more money that she knows what to do with. She can afford to lose this one thing. I would've never given those pictures to anyone—ever. I just needed to make her think I would so she would go along with it. I thought I had to put pressure on her to make sure she gives me what I need. She loves you. I thought if the pictures didn't work, then the threat of losing you would."

My dad is near panic and so am I. It's not a good combination. "That's why she said she would've given it to you freely if you'd just told her you needed it," I'm just now understanding her comment from that night.

This makes my father completely break down and tears are falling down his cheeks. "Yes."

"How the hell could you do this to us? I love her, Dad. I love her more than anything and I completely betrayed her." Wait a minute... "What else do you know about her being remanded to the mental hospital?"

He takes a deep breath, "That was all true, but the PI said the circumstances were very, very suspicious. She attacked her foster father, who was some well-known political figure but his name has been redacted from every document. Everyone the PI asked about it warned him off of it. Told him to leave it alone if he valued his life."

My response is like a lion's roar, "*You knew this when you showed me the pictures? When you let me believe a lie about her?*"

Dad nods his response. "I'm so sorry, son. I can't tell you how sorry I am. I love you, and I love Andi, and I hate myself for what I've done."

I don't even know what to do with this information. I don't know how to process all this shit.

CHAPTER SEVENTEEN

ANDI

"I'm not going," I state matter-of-factly.

"Oh hell, yes, you are, girl," Tania retorts, just as matter-of-factly, as she digs through my closet, tossing clothes all over the floor. "You have nothing to wear tonight."

"I've already said that," I point out to her, "and that's why I'm not going!"

The determination in Tania's eye can't be missed. She grabs my hand and drags me out of my house, ignoring my complaints. After hitting the Atlanta formal dress shops, we finally settle on a full-length gown with one long sleeve that covers my tattooed arm but leaves my other arm, shoulder, and back bare. It has navy blue and silver sequins set on black silk with a thigh-high split in the front. It is exquisite with the matching heels.

Tania and I go to our appointment with my hairdresser. I love the pink stripes in my hair. I got them because it helps get the kids at the youth center to trust me. But I was convinced, ahem, strong-armed, by Tania to get them covered up and go all blond for the board announcement tonight. I still can't believe this is really happening.

I've dreaded this day for so long—being thrust into the limelight and having all my secrets dissected by the media. Being judged for something none of them really know the truth about and knowing that no one would even believe me if I told them. I know it'll happen especially since Sam's private investigator found those pictures of me. Whoever the private investigator got them from will undoubtedly make the connection and sell copies to the highest bidder. I hope I've found a private island to seclude myself on by then.

Our hair is perfectly coifed, our manicures and pedicures are professionally done, and now our makeup is being expertly applied. The makeup artist is using stage makeup so it won't fade away under all the flashing bulbs tonight. It feels thick like rubber and I'm sure it'll hold up during a nuclear bomb blast. Whatever it takes, right? Tania's driving me home and insists I keep the air vents from blowing on my perfectly finessed coiffure. I roll my eyes and comply because she scares me a little when she's like this.

I've arranged for a limousine to take us to the Hyatt Regency. Tania is my plus-one tonight and she looks fabulous. The driver calls my cell to let me know he's just pulled up outside my house and Tania and I walk out my front door to go face the tenth circle of hell. With the clicking of the door shutting behind me, Tania and I are off to the ballroom in our more-than-Sunday-best clothes.

Exiting the limousine, the flashes of light are absolutely blinding and they're going off from every direction. The photographers are yelling my name and questions I can't really understand because the roar is so loud. I'm glad there are ropes up to keep them back, otherwise I'm sure I'd be swamped by them right now. My family's lawyer, Bill Stanton, warned me it would be this way, so Tania and I keep our best smiles plastered to our faces and ignore the questions.

It's much more subdued inside the ballroom. There's a small band playing classical music in the corner and the tones carry lightly throughout the room. Wait staff walks the room with trays of various types of hors d'oeuvres and flutes of champagne. There's also a buffet table with small trays and finger foods but I don't see anyone eating. Everyone looks too pretentious to dare pile a plate full of food at a gathering like this.

I dare Tania to do it and threaten to call her all sorts of names for the rest of her life if she chickens out. Like me, she doesn't cave to peer pressure and threatens to call me worse names regardless of some stupid dare. This is why I brought her—she can make me laugh no matter how deep I am in my own pity party. We mingle for about thirty minutes before I run into Bill, who is really the only other person here that I know.

We chat for a few minutes before he escorts me around the room to introduce me to my father's old associates, and of course, the chief executive officer of MaxMorgan Music. The CEO will be making a huge announcement tonight and I'm so glad this will soon be over. I've been very anxious over the decision I had to make, but it seemed easier to make after the last night I was at Luke's parents' house. Tonight hopefully closes that chapter. And here I am thinking about Luke again. My heart is still broken and even though I try to tell myself I won't look back, that's exactly what I keep finding myself doing.

A few reporters have been allowed inside the ballroom and they're taking pictures as we make our way forward. My confident smile is plastered in place and I'm consciously avoiding fidgeting in front of the cameras. I draw in a sharp breath when the current CEO of MaxMorgan Music finishes his introduction speech and calls me to the podium.

Crazy Maybe

"Thank you all for coming tonight. I know most of you personally knew or worked for my father and I appreciate the support you're showing by just being here. After careful deliberations with key executive officers and legal counsel, we have come to an agreement for the future of MaxMorgan Music."

The term *you-could-hear-a-pin-drop* comes to mind.

"MaxMorgan Music will remain fully intact but I will not assume CEO responsibilities. That position will remain in the capable hands of our current CEO. I am very proud of the company my father built and the many employees and executives have cultivated into a prestigious, lucrative corporation. In no way do I want to detract from that achievement. While a part of me desperately wants to hold onto my father's legacy, I know that's not a reasonable expectation.

"MaxMorgan Music will remain a privately owned company and my interest will be sold back to the company for an undisclosed amount. I have accepted a contract position within the company to identify and sign new musical talent and I am looking forward to being a contributing member of the staff. Thank you for your support and dedication to the future of MaxMorgan Music."

I step away from the podium and ignore the questions the reporters are yelling to me. The public relations director takes the podium and informs the media that she will be glad to answer any business-related questions but that I will not be taking any business or personal questions at this time. Her blunt, no-nonsense statement leaves no room for argument.

Bill Stanton and the lawyers for MaxMorgan Music escort me to a private room where I'm given a copy of the papers that finalized the deal I just announced. We shake hands and exchange pleasantries. My contract

153

Crazy Maybe

position basically means that I can work when I want to and I'm paid on a per-case basis. The money doesn't really matter to me, especially since after selling the company to a handful of specific private investors, I'm now a billionaire.

The only thing is, I've never felt more alone in my adult life.

CHAPTER EIGHTEEN

ANDI

Tuesday morning, I arrive at Bill's office to finalize the transfer of the property to Sam. I'm dreading this meeting and I'm looking forward to it at the same time. I dread seeing Sam and Linda again after our last time together. I had started seeing them as my own family and now having them, and Luke, ripped from my life has been harder than I could have ever imagined. The only reason I'm looking forward to it is to get it over with and get on with my life. I need complete closure on everything to do with them and Luke.

The only thing I can't bring myself to do is cut Brandon out of my life. He's been too good to me and I would never do that to him. He calls or texts every few days to check on me and asks if there's anything he can do to help. His support means a lot to me when I have very few people I can truly count on. I sort of wish he was going to be there today. Even if he sat with his parents, at least I would still feel his support of me.

So imagine my surprise...and horror...as I step into Bill's conference room and find Luke, Sam and Linda there waiting for me. This is just *perfect*. I sit on the opposite side of the table from them and avoid eye contact. We're all obviously more than uncomfortable since no one speaks until Bill and another man walk in the room. Bill introduces him as the Woods' lawyer and he shakes my hand. He has a weak grip and the vibes I get from him make me want to urgently wash my hands. With bleach.

Bill and Sleazy, as I've nicknamed him, give a stack of papers to Sam and me and Bill takes the lead in explaining what each paper is. When Bill first learned of this property transfer and the reasons behind it, he vehemently disagreed with my decision to just give it to Sam. I don't want his money, I don't want his company's money, and I don't want his bank's money. I didn't give Bill a choice–I just told him to make it happen as fast as possible after my birthday.

So here we are the morning after my birthday. There's some strange rule–something about property or taxes, I don't know because I'm not really listening. But apparently Sam has to pay *something* for the property, some amount of money regardless of how little. It's asinine but we'll make it happen anyway. Everyone is waiting for me to answer Bill's question about the amount I want to list.

"One dollar," I respond to Bill, flatly. I purposely don't look at anyone whose last name is Woods, even though I can feel all of their eyes on me. Bill's lips form a tight, straight line and I know he wants to argue. I arch one brow at him, daring him to push me, and he nods curtly and fills in the blank with his handwritten note.

We make a few more adjustments to the papers and Bill calls his assistant in to update and reprint the paperwork for us to sign and seal the deal. While we're waiting, Bill turns up the volume on the flat screen TV at the other end of the room to listen to the news. I look briefly at the TV when I hear my name mentioned and I see the footage from the gala last night. I quickly look away and from my peripheral vision, I can see Luke and

Sam both staring at the TV. The reporter's next statement catches my attention, though.

"Just last night, Andrea Morgan reportedly became a multi-billionaire after selling her father's company to private investors. Today, we see Andrea from a totally different perspective in these photos obtained by *The Biz Insiders.*"

I look back up at the screen and see the pictures of my 15-year-old self in the mental hospital. The very same pictures that Sam dug up on me. I've obviously been crying and I'm vigorously fighting with the orderlies. In this particularly lovely shot, I'm wearing a hospital gown, so it had to be the day they transported me there and had performed all sorts of wonderful tests on me before they would let me wear my own clothes.

The reporter is regaling the lies that my foster family told to get me locked up in that hospital like it's the gospel. Just remembering those days is bad enough, but the myriad of emotions running through me watching this unfold for the world to see is overwhelming. I'm literally watching as my reputation is completely mauled by people who have no clue what they're talking about.

The reporter continues with her lies, "Andrea was thrust into notoriety by her association with the world-famous company, MaxMorgan Music, started by her father. Both of her parents were killed in a car wreck when Andrea was only 6. She was placed into foster care and soon was taken in by a loving, prestigious family. It was then that Andrea's mental illness made itself known when she attacked and attempted to kill her foster father.

"The generous family who took her in declined to speak on camera and court documents have been sealed because Andrea Morgan was a minor, thus preventing us from identifying the family. However, their continued concern for her is impressive and commendable.

"The family's spokesperson provided the following quote, 'Andrea cannot be blamed for what happened. She experienced too much trauma in her youth and we should've seen the signs earlier and sought help for her. Our only regret is that Andrea ever had to leave our home.'"

"*Turn. It. Off,*" I say forcefully to Bill. From the redness of his neck and face, his narrowed eyes and the clenched jaw, I'd say he's about half as angry as I am right now.

Sam finally speaks, "Andi, I'm so-"

I cut him off mid-sentence with my words and with my eyes. "*Don't.* Don't say you're *sorry.* You have *no idea* what you've done–and I'm not even talking about what you've done to me."

Sam opens his mouth to answer, then closes it without saying a word. He finally says, "I don't understand."

"Yeah, well, that's pretty obvious," I deadpan.

"I didn't leak those pictures, Andi."

"You didn't have to, Mr. Woods. The private investigator could've done it. The person he got them from could've done it. Anyone who that person told could've done it. There's no telling how much money they made off those pictures. This was set in motion the second you hired that PI to investigate me. Another thing you don't understand, Mr. Woods, is that because this has been leaked, *you and your family* are now in danger, along with others who are *innocent.*"

I think I've done pretty well at keeping the emotion out of my voice in this exchange. I'm dying to explode right now–start ranting, raving, throwing things, breaking shit. But I sit here with my fists balled up so tightly that my fingernails are digging into my skin. The family's "statement" disgusts me. They are so full of shit. That *family,* and I use that term loosely, never cared about my traumatic childhood or me. They're scrambling to cover their sins right now.

"Bill, I need to finish this now. I have other things to do today." I state calmly.

We sign the papers and the property is now Sam's. Bill asks everyone to wait as he steps out of the conference room and within a minute is back with Hugh Donovan, of Donovan Enterprises. He is a huge name in commercial property development and I've secretly negotiated a deal with him on Sam's behalf.

I have inherited other properties he wants to develop and I agreed to work with him on it if he would do this for me. He's here to offer Sam and Linda an enormous amount of money for the property I just sold for a dollar and for all of Sam's adjoining property. The insane amount of money will more than set Sam and Linda up for life. I know I have no obligation to help them, but I can't help but think Sam must be pretty desperate to do what he did.

Hugh makes the offer and the blood drains from both Sam and Linda's faces. Sleazy grabs up the paper and quickly reviews it. He looks at Sam and nods. Sam and Linda whisper amongst themselves while Luke gives me curious looks. I won't look at him, though, because he can read me all too well. Sam agrees to Hugh's proposal, they sign and close their own deal.

Hugh shakes hands all around the table before giving me a pointed look before he leaves. After a few minutes of Sam, Linda, and Sleazy talking about Hugh's sudden offer, I look at Bill and incline my head toward the door, "I'm going now." The others hear me and stop talking. We all stand and I finally look at Luke. He looks like he's about to say something to me, so I quickly turn and walk to the door.

I stop at the door and suddenly feel the need to make a statement to Sam before I leave.

"Mr. Woods, you've obviously wanted this for a long time. With your newfound wealth, hopefully you'll find your friends are more loyal than some of mine have been. Be careful what you wish for...because you may get more than you bargained for."

LUKE

I've been staring a hole in Andi but she won't look at me. I know she's uncomfortable in this conference room with us–my mom, dad and me–and I can't blame her. I insisted on coming after what my dad told me he'd done and because she won't answer my calls. My dad's lawyer is in Bill's office looking over the paperwork before presenting it to Andi. All this over a damn piece of property.

My dad has been a nervous wreck all morning. I haven't helped his anxiety in this situation, either. I'm still so pissed at him for what he did to Andi and I told him repeatedly all the way here. He didn't even argue–neither did my mom. I found out that Mom didn't know what he'd planned until she was sitting in the room. That's why she was crying. She felt like she had to support her husband but ended up hurting Andi and me in the process.

Crazy Maybe

I would be in love with Andi even if she hadn't done all the things she has for me and for my parents. But knowing how generous and loving she is, it makes me even more furious with him. I have so much to prove to her and to make up to her. I just have to find a way to get her to damn listen to me. She has every right to be mad. And I have no right to whine and complain about how she won't listen to me. Isn't that exactly what I did to her?

I'm deciding on how to start a conversation with her when the lawyers walk in and take over the room. If it weren't completely inappropriate to change the subject, I would jump in and start talking to her. I decide against it when they said she has to set a price on the property. Her tone of voice says *don't-fuck-with-me* and I can't remember ever hearing her sound this hard before. I continue my analysis of her body language and blatant avoidance of making eye contact with me when I hear her name coming from the TV.

I turn my head to see pictures of her from her birthday celebration last night. It isn't the first time I've seen them. I stayed glued to the TV and internet last night just to catch glimpses of her. My god, she looks beautiful in that gown. The first thing I noticed, though, was the pink splotches were missing from her hair. Then I noticed the gown's long sleeve covered up her tattooed arm. The only tattoo that still showed was the one on her shoulder blade. It's a small, colorful phoenix and it's so sexy on her.

Then the image changes from my beautiful, confident vixen to a scared, young girl in a hospital gown, fighting with the staff at the mental hospital. They flip through all the pictures of her in that damn place, all the pictures that my dad has at home right now. They better fucking be at home anyway. I'm so fucking stunned to see these images on the huge flat screen TV that it takes my brain a second to register what the reporter is saying.

"*Andrea cannot be blamed for what happened. She experienced too much trauma in her youth and we should've seen the signs earlier and sought help for her. Our only regret is that Andrea ever had to leave our home.*"

Andi speaks and stuns the hell out of me. "*Turn. It. Off.*" I take back what I thought earlier–*this* is the hardest tone I've ever heard her take before. My dad tries to apologize to her but she won't hear it. I can't say I blame her. It's a little hard for "I'm sorry" to take away all the damage that's been done. But I wish she would accept his apology because it would give me some hope that she would accept mine.

But she doesn't. In fact, what she says next cuts me to the bone so I know it does my dad, too. He looks stunned. He never really thought through the consequences of what he had planned. He must have seen this whole thing going very different in his mind. Andi's statement that she wasn't even talking about what he'd done to her worries me. That implies my dad's actions are worse than we know.

When Dad assures her that he wasn't the one who leaked those pictures, I think he was trying to tell me, too. Because if he had been the one who did that, I don't know that I could ever forgive him for that. Even if he is my dad–that would just be too much. I wish I knew what all this is really about because I see the pure panic in Andi's face. Her words confirm the danger involved. But she also says that people other than her or my family are now in danger.

What. The. Hell. Happened?

Crazy Maybe

She's so ready to bolt but something is keeping her here. She's signed the papers, the property is my dad's, but she's still sitting here. Bill suddenly gets up and within a few seconds is back with another man. When I hear his name, I instantly know who he is. And I know that the only way he could know about this meeting is either through Andi or her lawyer, because my dad's company is not in this man's league. This man is more in Donald Trump's league.

Andi suddenly looks a little self-conscious. She's fidgeting and keeping her eyes averted from me so that I can't see them at all. I can't see what kind of look she has, because she doesn't have a poker face at all–her eyes always give her away. That makes me even more suspicious and I know somehow she's arranged this meeting with my dad and Donovan. She keeps amazing me.

When I glance at the offer from Donovan, I know for a fact that Andi arranged this. The amount is insane and there's no way a man with his experience and resources would give that much for all the property my dad now owns. Even though it's prime real estate and is the equivalent of the entire block. Donovan would find a way to squeeze any opponents and get it at the bottom dollar. He didn't make his money and reputation by being this generous. Andi is generous to a fault, even when she has no reason to be.

Andi tries to make her exit as soon as Hugh leaves but I have been waiting for this. I stand as she does and my parents rise from their seats. She finally looks me in the eye and I'm ready myself to talk to her but she whirled around and rushed for the door in a split second. She suddenly stops and the hurt in her voice is like a dagger in my heart. I know she directed her statement at my dad, but it applies to me, too.

Crazy Maybe

"With your new found wealth, hopefully you'll find your friends are more loyal than some of mine have been."

Then she's out the door and walking swiftly toward the elevators. I'm on her heels before I know it and my hand reaches out to grab hers.

"Andi," I say on a whisper.

She turns to me and I see tears in her eyes, though she's fighting hard to keep them from falling down her cheeks. My hand cups her cheek and for just a few seconds, she leans her face into my hand and closes her eyes. A single tear rolls down her cheek and I wipe it away with the thumb of my other hand. She suddenly tenses and jerks her head up, out of my caress.

She swallows hard, "What do you want, Luke?"

"I want to talk. I've called, sent texts, and even came to your house. I'm just asking for time–time to say the things I need to say and time to hear whatever you have to say to me. Please."

Her eyes slowly roam around the empty hallway, taking time to thoroughly study the carpet and the elevator buttons, before she softly replies, "Our *time* has passed, Luke."

All the oxygen in the building has suddenly been sucked out because *I. Can't. Fucking. Breathe.*

"No," I say on what I'm sure the last bit of oxygen reserves I have in my lungs.

"It's too late, Luke," she replies with a choke.

The elevator dings, the door opens and she walks backwards until she's inside it. Our eyes remain locked on each other as the doors close. I don't care that we're on the 16th floor. I hit the stairs and take them two...or sometimes five...at a time until I'm busting out the door into the lobby. The security guard at the front desk startles at the sound of the door slamming into the wall as I run to the elevators.

My chest is heaving but not from the physical exertion of running down the stairs but from my heart that's splintering into a million pieces inside me. I reach the elevator just before the doors open and I get my speech ready to make her listen to me. If I have to carry her out of her thrown over my shoulder like a fucking caveman, I will do it. I block the doors and get ready for a fight...but she's not there.

CHAPTER NINETEEN

ANDI

Time? He wants time to talk–now? After my psychiatric-patient pictures have been splattered all over the news and internet, he decides he wants to talk to me. After his father tries to blackmail me to get the property he wanted, now he wants to talk. After he left me at his parents' house, broke his promise, broke my heart, and just fucking walked away from me, now he wants to talk.

A thought takes root in my mind…something I haven't considered until now. *He was in on this from the start–that's why he reacted that way.* His dad gave him his planned out that night–a way out of our relationship and away from me. It makes sense to me now. Why else would he not even ask me any questions? Why else would he drive off and leave me stranded with the very people who were blackmailing me?

He's the one who needs to be in the psych ward, dammit!

My anger hits a boiling point and I hit the button for the next floor and get off the elevator. I make my way back up to the sixteenth floor to give him a minute of my time. I'm solely intent on telling him what's on my mind and not giving him a chance to say anything. But he's not there when I exit the other elevator and I run into his parents, who are more than a little shocked to see me again so soon.

166

Crazy Maybe

I brush past them without a word and barely a glance as I walk toward Bill's office. I'm still looking around for Luke because I'm intent on finishing this now. *Closure.* Not finding him, I go back to the elevator and I'm relieved to see his parents have already left. I hit the button for the sixth floor to take the bridge to the parking lot. My phone beeps in my purse, telling me I have a text. It's from Luke.

L: Andi...please

U and ur dad got what u wanted. Stop pretending now & leave me alone.

L: NO, Andi, that's not

He didn't finish his text but now my phone is ringing. He's calling me to finish his sentence and have this conversation out verbally but he's shit out of luck. I have nothing more to say to him. I decline his call and every consecutive one after that until I turn my phone off to be left alone. I consider stopping by the cell phone store to get my number changed but decide I am way too mentally drained to do that today. I make a mental note to do it later.

When I get home, Christina, Tania, and Katie are waiting for me in the driveway. Thankfully they're in one car so I open both garage doors and tell Christina to pull her car inside. If Luke comes by and sees a car here, I know he won't leave. I make another mental note to call that real estate agent that I've been meaning to call but have been putting off.

Procrastinators unite – tomorrow!

My girls don't have to ask—they know where everything is and what I need. They make quick work with the margarita machine and soon we're all headed to Margaritaville with Jimmy. I give them a recap of my day and I'm infinitely grateful that they don't need all the details of my mental hospital stay to believe me when I say it was all based on a lie. They know me well enough to let me have a little breathing room and time to regroup.

Christina turns on my iPhone to put it on the speaker dock and one text after another comes through all at once. Followed by notifications of numerous voicemails. We ignore them, turn on the music and turn up the volume. The hot tub on my back porch has never felt better than it does right now. We're all in it, only leaving the hot water and relaxing jets to use the margarita machine and refill our pitcher. Several times.

I'm thankful to have a large house with multiple bedrooms and bathrooms because everyone will be staying with me tonight. Actually, we have done this pretty frequently, so every one of them has some clothes here. And whatever they don't have, they know they can just take mine—except my toothbrush, of course. It feels a lot like when we were in college and all shared a four-person dorm room.

I don't know what I'd do without my fun and supportive best friends.

Friday night at the club with my girls, I plan to get my drink on and try to feel better. I still haven't talked to Luke or responded to his daily text messages. And I obviously haven't changed my number yet. But I have started back at the gym instead of letting him run me off from one of the few places that have ever felt like home to me. I am glad that we've somehow missed each other all week, though. I'm not getting into this in front of Mack and the guys.

Crazy Maybe

Tonight is my real birthday celebration, though–with my real friends. We meet at a small sports bar before heading to the club later. After my last performance, I left the club before finding out if I had advanced to the finals or not. At the time I didn't really care, but when Mitch sent me a text to let me know I'm one of the five finalists set to perform next weekend, I have to admit I was excited. So now I have to figure out what song I'm going to sing. I have an idea but I need to work out the details in my mind first.

It's still early, but the restaurant-slash-bar is already pretty full. The two TVs over the bar are on the local channels and we're sharing some appetizers when I hear the reporter saying my name again. I roll my eyes as I say, "I thought my 15 minutes of fame was over."

The silence at the table is suddenly deafening. I look up to see Christina, Tania, and Katie's stunned faces. I whip my head around to the TV and they're showing the youth center. I'm being investigated for my involvement with the kids and what kind of influence I am on them.

There's a social worker that has never met me, giving an interview and reciting all the ways that I may be a threat to the children. They're questioning who approved me to work there. They cut to a parent who is asking if I will be suspended until an investigation can be conducted.

They don't even know that it's my personal money that funds that youth center. They've never questioned my involvement or my motives before this week. They've never cared that while some of the parents were too high on drugs to care for their own children, I was feeding, clothing and protecting them from the dangers of the neighborhood. Or when the parents were working multiple jobs and long hours just to try to make ends meet, I was helping their children with their homework and doing everything possible to keep them in school. But suddenly, I'm the monster who has been hiding in plain sight and feeding on their children without them even knowing it.

The reporter is holding up the front page of several different publications–magazines, tabloids, and newspapers–with various headlines but all about the mental hospital, the youth center, or my alleged attack on my foster father. It's sickening how the vultures have descended upon me and have torn me apart without the first shred of evidence. The term "innocent until proven guilty" has never really rang true with me– why else would someone have to *defend* themselves? It's more like "guilty until proven innocent, but even then doubt will always remain."

I bury my face in my hands for a minute. I am not retreating, I am not giving up, and I am not caving in. I am simply refortifying and readying myself for all-out battle. I can't avoid this any longer–it's impacting the youth center now and there are too many kids who need support. If my former foster family has any foster kids now, they need to be protected more than anyone I know. I steel my nerves and take a deep breath as I raise my face to my girls.

"It's about time to head to the club," I firmly state.

Our usual table is inhabited by the usual suspects– Shane, Will, Brandon and of course, Luke. He has his back to me and doesn't know I'm here yet. So I walk to the DJ booth and tell him to queue up a song for me. I had a few drinks at the pub we just left, I'm pissed, and I'm really fucking hurt, so I'm going to take it out on the stage. The song, *Just A Fool*, is actually a duet between Christina Aguilera and Blake Shelton, but tonight I'm singing it solo. And I'm singing it with every bit of emotion I have bubbling just below the surface of my cool façade.

The lyrics are perfect for me right now. I obviously feel like a fool because I can't get over him and I can't let him go, but I know I should. I feel like I'm weak for wanting him to make this all up to me. For even thinking I could forgive him if he would just do something to take this pain away. Love feels like a cruel joke and no one has hurt me in the way that he has. I just want to forget about love and about him, but somehow he's in every thought I have and every move I make.

I leave the stage and a friend from the gym I haven't seen in a while stops me and asks me to dance with him. Another slow song is playing so I step into his embrace and we take the opportunity to catch up. He asks how I'm holding up, knowing how bad my life sucks right now, and I give him a noncommittal shrug of my shoulders. Christina taps on my arm and her gaze suddenly shifts and I turn to see what she's looking at.

Oh. It's Luke and he is charging forward like a bull, hell-bent on his destination. Which happens to be me at the moment.

"Andi," he barks at me.

"Yes," I reply smugly.

I watch intently as he grits his teeth and clenches and flexes his hands. His anger is barely contained and he's working hard at restraining himself. I know I'm not helping it but I'm no more in the mood to be fucked with right now than he is.

"I need you to come with me," he finally says.

"No."

He nods his head, seemingly understandingly, until I realize that I read him completely wrong. He just decided he wasn't going to argue with me. In the typical method of the men in my life, he picks me up with ease, throws me over his shoulder, and charges back to the front door. People watch with amused expressions as I scream obscenities at him like a lunatic until he reaches the door. Then I realize we're going outside and there may be cameras that catch me actually acting like a lunatic, so I stop.

"Luke—do not walk out that door with me over your shoulder. I'm in the news enough as it is. I don't need to add any more to it," I say in my sternest voice possible. This stops him in his tracks and I know he hears the words I didn't say—*thanks to your family*.

He puts me down but doesn't let go of me. "Then walk with me like a normal person would."

I sigh heavily, not hiding my dislike of his demand and respond with the typical pissed-off female response. "Fine."

CHAPTER TWENTY

LUKE

Damn, infuriating woman! I've called, left voicemails, sent texts, banged on her door at all hours of the damn day and night. No answer—not even one! The last thing she said to me implied that I was only with her to help my dad get what he wanted. That not only hurt, but that also infuriated and insulted me. Then she ignores me and won't even let me fucking respond to that fucked up statement. What the hell?

Shane has been barely speaking to me for the past couple of weeks. He's known something has been really wrong. He's not stupid by any means. He's known all this shit with Andi has something to do with me. I finally broke down and told him everything today and I swear I thought he was going to tear my head off. I'm not afraid of any man but I know I would've deserved this ass whooping. He broke a bunch of shit in the gym to work out his anger and avoid breaking *me*.

He did ultimately threaten to have my balls stuffed and mounted if I didn't make everything right for Andi. I believe he would carry out that threat. He really does love and protect her like a brother should for his sister. Like I should have as her friend and her lover, but when the pressure was on, I caved. The press is getting bad around her and we're both concerned about what kind of toll it's taking on her. Her strength amazes me.

I'm waiting inside the club because I know she'll be here tonight. Shane told me he's meeting the girls here

Crazy Maybe

so I am taking full advantage of it. We were waiting here for them when her face was all over the TV screens and when I heard all the people, who don't even know her, tearing her down, my protective instincts went into hyper drive. Then she walked right by our table and went straight for the stage. I've had to use every bit of my willpower to keep from storming the stage and carrying her off so we can be alone.

That song she's singing is killing me. *Killing me.* She's pouring all of her pain into it and singing about what a fool she is over me–because she thinks I used her. She thinks the reason I didn't stand up to my dad is because I was in on his blackmail scheme. She thinks every second I spent with her was a sham and that I'm not sitting here with my heart bleeding out inside me. *Killing me* one damn word at a time.

Shane stands up and he is one pissed off brother. He glares at me and I swear he was about to break my jaw when Katie stands up, takes his hand and leads him to the dance floor for a slow dance. The others follow suit and leave me here to stew and wallow alone in my pitiful state. All of my willpower drains when she finishes singing and starts dancing with some other man, who is too happy to have her in his arms. So, I stomp toward her and demand that she come with me.

And, of course, being as stubborn as she is, she refuses to come with me. So, being as stubborn as I am and refusing to let one more day go by, I nod my head to my own conclusion that I will resort to kidnapping her and deal with the consequences later.

I throw her over my shoulder and carry her off the dance floor. People give us curious looks but no one interferes. I guess my *don't-even-fucking-try-it* face is on full strength tonight.

It's only when I hear the voice that she uses with the kids who get out of line at the center that it registers I'm about to walk outside with her thrown over my shoulder, against her will, and she's obviously pissed off about it.

I reconsider my kidnapping idea since there may be cameras outside that capture my crime. The damn reporters have been following her everywhere lately. Mitch has done a good job of keeping the fuckwads out of the club.

I put her down but I don't let go of her. I can still kidnap her and make it look like we're holding hands. Once I have her at my place, I just won't let her go until this is resolved. I'll take good care of her for the next forty or so years until she decides to forgive me. Then we'll live happily ever after. She agrees to walk with me like a normal person so I take full advantage of it by linking our fingers together and holding tight.

I lead her to my truck and help her into the passenger seat and lock her door before closing it. I quickly round the front of the truck, climb into the driver seat and buckle her in while she looks at me like I'm crazy. I may be a little nuts right now but it's her fault if I am. If she'd just answered my calls, my texts or even her fucking door, I wouldn't have to resort to committing a felony right now.

"Luke. What the hell do you think you're doing?" She asks in annoyance as I start the truck and put it in drive.

Think fast. "With all the press coverage, I thought it would be best to keep moving so no one films us talking and twists it for another story," I lie. I'm kidnapping her and the longer I can keep her from realizing it the more likely I am to succeed.

Crazy Maybe

She nods tentatively, like she's considering my reasoning but isn't completely sure of my sanity. I sneak a look at her when I check the adjacent lane for traffic.

"So, you're just randomly driving then? No destination in mind?" She asks calmly, but I know that tone she's using better than she thinks I do.

Shit. "Yes." *No.* "I'm just driving the roads I know well. In case I need to make a sudden detour." *Sounds reasonable.*

"What do you want from me, Luke?" She sounds exhausted now–weary with me. It suddenly occurs to me that I have to somehow get her out of the truck without her throwing a fucking hissy fit on me. That would draw way too much attention.

"I want to talk to you, Andi. And I want you to listen to me. And I want to help you," I reply and even I can hear the pleading edge of my voice.

"If I agree to this, will you leave me alone then?"

"Yes." *No.*

She sighs heavily again, telling me she's pissed that she's being forced into it, but I'll take it any way I can get it.

"Fine."

"Your house or my apartment?" I say casually. I really don't care which one she chooses but her house would be easier because she doesn't have close neighbors.

"My house," she replies without hesitation or issue.

The kidnapping stars are aligned and winking at me tonight.

Her phone beeps and she pulls it out to check her text message. She quickly types a response back and I mentally note that all of her fingers are, in fact, not broken, thus she could've answered any of the hundreds of messages I've sent her.

"Your friends worried about you?" I ask with a smile, though I just really want to know if some fucker is texting her.

"Yeah, they asked if you kidnapped me," she says pointedly.

I stifled a choke to avoid giving away my plan. I chuckled at their joke. "And what did you tell them?"

"I said that still remains to be seen," she cuts her eyes at me, "but that I'm fine for the moment."

I give her my best smile, "You know I'd never hurt you, Andi." *Kidnap you, yes. Hurt you, never.*

"Maybe. But that's not what they asked, is it now?" She cleverly replies. My little vixen is very shrewd.

"Here we are," is my only response as I pull into her driveway.

I've never been so glad to reach a destination in my life. I jump out of the truck and rush to open her door and escort her inside, astutely cloaking my excitement at being at her house with her in tow, and all without the need of chloroform to achieve any of this. All in all, it's a good night.

We're inside now and she's walking toward the chair, but I want her to sit with me so I gently steer her toward the couch. She sits at one end and I know she expects me to sit on the other end, but when I sit I leave no space between us. She looks a little perturbed at this but she turns slightly toward me and waits patiently.

"I'm not really good at this, Andi, so first let me say *I'm sorry* right now in case I say something wrong." She nods but doesn't say anything.

"Saying I'm sorry isn't enough, even though I mean it. I'm infinitely sorry for what I've done, but there are a few things I want to explain that will hopefully help you understand me." She looks interested in hearing what I have to say so I continue.

"Several years ago, I started seeing this girl, Megan. We were together for a while and we were pretty serious. Her father, Carl, owned the gym where I was working out and that's where we met. My father's business was doing really good and he had a lot of high-profile development projects going on. So, during a family get together one night, Carl mentions in casual conversation with my dad that he has some plans to revamp his gym. They talk shop for a little while and before long, they have a verbal agreement for my dad's men to do the work for Carl.

"Turns out, it was a lot of work and it took a lot of resources away from the other projects my dad had going on. He lost a lot of money doing work on the gym and had penalties against him for not finishing his other projects on time. I found out way too late that Megan only wanted to date me–or Brandon–to get my dad to do the work for her dad for free. She had been flirting with Brandon behind my back the whole time she was with me. I walked in on them kissing one day and that was the end of us and it almost tore apart my relationship with my brother.

"It has taken a long time for me to forgive him and it was actually because of you. He's tried to tell me for years about that day and I wouldn't listen to him. I think I always knew deep down but I didn't want to face it. She had kissed him and he pushed her away. But when I saw them, I didn't see him push her away so I've blamed Brandon all this time. But Brandon said something to me that really shook me. He told me to stop using Megan as the standard I use to judge other women.

Crazy Maybe

"I did that to you. When Dad showed me those pictures and the court document, I put you in that category. Andi, I've always felt guilty for how Megan and Carl's scheme hurt my dad's business. If it weren't for me, he would've finished those big projects on time and wouldn't have lost so much money. When he showed me those pictures and told me that stuff about you, I immediately jumped to the conclusion that you were using me for something and lying to me about who you really are.

"I was completely in the wrong for that, and I am sorry, even though I know that won't make up for how much I hurt you. But I swear to you, *on my life*, that I had nothing to do with my dad's scheme and I didn't know anything about it. He knows without a doubt how mad I am at him right now. Brandon's mad at him, too, and he feels really bad about everything. The only time I've ever seen that man cry is when he talked about how he'd hurt you and me.

"I know I broke my promise to you, Andi, and as much as that hurts you, it hurts me. It hurts me every single day. I will spend every single day of the rest of my life doing everything and anything within my power to make it up to you. No matter what it takes or what sacrifices I have to make—you are more than worth it. This whole mess is no one's fault but my own. No matter what my dad—or anyone—said, I should've stood by you. I will never make that mistake again."

"Is that why you never thought your family accepted your career choice?" Her voice is so soft but it is full of emotion.

I nod, "Yes. I made a terrible choice in the girl, right? Not only did I catch her with my brother, but she and her father screwed my dad over. I got the brunt of that blame from the family. So when I didn't follow the

179

family's advice and go into business, or real estate development like my dad, everyone automatically thought I'd fail again."

"*You* thought you'd fail," she states. It scares me sometimes, how she sees so much of me that no one else sees.

"It doesn't make it right or excusable, but I hope you better understand my reaction now." It's a statement, but I raise my eyebrows in question, looking for an answer.

She considers me for a minute, her astute eyes boring into my soul again before she answers. "Yes, I understand better now. I still wish you would've listened to me, though...," her voice trailed off with her last statement.

"Andi, I should have-"

"Luke, wait. I wish you had let me explain *that* night, but I should have told you about it before then. I have to take my part of the blame in this. I wanted to tell you, I really did, but I was selfish. I was afraid I would lose you, so I kept putting it off, wanting just a little more time with you. You never should have heard it from someone else first. I'm sorry for not telling you when I first realized how important you were to me."

The tears are glistening in her eyes after her apology. My mind caught her words–'*but I was selfish*'– and all I can think is how she's the most *un*selfish person I've ever known.

"Andi, you're not selfish. You are the kindest, most giving, and most loving person I've ever met. How can you say you were selfish?" I ask sincerely.

"Because you had a right to know. If you wanted to be with me, you had a right to hear from me exactly what you were getting into. I just wanted to keep you a little bit longer. Every day, I just wanted one more day with you." She's wiping tears away as soon as they fall, trying to maintain her composure.

Could I be any more of an idiot? I let this wonderful creature get away from me.

She continues talking and wiping the stray tears away, "I never dreamed it would come out the way it did. But with my twenty-fifth birthday coming up, I knew it would probably come out somehow. I'm really sorry if I caused problems between you and your dad."

"Baby, no, *none* of this is your fault. I don't know what happened, why they put you in that hospital, but I believe you. Unconditionally, I believe you—you said it wasn't what it looked like and that's all I need to know."

I feel a little uneasy for a few minutes because she looks like she's in shock. Without warning, she breaks down in sobs and I wrap my arms around her. She hugs me tightly and I hold her for a few minutes while she cries. Like a dam has been released, her whole body shakes with sobs and it breaks my heart again. Even through the pain, it feels so good to hold her again that I completely understand what she meant when she said she just wanted one more day with me. Every day, I just want one more day with her.

"I have no right to ask this of you, Andi, but I can't help it. If you're selfish, I guess I'm just fucking greedy. *Please* forgive me. *Please* take me back. I miss you so much. I love you—so damn much," I resolve, that whatever I have to do or say to earn her love again, I will gladly do it.

She pulls away from my arms and looks down at our hands as she entwines them. I'm watching her and I feel my heart in my throat because, from the look on her face, I don't think I'm going to like her answer.

"Luke, thank you for explaining what all happened with Megan. It means a lot that you shared that with me. It does help me understand why you reacted that way. I do forgive you and I want you to forgive your father. He made a mistake but he's a good man. He did that for his family so it's hard for me to fault him for that," she stops talking for a few seconds.

"Why do I hear a 'but' in there?" I ask calmly but I'm really about to jump out of my fucking skin.

She looks up at me, blinks back the unshed tears in her eyes and resolutely declares, "But, I can't take you back, Luke. We can't get back together."

"You don't love me anymore?"

"No," she whispers, staring at our hands.

"You don't mean that." I don't believe her. Her words say one thing but I can see it in every fiber of her being. She's lying—and she doesn't lie very well. My beautiful little vixen.

The irony of the situation isn't lost on me. I can tell she's lying—it's so obvious in everything about her because she's not a good liar. That should've been my first clue when she tried to convince me to listen to her to begin with. Fuck—I am a moron.

"Look me in the eye and say the words. *'I don't love you, Luke.'* Say it, Andi," I demand. She cries harder and her tears are soaking my hand from where they're dripping off her beautiful face. "Say the words to my face, Andi."

I barely make out the words of her whispered response, "I can't."

CHAPTER TWENTY-ONE

ANDI

This is the hardest and the worst thing I've had to do since the night that landed me in the psychiatric hospital. But I know what danger lurks out there, waiting to pounce on me, and I can't put Luke and his family in the crosshairs. If anything happened to them because of me, I wouldn't be able to live with myself. Pushing him away is the only way I know I can even try to protect them from what's inevitably coming.

Luke's calling bullshit on me saying I don't love him anymore. Actually, I didn't even say those words. I just said 'no' when he asked me if I did. He knew that was a lie–that's why he's trying to make me say the words to his face. I can't do it. No matter what's happened, I can't do that. If this whole mess goes as badly as I'm afraid it will, I can't die with those being my last words to him.

I let go of his hands and stand up. I don't know what the deal is but when I cry, I can't breathe through my nose if I'm sitting down. I have to stand to get my sinuses cleared enough to breathe. When I stand, he stands and I almost chuckle. I had a feeling he was kidnapping me when he led me to his truck. But he's right about one thing. I know he would never physically hurt me.

I start pacing and he moves into position to block the door and prevent me from making a run for it. That wasn't my plan but I'll let him keep his illusion of control

183

over the room. I have bigger fish to fry right now. Like convincing a very large man that he needs my protection when he's the one who gets in the boxing ring with other large men and beats the crap out of them. This should go well.

I stop pacing and look at him, giving him a clear indication that I'm telling him the truth. "You're not going to like what I have to say."

"And that's different from just now…how?" He asks dryly, with a hint of the sarcastic humor he knows I love.

And I chuckle, a little. "Luke, I can't tell you that I don't love you. You already know that."

He smiles knowingly, "Then tell me you do. I will accept that, too."

"I do love you. I never stopped loving you," I finally admit–to him and to myself, "but we can't get back together, Luke." I'm on the verge of a real nervous breakdown here but I need to make him understand.

"And why is that, Andi?" he asks as he takes on his menacing fighting stance, fully blocking the door and looking very intimidating. This will make it harder to argue my case.

"Promise not to laugh?" I ask and can't keep the blush from creeping up my face.

He looks slightly amused already at my request, "This should be interesting. I promise I will do my best to not laugh. But I won't break another promise by saying I won't laugh when I don't have a clue what you're about to say."

Fair enough.

"I have to protect you."

His lips twitch and he sucks his cheeks in like he's making a fish face for a second before looking down at his feet. He's working hard to keep from laughing and to keep his promise to try not to laugh.

Crazy Maybe

"Go ahead," I concede, and he releases a hearty laugh that rumbles through his expansive chest. And that laugh sounds so good, so right, and it makes me miss our time together so much more.

"I'm sorry, baby, really," as he tries to regain his composure. He wipes his hand over his mouth as if it will wipe the huge, shit-eating grin off his face. "Care to explain that revelation?"

I'm suddenly serious and he takes the cue. "Luke, this is really hard to talk about, okay? I know it sounds funny and I know I'll have a hard time convincing you that I have to protect you, but-"

"First of all, I'm sorry for laughing. It's obviously not funny to you. It was just the way it sounded at first."

"I know—I don't blame you for that," I quickly explain.

"As much as you obviously want to protect me, I want to protect you, Andi. I don't understand why I need protecting, though."

To tell or not to tell, that is the question.

"Can you sit down and let me explain? I promise I won't make a run for the door," I add with a smile. He doesn't even pretend to not know what I'm referring to as he takes a seat. The one closest to the door.

Let's start with the shocking truth and see if he runs for the door. If not, I'll know I can finish the story. "The night I was put in the psychiatric hospital, I did attack my foster father with a knife and I would've killed him if I could have. But not for the reasons they say I did it."

He's shocked at first, but I don't blame him for that. He probably thought it was some kind of accident that went terribly wrong. "Okay, baby, go on." There's no judgment in his voice. No disbelief. No suspicion.

"It was just before my fifteenth birthday and I was the oldest of the foster kids. There were several—all

185

girls," and his face hardens, as if he is guessing what comes next. "There were five of us in all and the others were all between six and ten years old. Our foster mother wanted nothing to do with us and I was responsible for babysitting, helping with homework, baths–all that kind of stuff.

"One day, Maria, who was nine, had been sick all day. She had a fever and could hardly get out of the bed because she felt so bad. I'd given her medicine and fed her soup every few hours. I got up during the night to check on her and give her more fever-reducing medicine. When I opened her door, I found our foster father...raping her.

"Suddenly, everything made sense – how they only took in young girls, how shy and afraid of other people they were, why he looked guilty when I'd caught him in the girls' rooms before, and why the foster mother never wanted anything to do with the kids they got so much adoration for taking in.

"I had left a knife in her room from where I had peeled an apple for her earlier that evening. I picked it up and rushed toward him, intending to kill him for raping her, especially when she was so sick she couldn't fight back. I mean, as if her being sick made it worse, right? It was bad enough already but for some reason, knowing how sick she'd been and how little he cared about that just made it worse.

"I guess that *is* crazy thinking, isn't it?

"I don't regret it, though. And I never will. They convinced the authorities that I was mentally unstable because I had been bounced from one foster home to another before they took me in. They had me locked up for a year in that mental hospital where the staff tried to convince me *every day* that I was crazy. Sometimes I felt crazy, trying to convince them that I was sane and what I'd seen that night. I begged them to check the other girls but they ignored me.

"When the foster mother came to the hospital under the pretense of visiting me—to give me her *'forgiveness,'* all she wanted to do was make sure I knew my place. When I asked her why she didn't protect the little kids, do you know what she said to me? She said, 'Whom do you think gave him the idea? He wanted *you* for a long time, but I convinced him the younger ones would be easier for him to control.'

"Maria was raped at nine years old because *his wife* convinced him I would be too much trouble. She suffered what was originally meant for me. When I turned sixteen, since I was a ward of the state, I could be released and taken out of the foster system. That's when I got in touch with Bill and he helped me get my trust fund.

"After college, I started the youth center downtown to help other kids in bad situations. No one else knows it's my money that funds the whole program. I just wanted to help kids—because of how I left the other kids in that house to fend for themselves.

"The problem is he's a big political figure now—even more than he was when I lived with them. No one will believe me now. You can bet he's behind the smear campaign going on around me right now. And anyone who's with me will be drawn into this mess. I can't let that happen to you and your family, Luke."

I don't realize that I was frantically pacing as I explained the situation to Luke until I saw him leaned up, like a barricade, against the front door.

CHAPTER TWENTY-TWO

LUKE

Wow.

This is some crazy shit but I completely believe her. I can see her stabbing some asshole for hurting a child and not feeling bad for it. I don't blame her at all. And this is one more reason why I love her and I've fallen more in love with her in the last few minutes, if that is even possible.

She knows me too well. She was only half-joking when she said I didn't have to guard the door. She knew I had ulterior motives of getting her here. She gave me a chance to redeem myself when she announced that she had tried to kill the man but not for the reasons they stated. I could see it in her eyes–she was silently praying that I would trust her. And the way she couldn't lie to me and say she didn't love me? I fucking love that about her.

But when she said she had to protect me, I didn't know how to feel about it. At first, the way she said it, struck me as funny. I mean, I'm standing here looking at this petite, beautiful woman who owns my heart. She's built and has her feminine muscles from her own workouts, but she's not freakishly strong. I'm in training for heavyweight boxing and have been street-boxing for years. I routinely take on men who are over two hundred pounds of all muscle...and she wants to protect me?

I fucking love her.

Crazy Maybe

I have to admit, I was a little worried when her panic level kept rising while she was recounting what had happened all those years ago. She had a far-away look in her eyes and she was pacing erratically. I didn't think she's consciously try to escape from me but I was a little nervous that she would take off running out the front door from a full-blown panic attack. So I quietly moved around the room until I was leaning on the door to block her, just in case.

She seems to have realized this now because she's stopped talking and pacing–and seems to really see me. She smiles tenderly at me and says, "I'm okay, Luke. I'm not planning to bolt."

I push off the door and walk slowly to her, trying to not look threatening in any way. She watches me approach and doesn't move, doesn't back down in any way. I cup her face gently with my hands and peer into her eyes. "I love that you want to protect me. I love that you shared this with me and that you trusted me with it when you haven't trusted anyone with it before. But more than anything else, I love *you*, Andi. And there's no way I would let you shield me and put yourself on the line. I'm with you, remember? I'm with you."

"We're about to have a disagreement about this, Luke," she replied coyly and gave me her sweetest smile.

"You can disagree all you want, as long as I get my way and you don't try to ever leave me again," I reply with my bedroom voice.

Andi laughs out loud at this and I know without a doubt that I am completely wrapped around her little finger. All that she's been through in her life flashes through my mind and I silently vow to her that no matter what the future holds, I will be there every day to do

189

everything in my power to make sure she's laughing and happy.

"Luke," she says as she leans into me, "I'm really sorry to have to do this, but it's for your own good."

"What are you talkin-," her front door opens and in walks Shane, Will, and Brandon. *Oh shit, this is not happening!* "Andi," the warning is clear in my voice, "what have you done?"

She rubs her hand across my jaw, feeling the stubble of my 5 o'clock shadow and looks at me so lovingly. "I'm protecting you, Luke."

And with that, all the guys grab me from every direction and I fight like a wild animal. A lot of good it does me. Will the Giant grabs me from behind in some wrestling move and now I can't move my arms to fight back. Shane and Brandon have my legs and they're carrying me toward Andi's back door. I'm yelling all kinds of obscenities and names at all of them. Even threats of removing the important parts of their body that are directly related to their manhood don't faze them.

When we reach the back deck, I notice a rope is conveniently waiting and I look at Andi, who is grinning like a damn Cheshire cat. Shane and Will hold me down on the lounge chair while Brandon uses the rope to tie me down to the chair at my arms and at my legs. After they're satisfied with the knots, the four traitors sit down opposite of me as Christina, Tania, and Katie all file out to gawk at me and my predicament.

Laughter erupts from everyone, including me, when Christina exclaims, "Now *this* is a party!"

Andi moves over and sits in my lap, knowing I'm unable to move my arms to touch her, and smiles that same shit-eating grin at me. "This was *just in case* you decided to kidnap me after all," she laughs, gesturing to

190

all our friends who are now pulling out food and drinks from Andi's kitchen.

"You knew they were going to do this to me?" I ask Andi, deceptively calm.

She's still smiling, "Mmmhmmm," she nods.

"So this was all planned?"

"Yep." She's so damn proud of this little covert coup against me. "Remember the text in the truck?"

"I see. Untie me, Andi."

"You have to promise me something first," she says, still smiling but a little hesitant now. As well she should be.

"I will promise you something, Andi," I state confidently, "I will promise if you don't untie me *right now*, it will be *much worse* for you when I do get untied." I am still calm but there's no doubt in her mind as to what I mean.

She laughs nervously, but the mischievous gleam in her eyes is shining bright, "No, Luke. You have to promise you will behave and be nice if I untie you. Otherwise, I will just have to hand-feed you every meal until you promise me you decide to be a good boy."

I smirk, "Okay, Andi." She won't accept that. She makes me say the words verbatim.

"I promise I will behave and be nice if you untie me now," I recite after her. So she unties my legs first. Then my hands last. And she's kept her eyes trained on mine the whole time. I stand up, moving my arms and legs around to get the blood flowing again. Then I give her my mischievous grin and she squeals.

"NO, LUKE! YOU PROMISED!" She's laughing and backing away from me with her palms up between us.

"Silly woman...didn't you notice my arms and legs were crossed when I said that? Automatically makes it null and void...so I'm not breaking my promise, now am I?" I respond in a low, threatening whisper despite the smile that is splitting my face in two. I'm closing in on her as she turns to run from me–in her heels.

I wrap my arms around her and tackle her full force and we land in the deep end of the pool. When our heads emerge back up through the water, she's sputtering water and laughing hysterically. She playfully swats at me as she admonishes me, "You lunatic! You are crazy!"

I wrap my arms around her and hold her afloat, "I am crazy...crazy about you."

ANDI

I knew I'd pay for that little trick but it was well worth a little dip in the pool to see him tied up to the chair like that. The look on his face was priceless. I don't know what he thought we were going to do with him but it certainly wasn't this. I've just washed my face and I'm changing into my bathing suit for a real swimming party and I can't help but laugh again every few minutes when the scene replays in my mind.

I go back outside and most of the gang is already in the pool. My girls already had a bathing suit at my house from our hot tub party and the guys brought theirs, plus one for Luke. I put towels out for everyone and smile at Luke, who's stalking toward me in a cat-like prowl right now. He wraps his arms around me and pulls me in for a bear hug. I love his hugs, so much that

I moan in pleasure and feel his smile against the side of my head.

"Does this mean I'm forgiven and we're back together?" Luke whispers in my ear.

"You're forgiven, Luke." I can't stay mad at him, especially when he apologized so sweetly, explained everything to me, and then was such a good sport after our little practical joke.

Most people would think I should stay mad at him and hold a grudge for how much he hurt me. But one thing that I've learned the hard way is that life is too short to stay mad at the ones you love. And I do love him.

"But we're not back together? Because you have to protect me?" He's only half-joking and we both know it. He wants me to say we're back together but the stubborn man doesn't think he needs to be protected. Even though he doesn't know what he's up against.

I bang my forehead in frustration against his massive chest as his laugh rumbles through it. "Do we need to have another disagreement about this?"

"No, no argument here. I will let you protect me as long as you say we're back together. That's a fair compromise, don't you think?" He's murmuring in my ear, his lips are grazing my earlobes and sending chills through me. *Smooth talker.*

When I look up into his eyes, I can see it-he knows he has me. There's no use in denying it. Or in denying myself of what I really want.

Him. I just want him.

"So, Andi, how do you know Luke doesn't just want you for your money?" Brandon calls from the pool. He really is a great brother to Luke and right now I'm really appreciating that he just got me out of answering Luke's question.

Crazy Maybe

"Shut the fuck up, Brandon. You know better than that. And I've told you a million times–*you can't have her!* Find your own girl" Luke yells back at Brandon as I laugh.

"Think he's funny?" Luke says, turning on me with that evil glint in his eye. I immediately start backing up but he keeps advancing on me, slowly but surely gaining on me.

"Yeah, I think he's funny," I answer casually.

"Huh. You think it's funny that he's badmouthing me?" He tilts his head down and his eyes track my movements from under his furrowed brow.

"I think it's funny that he's giving you a hard time," I clarify. I'm still slowly moving away from him because I know he's up to something.

"A hard time," he repeats thoughtfully and picks at the finger foods we set out on the outdoor table. I start to answer but like lightning, he grabs me and holds me above his head while walking toward the pool.

I'm laughing and screaming, "*No, Luke!*" with his every step. He has the biggest smile on his face and he's really enjoying this way too much.

He starts to throw me into the pool but at the last second, he drops me and I'm free falling for a couple of seconds before I'm cradled in his arms like a baby. He throws his head back in a full-out laugh at the shocked look on my face and the sharp gasp of air I just inhaled. I totally thought I was going to hit the concrete full force. My heart is about to beat out of my chest but I can't help but laugh!

"You just wait, *Lucas Woods!* You will pay for that! *Next time*, I won't untie you!" I threaten him, for all the good it does.

He puts my feet down and wraps his strong arms around me. "I would never let you fall, baby. Speaking

194

of being tied up...maybe we could use those ropes tonight? In your bedroom?" He wiggles his eyebrows suggestively at me.

"Oh, I think I can definitely put them to use tonight, Luke." I coyly answer, but I seriously doubt my idea is the same one he's thinking of right now.

He narrows his eyes at me, "Andi," but before he can finish that threat, I catch him off guard and push him into the pool. He surfaces and smiles that mega-watt, panty-dropping smile and all I can think of is how gorgeous this crazy man is. I am so in love with him and I don't want this to end.

CHAPTER TWENTY-THREE

LUKE

Showered and changed into more comfortable clothes, we're all piled up in Andi's den watching movies on her huge, plasma TV. Looking around the room, I feel like the luckiest man alive. I have the best group of friends, and in my lap, snuggled up lovingly to me, is the most wonderful woman I've ever met. That's ever walked the face of this earth. And she's *mine*–even if she hasn't said it yet.

My arms are wrapped protectively around her and we have this couch to ourselves. Luckily, Andi's house is huge, so her den has enough room to fit several couches and recliners. She purposely set this room up to be very cozy and lived-in because she loves having friends over. Growing up without a real family has made her want to keep the people she loves very close and comfortable.

Andi sits up to grab a blanket to cover herself up with because in the summer she keeps her house the same temperature as the bottom of a fucking deep freezer. She's wearing a thin, cotton tank top with spaghetti straps and a short pair of cotton pajama shorts, so I'm completely fine with her covering herself up while all these other guys are in the house. Especially Brandon. She's obviously cold because her nipples look like little pebbles under the thin material of her top.

Crazy Maybe

While she's up, she grabs the remote control for the lights and turns them off so we can watch the big screen in "movie-theater style," as she puts it. Also fine with me, because my girl will be all snuggled up to me in the dark. Under a blanket. All alone on this comfortable, overstuffed leather couch. *Hell, yeah!*

While she's still up, I take the opportunity to stretch out on the extra wide couch. When she turns around with the blanket, she smiles shyly and lies back down with me on the couch, her back to my front. I cover us with the blanket and wrap my arm around her front, being sure to rub across her best parts as I finally still my hand on her stomach. I nuzzle into her neck and strategically place kisses right where I know she likes it. She arches her perfect little ass into my already growing hard-on and in an instant I am the man of steel.

Without turning my head, I look around the room to make sure no one is watching us. I chose the best location in the room. Our couch is on the back wall and everyone else is coupled up but with their backs to us. The guys picked an action movie with a little bit of romance weaved in for the ladies. With Andi's awesome surround sound system, it sounds like we're in a theater and it's just as loud. I fucking love it.

I both feel and hear her whimper a sexy little moan and I push into her from behind. My finger is tracing lazy circles on her silky smooth skin. I can't fucking take it anymore—it's been too long since I've held her. I'm not a fucking exhibitionist by any means. I don't want anyone else seeing my girl like that. But I fucking need her so I'm determined to find a way to make this happen. She's going to kill me but it'll be so worth it.

I slide my hand up to her hipbone and around to her plump little ass. I slip my hand into the back of her shorts and find that sweet spot between her legs. Her

197

whole body tenses for a few seconds and I'm sure she's wondering what I'm doing. Well, there's no way she doubts what I'm doing–but she has to wonder if I've lost my fucking mind. *Yes, yes, I have.*

I push one finger into her and find her already wet for me. *Fuck!* With my finger now soaked from the sweet nectar that is all Andi, I move it around her velvety folds, spreading her wetness. I can't hold back the growl I let out in her ear and I feel the cold chills across her skin from it. There's no denying her reaction to me–the way her body answers to me. *She is mine,* dammit!

I hear a muffled gasp from her when I plunge one finger deep inside her and it spurs me on. I add a second finger and feel her inner walls clenching around my fingers. Her breathing is labored and she's gripping the couch with one hand while the other has the blanket clenched at her mouth. She becomes more and more animated as my finger speed and forcefulness increases. I feel a sudden warmth of wetness flood my hand and I hear a muffled squeal come from the sexy vixen lying with me. But I'm not done with her yet.

Pulling my hand free from between her legs, I push her thin cotton shorts out of the way and free myself from my cotton lounge pants. With the late hour and all the evening's activities, it looks like everyone has fallen asleep watching the movie. I move one of my arms under her head while I position the head of my manhood at her wet entrance. Leaning in to her ear, I whisper to her, "Tell me we're back together, Andi." I slide my hand down her body, taking in each curve slowly, until I reach her swollen nub. She inhales a sharp hiss when I press my finger against it and softly give her the command again.

"Andi, tell me you're *mine.*"

Crazy Maybe

I nearly lose it like an inexperienced teen when her sexy whisper resounds in my ears.

"*Always*," she replies on a raspy exhale.

I push into her velvety wetness and immediately have to hold still. This isn't exactly how I wanted to make her mine again but I can't fucking wait another second. Seeing her in that bathing suit earlier just about made me take her right then and there, but lying here beside her with only her fucking thin cotton pajama tank and shorts is more than I can be expected to take. After a few seconds of getting myself under control, I start moving slowly, in and out of her sweetness, while still applying pressure on her nub with my fingers.

"Fuck, baby, you feel so good," I whisper to her, barely audible, but I know she heard me. She arches her back a little more, giving me better access to her and I push in harder and deeper. Increasing the tempo, her inner walls squeeze me and I feel a shudder run through her body. I know she's oh-so-close.

"That's right, baby," I whisper to her. That's all it takes for her to clench me harder as she peaks, stifling her moans into the blanket just clenched in her hand at her mouth, and her body milks me.

Andi starts to get up but I tighten my arms around her and hold in her in place. I'm still buried deep inside her and I'm not ready to let her go yet. "I love you, baby, so damn much," I repeat while placing kisses on her neck and shoulder. She whispers back, "I love you, too," and I know without a doubt she means it. Reluctantly, I let go and give her time to get to the bathroom before I wake up the troops and send them off to the bedrooms.

They're adults–I let them figure out their sleeping arrangement. I can't wait to be completely alone behind a closed, locked and barricaded door, with Andi.

Unless Andi's life is in danger, not one motherfucker is allowed to interrupt us until sometime tomorrow or it'll be their head.

ANDI

I've lost my damn mind. It's a delayed reaction from all those drugs the nurses pushed on me in the psychiatric hospital–a flashback or some shit like that. There's no other explanation for why I just had sex with Luke, in my den, on my couch, with all of my friends in the room! But, in my defense, the thrill of possibly getting caught was fucking hot! I'm starting to think that Luke may be a bad influence on me. Now I just have to leave the safety of this bathroom, face my friends and pretend nothing happened. Piece of cake.

Shit, I can't do this.

With my hand shaking, I grab the doorknob and slowly make my way back to the den. The den that is now empty and dark. I turn and find Luke walking toward me. He easily picks me up and I wrap my arms around his neck, and I softly place kisses along his jawline. He effortlessly carries me up the stairs to my bedroom and deposits me on the bed. His big hand cups my cheek and I welcome the warmth of his touch by leaning my face into his hand.

He bends to kiss me and at simultaneously grabs the hem of my pajama top. He slowly pulls it up to my chin and only breaks our kiss to remove it completely. He wraps his hands around my shoulders and gently coaxes me up. Bent at his knees, he slowly pulls my shorts down and I'm now standing completely naked in front of him.

As he stands, my hands develop a mind of their own as they reach out to touch his bare chest and stomach. The muscles on his torso are so defined and beautiful, I can't help myself. I run my fingertips over the lines and ridges of his muscles before reaching the waistband of his pajama pants. Lowering to my knees as I relieve him of his clothing, his impressive erection springs free and is conveniently positioned right in front of my face.

The intensity in Luke's eyes when I take him in my mouth is palpable. I maintain eye contact as I take my time lavishing attention on him. My tongue circles it twice before I drop to the base and lick my way back to the top. Then I open wide and take him in until he hits the back of my throat.

I relax the back of my throat to take him a little deeper. He groans loudly as he grabs my hair in his fists on both sides of my head when I first hum then mimic swallowing, flexing and releasing my throat around him. He tries to stop me and I won't let him go.

His words come out clipped and strangled, "Baby...stop or...oh God...I'm going to-," and there it is. I've found the limit of his restraint as he releases in my mouth and I swallow it down. When I'm positive I've drained every last drop from him, I lean back to look at him and lick my lips. In the blink of an eye, I'm weightlessly flying through the air and onto the bed with Luke already hovered possessively above me.

Have I mentioned how much this man turns me on?

Then he completely stuns me.

"From now until I die, whatever hardships we face, we will face together, side by side. You will never fight another fight alone. There is absolutely nothing I wouldn't do for you. I love you with everything I am, baby. I will make you happy and I will give you everything you could ever want. You just can't ever fucking leave me-I *need* you, Andi, so much. I can't fucking live without you."

His voice is soft and low, but somber and sincere. His demeanor is kind but resolute. His eyes hold both adoration and purpose as they search mine, looking for affirmation that I believe him. His words are like fire and ice in my veins. They touch me like nothing else and remind me of what I've never had. He has just vowed to give me everything I could ever want or need in my life–love, security, support, loyalty, and desire.

I am not normally such a big crybaby but that seems to be what I'm best at lately. Because with his declaration, my eyes are leaking like damn Niagara Falls. The tears are streaming down my face but I can't tear my eyes away from his eyes. His face is mere inches above mine, his body covers mine, and his hands are framed around my face, lovingly stroking my cheek with his thumb.

"Luke, for the rest of my life, I will believe in you and support your dreams, regardless of the circumstances. You have all of me and I give myself freely and unconditionally. You will never have a single reason to doubt me because my heart, my body, and my mind belong to you now. I trust you like I trust no one else. Everything I have, everything I am, and everything I will ever be means nothing if I don't have you."

The tenderness and affection in his eyes is intense and tangible, and I know that they mirror my own. He kisses me softly and tenderly, making slow, sweet love to my mouth with his tongue. My, my, the man can kiss–he curls my toes every time. But this time, along with curled toes, I am completely melting underneath him. "I will never get enough of that," I murmur against his lips when he ends the kiss. I feel his smile against my lips as it spreads across his beautiful face.

This is the first time in my life that I've even wanted to share everything with anyone. This is the first time I've ever even wanted to depend on someone else since my parents died. Giving someone my full trust is foreign and uncomfortable. But I have to let him in for us to ever have a chance. I know I must do the one thing that's hardest for me—I have to let him protect me.

It's not that I'm a control freak. Okay, not a *total* control freak—only about certain things. The people I love have a tendency to disappear from my life. So, it's not a far stretch to say that I want to protect the ones I care about simply to keep them in my life. Knowing this and changing my behavior about it are two very different things. Just because I know what's best, or because I know what's causing a problem, doesn't necessarily mean I do what's right. Old habits die hard or some such shit.

I believe him when he says he will stand beside me during the uphill battle we have coming. I also know he has no idea what kind of bloodbath this battle will soon become and I have to tell him. I have to finish the story—for Luke as much as for me. I stare deeply into his eyes while all of this is running through my mind and he just watches me, with a somewhat amused but loving countenance on his face.

"What's going on in that beautiful mind of yours, sweetheart?" he asks with a warm smile.

"Luke," I say on a whisper, "there's one last thing I need to tell you about that bastard I stabbed." *Please, Luke, please don't run from me.*

"OK, baby. You can tell me." He hasn't moved or tensed a muscle in his body. His heart is open wide to me. I can feel it.

I nod and try to look down, away from him, but his finger gently tilts my chin up to maintain full attention. I release a calming exhale and really talk to him.

"I may need you to *patiently* and *gently* remind me to let you protect me sometimes," I state somewhat timidly. "I know this will come as a shock to you, but I'm a little stubborn and independent in that area."

His lips twitch and he really tries to keep the laughter in but it proves to be too much for him. I glare at him with all my might. Then he really loses his composure and is now laughing uncontrollably.

"Yeah, baby, that is a real shocker," he deadpans after his fit of laughing hysterics has subsided. "I will *patiently* and *gently* remind you," he adds lovingly. So much so that I can't help but smile back.

Then he takes his time as he kisses, licks, and adores every inch of my body before making love to me, slowly and thoroughly, several times throughout the rest of the night. He is so very thorough in his exploration of my body. Every move, every thought and every touch was meant for my complete and total satisfaction.

I'm so in love with him that I can't imagine what losing him now would do to me. And this is so not like me. I'm not the needy, clingy, crybaby female that requires a man to complete her. But I feel different about Luke. I think he could be the one man who could totally annihilate me if he left me. And that realization scares the shit out of me.

CHAPTER TWENTY-FOUR

LUKE

I've had *e-fucking-nough* of the paparazzi, the reporters and all these people they're interviewing. They fucking don't even *know* Andi but all they're doing is talking trash about her. It's been several weeks now and the smear campaign continues. She told me she had something else to tell me about that bastard the night we got back together but I haven't pushed her for the information. I don't even care what it is—she has my support no matter what.

Mitch is still doing a pretty decent job of keeping them out of the club so we can at least hang out with our friends. I get to watch my girl on stage singing songs to me—even if it's not for the contest. Like the other night when she sang Rihanna's *Umbrella* to me, she let me know that no matter how bad things get all around us, our love will always shield us. We will take care of each other and nothing will ever come between us.

She has an amazing voice but the songs she picks for me makes my chest, and my head, swell with pride. Most every other guy in the club wishes he had her, but she's all mine. She tells me and shows me every night in every way imaginable and a few that defy imagination. Hell, no, I'm not complaining. I will take my little vixen any way she wants.

The media has been bugging the piss out of Mack and Shane about Andi, especially since Shane is so close to the light-heavyweight title fight. They're trying to make a big deal out of Andi's involvement with his training so she's tried to stay away to protect Shane's reputation. Shane has told her over and over that he wants her at the gym because she helps him. She just keeps saying she'll end up causing him more trouble than she's worth.

Shane was madder than I've ever seen him about that. All I could do was smirk as he explained to Andi that she was more important than any fucking news story. She won't be "the cause of his career's demise," as she puts it. Shane still comes to see her at her house and at the club. Only when we're at the club, he does everything he can to get photographed *with* her–just to get a fucking rise out of her. It's hilarious.

I've been spending more time with her at the youth center lately and not nearly enough time at the gym. I haven't talked to Andi about a major decision I have to make yet, mainly because I'm still trying to come to understand it myself. After everything I've done to convince my family that I want to be a professional boxer, I'm not sure that's where my heart is anymore. I haven't changed my mind because of Andi, but being with her has helped me see a few things about myself that I didn't before.

Which is pretty damn hilarious considering I have an advanced degree in psychology. Guess my psychoanalysis skills work on everyone but myself. Working on the landscaping at the youth center has had an unexpected benefit. I've found that I actually enjoy building things with my hands. Even helping with building my mom's back yard sanctuary, despite her Hitler-like tendencies, was constructive. That's when the realization hit me–constructive feels better than destructive. Yes, that's me, the guy with the life-changing epiphanies, also known as the Dalai Lama.

"Hey baby," Andi gives me a kiss before she sits across the table from me. "How was your day?"

"Much, much better now that you're here," I say as I take her hands in mine. We decided to meet for a casual dinner at a small Italian restaurant where we're less likely to be hounded by people who recognize her.

She looks apprehensive. "Baby, what's wrong?" Translation: *Who do I need to beat the crap out of?*

She takes a deep breath and says, "Remember I told you there was still something I needed to tell you about the bastard?" She doesn't need to say more—*the bastard* is his moniker now. I nod and let her continue uninterrupted.

"I tried to give it time to see if he would leave me alone. I haven't talked to the press or anything. Bill called and told me *the bitch*," also known as the foster mother, "is involved and they're doing a joint press conference about this—to solidify their position and paint me as the emotionally disturbed one."

My hackles are instantly raised in defense. "When is this press conference?"

"Sunday morning," she says cautiously.

The last thing I want is for her to be afraid to talk to me so I visibly relax my shoulders and my jaw muscles. Which fucking hurt right now from being clenched so hard. I rub my thumb across the back of her hand, pick it up and kiss her palm. "I'm here, baby. I'm not going anywhere."

She suddenly looks fearful, "I need to tell you who he is, Luke." It comes out less of a definitive statement and more like a confession after a torturous session of waterboarding.

"You can tell me he's the fucking President of the United States and I'm still not going anywhere, Andi."

She winces and looks down at our hands as she says, "You're close, actually. He's the current Speaker of the House. Congressman Jackson Rhoades."

The Speaker of the House? The person third in line for the presidency and second only to the vice-president in case of a disaster. That man is *the bastard?* Andi is fidgeting and her eyes keep darting to the door. She pulls one hand away and reaches for her purse.

"Where are you going?" I ask her pointedly.

"You didn't sign up for this, Luke. Let me deal with this and when it's over, we can try this again."

She's fucking serious.

Remembering our conversation a few weeks back, I pull her hand back to my mouth and kiss it repeatedly. On her palm, on every knuckle, and then on every finger. "Sweetheart, remember you wanted me to patiently and gently remind you to let me protect you?"

She won't make eye contact with me but she nods. Then I see a tear escape from her eye and she quickly wipes it away.

"I'm not going anywhere, Andi. I'm with you, remember? We're under the same umbrella. We're crazy about each other. And I can't even sleep without you now–much less live without you. We do this together, my love."

Andi smiles hesitantly and takes a deep breath. I know she's weighing her options right now. Argue or accept what I said? Go off on her own and figure it out? Try to avoid me and keep me from kidnapping her again?

Crazy Maybe

"None of those ideas will keep me away from you, Andi. Just accept it. You know I'm not above kidnapping you again," I say matter-of-factly.

This earns me a laugh, because she really does know it, and she finally relaxes a little.

I've been staying at her house every night and only going by my apartment to get my mail. I've tried sleeping without her but it doesn't work. Later at home, I'm sitting on the couch watching TV and Andi crawls into my lap and curls up in my arms. I love it when she does this. She lays her head on my shoulder and wraps her little hands around my neck. Sometimes she falls asleep in my arms like this and I carry her upstairs to bed.

She's nervous tonight, though, and me holding her like this helps calm her. She surprises me when she whispers, "Thank you for not leaving me," as she closes her eyes and lays her head on my shoulder, nuzzled into my neck.

I'm so stunned I can't speak for a minute. I rub her arm gently and ask, "What do you mean, baby?"

"When I told you who he is. Thank you for not leaving me. I would understand if you change your mind, but I just want you to know that what you said means a lot to me."

I know she was in foster care. I know she was legally emancipated at sixteen and has been on her own since then. My mind *knows* these things but I don't think I've ever fully thought about what that includes. But when she says something like this, I'm forced to consider what that really meant for her, how scary it had to be for her, and how lonely.

She would still let me off the hook if I wanted to walk away until she dealt with this. What other choice

209

has she had her whole life? None–she's had to face everything all alone.

I squeeze her tighter to me and reassure her, "Baby, you never cease to amaze me. You never have to thank me for not leaving you. It'll never happen–I would never make it without you. I don't even want to think about it, much less try it."

My relationship with my parents is still a little strained. We haven't been back to their house together since that night and I haven't been back since they confessed to everything, except to work in the yard when they're not there. And that's really only because Andi went to the trouble of buying all that for them and I want to see it finished.

My thoughts drift back over every major event in my life and there's not one single event I can think of that my whole family wasn't there for me. Mom, Dad, Brandon, and Alicia–they've all been so invested in my life and shared every milestone and major event with me.

Andi's had no one considered family to be there for her, to show how proud they are of her, to support her or to even hold her when she was scared or sick. It brings my betrayal back to the forefront of my mind and I feel guilty all over again. She's told me over and over that it's forgiven and forgotten. She doesn't want me to dwell on it or bring it up anymore.

It's just that she asks so little of me…so naturally, I want to give her everything.

I think maybe she finally understands why I want– *need*– o be the one to protect her. I get that she's capable and she's proven that over and over. She has to let me in. She has to let me help her. I love her independence and strength–I would never try to take that away from her. But she also can't take this away

from me. We can do this together, side by side, as one.
We can't work as a couple any other way.

CHAPTER TWENTY-FIVE

ANDI

Saturday night at the club, we're all here and the contest continues. I'm still in the running even though I haven't practiced any songs. Just as well since Mitch decided to change the rules on us when we got here tonight. He claims that since we're in the "playoffs," he can change the rules at any time. So instead of getting to pick our own songs tonight, he's assigned us songs. And they're in a completely different genre than the five remaining contestants normally sing in.

For example, my song tonight is by Disturbed. Don't get me wrong—I love the song—but my voice is not accustomed to this style of singing. I probably won't be able to speak for a while after the song. But I have a few ideas for playing up to the song lyrics, so I'm not worried about it. Luke may actually enjoy a little silence when we get home tonight.

Home—I don't refer to it as my *house* anymore. I've tried to talk Luke into just moving in with me and giving up his apartment lease. He's been living off a trust fund his parents set up for him when he was born while he's pursued his boxing dream. There's no reason for him to keep paying for that apartment when he sleeps in my bed every night. I guess it's a way to hold onto his bachelor pad...just in case.

I hit the costume rack backstage and look for something to fit my vision for the song tonight. After a few alterations, and by that I mean I found the scissors,

I think I have a winner. I took a camouflage t-shirt and cut it off just below my breasts. I also cut the shoulders out to make it a tank top and make it a low plunging neckline. It's a size too small so it fits my B-cups very tightly. I also found a pair of tight, black Yoga shorts that will work nicely with my soldier theme. I use the bottom part of the t-shirt material to fashion a camouflage headband.

I've added the pink highlights back to my blond hair and I decide to leave it down. I thankfully wore black high-heeled boots tonight, so they will complete my look. I wait backstage as the guy before me, who would normally sing something closer to Disturbed, finishes a Kelly Clarkson song. I can't help but smile–he has multiple facial piercings, tattoos everywhere and he looks scary as hell, but he's singing one of Kelly's slow songs and crooning like a heartsick fool. I love it!

My turn now and I take the stage. As the sirens start at the beginning of *Indestructible,* Mitch puts the red lights on spin to add to the overall ambience of everything that is war. I march to the microphone and stand at attention with my hand at my face in a salute like a good soldier until the music begins. Then I take the microphone off the stand and begin the song.

As I finish the chorus, I see him. Him–*the bastard.* He's sitting in the audience behind Luke. He knows exactly what he's doing. It's a blatant threat that Luke doesn't even know is there. Jackson Rhoades is so dressed down tonight that I doubt his own wife would even recognize him. He's trying to blend in with the crowd but he also wants me to know he's here. He wants me to know without a doubt that he can find me and anyone I love. I know this because he and his wife, Delia, have already threatened me with this multiple times.

213

Crazy Maybe

I don't deal with being threatened very well.

I'm glad I didn't see him at first because the second verse of this particular song is fitting for him. I move to stand directly in front of him and sing every word to him. I even point to him to let him know that I will fight him with every fiber of my being. During the chorus, I point to myself and tell him that I am the one who is indestructible—not him. He is the enemy and he will be destroyed in the end. Saying this to him feels fucking fantastic, liberating, and empowering. He damn well knows it, too.

His face loses a little of the cockiness and smugness it originally held. He must have thought I'd cower in the corner and beg for mercy. Not a chance—I've been through too much to give him one ounce of satisfaction from seeing any apprehension in me. I suddenly realize I have been blatantly staring a hole through the bastard when Luke's movement catches my eye. He's turning around to see who I'm looking at.

I've never been so relieved to finish a song before now. I have to get to Luke before he either recognizes Jackson or thinks he's someone I'm interested in and makes a scene. Even if Luke wants to protect me, he doesn't need to go looking for trouble before we're ready for it. I jump off the stage from the front instead of going down the steps at the back. I reach our table and sit across from Luke so his wide shoulders and back will shield me from Jackson's view.

I immediately see the hurt in Luke's eyes. He didn't see Jackson or didn't recognize him, but he knows something is up. I take my cell phone back from Katie and discreetly show it to him. He nods in understanding and pulls his phone out. I hold it in my lap, under the table and out of view, and send him a text.

The bastard is here. Behind u. Don't look!!!

Luke looks up at me and he is visibly furious. He takes a few seconds to pound out a response on his phone.

L: Y r u not sitting w/ME?

My eyes implore him before I send my response.

He's threatening. I don't want u 2 b a target.

Luke's blue eyes are almost black with fury now. He pins me with a look of steel and I know exactly what he's thinking—that I'm not letting him protect me. So I send another quick text.

Element of surprise. He may not no abt u yet. Trust me. PLS!

Luke is staring down at his phone in his lap. His jaw is working again—grinding his teeth, clenching the muscles, and muttering swear words under his breath. He hasn't answered my text or even looked at me.

My phone vibrates in my hand.

L: I'm leaving.

While I'm reading it over and over again, and feeling positive that there will be more to the message that will come through my phone any second now, Luke gets up and walks out of the club. Not another word. No more messages. Nothing to indicate he understood what I meant or that he would even just trust me until we were out of sight so I could explain my reasoning to him. He just got up and walked away.

I'm now visible to Jackson and he's intently watching me. Somehow I mask the emotions that are threatening to take full control of all my faculties. I can't let him know that Luke affects me. To keep at least some semblance of sanity, I have to hold to the notion that he doesn't know about us yet. I'm also desperately hoping that Luke is actually waiting for me in his truck outside. I'm praying that he understood my message

215

and is just putting some space between us so it will appear I'm here alone.

I wait a few minutes before I get up to leave. I keep my eyes trained on Jackson's but I let how much he disgusts me burn through my glare at him. He takes a deep breath as I pass by him. He thought I was going to cause a big scene and get him busted for being in the club tonight. I thought about it, actually, but I feel an urgent need to get to Luke right now. I keep my pace casual until I get to the door and out of the bastard's line of sight, then I run to the area where Luke parked.

No!

Oh God, please don't let this be true.

He. Left. Me.

Again.

I walk around the parking lot for a few minutes to double check that he's not really out here somewhere. I just can't believe that he would really do this after everything we just went through to get back together. After everything he said to me. After the way he made love to me.

He wouldn't really do this, would he?

Would he?

LUKE

"Why the hell are you walking around out here in that?" Has she lost her mind? I'm really trying to not be mad. She's still in her costume from her song earlier and it doesn't cover nearly enough of her. We've already had that one run in with douche-Brad in the parking lot and I don't want anyone else getting any ideas about her. I'm concerned about her safety with *the bastard* being here tonight and she's running around alone and half-naked.

She turns and looks at me and her eyes grow wide. Note to self: she may be small, but she is strong! Andi just flew through the air and plastered herself to me. Thankfully, I caught her under her ass just in time because her legs are now wrapped around my waist and her arms are around my neck. And she's squeezing the breath out of me. Her reaction to seeing me is just now sinking in and my first concern is, *who hurt her?*

"Baby, tell me what happened. Did someone hurt you?" I keep my voice calm to try to calm her but inside my blood is hitting the temperature of the sun right about now.

She shakes her head 'no' but she's still holding on to me with all her might. She turns her face and buries it in my neck. I rub her back with one hand while holding her up with the other. "Sweetheart, tell me what's wrong. Why didn't you meet me behind the club like I said? What happened?"

She raises her head and I realize my neck is now wet. I draw my head back to look at her and cup her face with one hand while holding her up with the other. "Andi, tell me what's wrong," I demand a little stronger this time.

"I couldn't find you...I thought...I-," her words are clipped and she's trying to speak between gasps of breath. "I thought you'd left."

"What? Why? I sent you a text–told you to come out the back door after you changed clothes."

Crazy Maybe

"I don't have a text from you. Other than when you said you were leaving," she says as she buries her face back into my neck and squeezes my neck tighter.

I remove my phone from my pocket and pull up my text messages. *Failure to send.* Son of a bitch!

"Andi, look at my phone, baby," I coax her as tenderly as possible. She doesn't budge. "Please, baby, just look for me."

She reluctantly takes the phone from my hand with one hand but her other hand grips my neck tighter, as her legs constrict tighter around my waist. We need to settle this before I pass out from oxygen deprivation.

I can't help but laugh–a little–when I see my phone disappear behind my neck. She's looking at it over my shoulder so she can still hold on with both hands. I love her so fucking much.

"You thought I left you, Andi?" I ask softly. I know she does. I know her mind went back to the worst thing I've ever done, the day I left her at my parents when she needed me the most.

"I'm sorry I thought that," she whispers, "I didn't at first. But then I couldn't find you. I've been walking around looking for you."

I squeeze her to me even tighter now and I really didn't think that was even possible. My arms are wrapped around her, supporting her and holding her to me, as I walk back to my truck parked behind the club. After I open the passenger door, I place her on the edge of the seat but she's still facing me so I can lean into her, between her legs, and talk to her. She hasn't loosened the hold she has on me with her legs yet, giving me no choice but to stay close.

Holding her face in my hands, I give her gentle kisses on her lips, nose, eyes, and then all along her jaw. "You have nothing to be sorry about, baby. I will

218

never leave you. Never. It was an honest mistake. I didn't check the text and I was mad when I left the club. But not at you, baby."

She finally looks up at me, and my chest squeezes like a vice is wrapped around me when I see her red-rimmed eyes, bloodshot and puffy from crying. I still can't believe how someone so completely beautiful inside and out could love me as much as she so obviously does. How could I have ever doubted her?

"I was so afraid I'd...that I'd lost you again. When I saw you, I was just so relieved and happy that you were really here." Her voice is so soft and I can see that scared, lost young girl behind the strong, independent woman she's become.

"You will never lose me, Andi. If you ever try to leave me, I will follow you. Every day, Andi–*every single day*–I think to myself that there's no way I could be any more in love with you. And every day, I'm proven wrong."

She lays her head on my chest as I draw her in my arms again and hold her tight for several more minutes. We both just need this right now–the comfort of each other's touch, the reassurance that neither of us is alone, and the warmth of our intense love. This feels so right and so natural that it doesn't even scare me anymore. The *I'm-not-a-relationship-kind-of-guy* just found the one person in the world who could make him *want* to change that.

"You ready to tell me why I couldn't just drag *the bastard* out of the club and save us all a lot of trouble?" I ask as I nestle my face into her neck, just below her ear.

She takes a deep, calming breath and looks up to give me a faint smile. "Maybe he doesn't know about us yet. He was here as a threat to me, I know that much. We could have an ace in the hole if you don't drag him out here and beat the crap out of him."

"So I could be like a *007*-type of undercover spy?" I ask with a snort. This earns me her award-winning smile.

"Something like that, tough guy," she quips.

"To be honest, I'd rather just drag the bastard out here and be done with him. But I'm willing to try it your way first," and I mean it. I would rather fucking drag the bastard out here, stomp his ass and ship him off in a freight container where he can be a love slave to his eternally horny, male gorilla cellmate.

"Baby," I add with a kiss, "as much as I love having your legs wrapped around me, think you can let go now so I can breathe?"

She smiles ruefully and releases her legs from around me. I make a big show of exaggerated breaths and broken ribs until I have her laughing again. Music to my ears.

I'm not willing to risk her safety by going back in to get her clothes so I'll just have to suffer the view on the ride home. Now if I can talk her into torturing me with this view for a little while longer in her bedroom, I'll pass out from exhaustion a very happy man tonight. Knowing that tomorrow morning will bring a world of hurt back to her, tonight I will bring her every bit of pleasure I can muster from my considerable arsenal.

We step into her house and I lock the door behind me, set the alarm and stalk after her as she makes her way to her bedroom. Her taut ass swings side to side as she walks, unaware that I'm completely entranced by her. She's about to start undressing when I wrap my arms around her from behind and still her hands. "Have I told you how hot you look in this outfit?"

She sighs in pleasure as I run my tongue up and down her neck, stopping to nip and kiss along the way. My hands love the feel of her body, moving up from her stomach to cup her breasts. She moans out loud when I rub the pads of my thumbs across her nipples, causing them to pebble under my touch. I move my hands under her barely-there shirt, *"You're not wearing a bra under this flimsy thread?"*

"No," she moans and tilts her head back as I continue rubbing her sensitive buds.

"If I'd known that..." I can't even finish the thought. I would've already taken her. I would've snatched her off that stage and away from all those eyes. I rip what's left of the shirt off of her, fully revealing her beautiful breasts. She gasps in response.

My hands flatten against her stomach and glide over her soft, supple skin until they reach her barely-there shorts and the V between her legs. One hand slides between her legs and I rub her from nub to ass and back again. I growl when I feel the wetness through her shorts and press my growing erection into the middle of her exquisite ass. Moving the fabric aside, I push one finger deep into her wetness. *"No panties either?"*

She shakes her head no.

Fuck!

I grab one side of the shorts and completely rip them from her body, too. She cries out in ecstasy and I grab a fist full of her hair to pull her face back to me. My mouth covers hers and my tongue pushes lightly on the part of her lips, urging her to give it passage. She obeys and I completely overtake her mouth, invading it with my tongue and owning her with it. She responds with full fury and need.

Crazy Maybe

I walk her to the bed and gently push her head forward until she's bending over at the waist with her hands on the bed. "Stay there, just like that."

"But-"

"Stay. There."

"Okay."

I step back and shed all my clothes in an instant. I am so damn hard now I could cut diamonds and still shatter a Ginsu knife with it. I gently thrust my hips to rub along the crease in her ass. She's panting and writhing in anticipation and it turns me on even more. I reposition myself to her soft folds and gently rub it back and forth, barely penetrating as my hips surge forward. With each thrust, her eagerness increases and she pushes her hips back in an attempt to take me in her.

I pull back and she groans in frustration. I run my hands across the small of her back and one finger gently trails her from the top of the crease in her ass, along her rosebud, across her wetness to her waiting, swollen nub. She sucks in a sharp breath and her whole body tenses and her back arches. She's so fucking ready for me. Using my middle finger to apply circular pressure on her nub, my thumb plunges in and she immediately clenches around it. I move my thumb slowly in and out of her, hooking it and hitting her sweet spot with each movement.

When I feel she is so close to her first orgasm, I stop and she growls loudly at me, *"Ugh! Don't stop!"* I smile widely even though she can't see me. I drop to my knees and start again with my tongue. She cries out as I take it in my mouth and suck on it, then lightly graze it with my teeth. Then I plunge two fingers deep into her, moving fast and hard. She screams my name with her first full-blown orgasm and her knees start to buckle below her.

Crazy Maybe

Using my hands on her hips to steady her, I tell her to lean over and put her weight on the bed again. I stand and run my hands over the sexy, muscular globes of her ass. "Are you ready for me?"

"Fuck, yes, Luke!" My sexy little vixen.

"Hold tight, baby." I see her hands grab the comforter tightly, waiting for me. I crave the wet, velvety feel of her wrapped around me. She always stretches to take me in and fits me like a glove. I can't wait any longer to be inside her.

I push in slowly the first time so I don't hurt her, "Oh God, Luke!" My hips rock back and forth, faster and faster, as she takes all of me into her.

"You like that?"

"I *love* it," she purrs back at me over her shoulder. She's so responsive to every touch and word tonight and the sounds she makes drive me wild. I feel her shudder as she tightens around me over and over again until she tells me she can't take anymore. We finish together, with Andi screaming my name as my fingers dig into the perfect skin on her hips until I'm completely spent inside her. I gently pull back and watch as her arms give out and she falls flat on her stomach. She has the most beautiful smile on her face.

She's just dozing off and jumps when water drops from the wet washcloth in my hand falls on her back. Raising her head from the bed, she looks over her shoulder at me and I give her a sheepish smile. I really didn't mean to do that but since she's awake, I roll her over to her back and gently rub the cloth between her legs to clean her up. She rubs her hand along my jaw and quietly whispers, "I love you."

"I love you, too, baby." I take my place beside her and she rolls over to face me. I am mesmerized by the love shining in her eyes and I'm struck by how lucky I am to have her in my life.

"I've been thinking," she whispers.

"Uh-oh," I tease.

She smiles before she continues, "I don't want you to play 007 with Rhoades. He always has security around him. I can't believe he didn't have it in the club. But when he's in political mode, you won't be able to get close to him. Maybe I should just do a press conference...let them ask their questions and get it all out there."

"Why do you want to do that?" I can't keep the concern from my voice.

"Because the parents are trying to keep the kids away from me at the center now. They think I'm some psychotic monster." Her voice is filled with pain and it makes me want to jerk Jackson Rhoades up by the balls even more.

"If you decide to do the press conference, I will stand by you. We need to think through all the backlash you could get though." She suddenly has a thoughtful, concerned look on her face and I know she's not thinking of how the backlash will hit her. She's thinking of how it will hit everyone *except* her.

"Maybe we should go see your parents tomorrow." She's looking off over my shoulder in deep thought as she makes her statement.

Well...*that* came out of the damn blue.

CHAPTER TWENTY-SIX

ANDI

Once everything I've gone through comes out into the open, I think Sam and Linda will feel guilty and have a really hard time with their part in it. Even though Sam betrayed me, he did it for the sake of his family. While it still hurt like hell, I can't completely blame him for wanting to protect his family and his business. I want to be the one to explain it all to them before I talk to the press. I don't want anyone in Luke's family to be blindsided by this whole mess.

Luke was surprised when I said we should go to his parents' house. I know he hasn't spent much time with them since Sam admitted what he did to us. I don't want to be the cause of a family fight so I want to put this behind me as much as I want Luke to put it behind him. He's never known what being orphaned really feels like, or what having no family really does to you. I don't wish that on anyone. So, I talked him into going for a visit today. He doesn't look thrilled.

He's been quiet on the short drive over but the scowl hasn't left his face. It gets worse as we pull in the driveway and he turns off the ignition. Without looking at me he says, "We don't have to do this, Andi. We can still leave."

It's taken me a week to convince him to do this and I'm not backing down now. I squeeze his hand, "Tell me why you don't want to do this, Luke." I can feel the

Crazy Maybe

sadness I see in his eyes when he finally makes eye contact with me.

"Because I can't believe what my parents did to us, and..." he exhales a long, sad breath, "I can't believe what I did to you. Here. In this house."

I know a thing or two about regrets and I know that is what Luke is feeling right now. But I also know a thing or two about loss and I can't be the reason he loses his family. I may have mixed feelings about what his father did, but I have no doubt he loves Luke. This is the right thing to do. I just have to convince this stubborn man who stole my heart.

"We've all done things we regret. What matters is how we heal the ones we've hurt. Some say it should come easy if it's real love but that's just not true. Love is never easy-love hurts sometimes. It causes insecurities and jealousies. Relationships take work-*love* takes work. And happiness requires forgiving others. I forgive you. Your parents need you to forgive them."

Luke pulled back, leaning his back on the door, and smiled at me with a slightly amused look. He shook his head and ran his hand through his hair, making it look messy and even sexier. "I'm always amazed by you, Andi."

"Why do you say that?"

"I'm supposed to be the shrink here."

"*Shrink*?" My confusion is obvious. I have no idea what he's talking about.

He's hesitant to answer me at first and I'm sensing I may not like his answer. He grabs both my hands in his, as if he's sure I will bounce from the car and never been seen again. He finally explains, "I have an advanced degree in psychology. I'm a counselor, Andi. Or I was."

226

Crazy Maybe

I am speechless. How could I not know this about him after all this time? And all that has happened between us. And all that he knows about me. Before I can respond, he continues.

"I can't even guess what you're thinking right now but I didn't keep this from you intentionally. My career choice is part of the problems with my parents. They think I should be Dr. Woods but I wasn't happy in that role. Look, I know we need to talk about this more, but can we finish this later?"

Too many suspicions are taking root in my thinking right now and I'm really trying to not jump to conclusions without hearing him out first. I stare at him like it's the first time I've seen him for what seems like several minutes as different scenarios play out in my mind. I finally nod in agreement with his request to finish this later. Pulling my hands from his, he reluctantly releases me and I exit the car without another word. Confusion seems to be a permanent state of mind lately.

Once inside the house, I hear voices coming from the formal living room and I freeze when I hear one deep, masculine laugh carry through the foyer. Luke is holding my hand and at first he doesn't notice I've stopped walking. He stops walking with a jolt when I don't budge from my spot.

"No," I whisper anxiously, "It can't be," even though I know it's true.

Luke is studying my reaction when he hears the laugh then notices the goose bumps rising all over my skin. He's about to speak when my feet suddenly start moving of their own accord and carry me toward the laugh of my nightmares. I don't stop until I reach the living room doorway and see the devil incarnate sitting with Sam and Linda. I feel Luke stop behind me and his hand settles on my waist, giving me his strength.

227

Crazy Maybe

"Luke, Andi-what a surprise. We weren't expecting you. Come in!" Linda sounds genuinely excited to see us as she rushes to embrace each of us. I hug her but my eyes never leave *the bastard's.*

Linda tries to pull me into the room but my feet feel like they've been cemented to the floor. "Let me introduce you to another surprise guest. This must be our day for company," Linda continues, ever the polite host.

Behind me, I feel Luke tense, like a snake coiled and ready to strike. Only he's about to strike at the worst serpent I know. I finally move into the room but I will not sit and pretend this man has done nothing. Luke and I are both openly starting at Jackson as he finishes his conversation with Sam.

"I've selfishly taken enough of your time today, Sam. You and Linda have been too kind to indulge my unannounced visit. Please accept my apologies. I should be going and let you enjoy some family time," Jackson's political charm and wit oozes out of every pore but I know what filth it really is.

Sam and Linda object to his apology and urge him to stay longer to talk with us. Jackson knows better, though. I can see it in his eyes and he can see it in mine. He's not willing to risk being exposed right now. He must not have his plan fully vetted yet. Whatever it is no doubt involves Luke and his family now. The press conference he was supposed to hold today must have been a ruse to distract me because he is definitely not in DC to answer questions.

Jackson stands, moves toward me, and his body language says he's about to extend his arm to shake my hand. I recoil from his close proximity while at the same time Luke steps in front of me to block his attempt. Jackson's brows furrow and his face registers his uneasiness about the whole situation. Sam and Linda watch us curiously as Jackson says his goodbyes. Sam walks him out and Linda turns to Luke and me with her eyebrows raised in a silent question.

Luke's arms are crossed over his massive chest and he's still in his fighting stance. He hasn't come down from the adrenaline high yet. His eyes are hard and his jaw is set as he says, "Wait until Dad gets back." Linda nods in agreement and offers us a drink. As tempting as that sounds, I don't really think now is the time.

Sam returns to the living room just in time to keep Luke from wearing a path in the hardwood floor from his pacing. Luke wastes no time with idle chit-chattery, "What in the hell was *he* doing here, Dad?"

Sam looks stunned and asks, "Do you know who *he* is, son?" His authoritative tone says he thinks he knows something we don't.

"We know who he is, Mr. Woods. How do you know him?" I blurt out. This is the first time I've spoken to them since that horrible day at the lawyer's office and I have to admit I'm having a harder time with it than I thought I would. Especially since Satan was just a guest here.

Sam looks taken aback but stammers out an answer, "Well, we don't really know him, Andi. He was a politician here for a long time before moving up in the DC world. He said he's trying to get back to his grassroots beginnings. He heard about the development deal I have with Donovan and wanted to work with me on improving economic conditions in Georgia."

"So the *Speaker of the House* just showed up here, at your house, out of the blue, to talk about a real estate development deal you have with *someone else*?" I am more than skeptical and it's obvious in my pissed off tone of voice.

Sam looks confused for a second but then reality seems to dawn on him. "It does seem strange when you put it that way. Why do you ask?"

"Dad, you better have a seat," Luke says flatly. He knows this is going to be a long discussion.

After two hours of telling, retelling, repeating, explaining, and generally regurgitating every detail of the whole sordid mess, Sam and Linda sit speechless for several long minutes. Sam lowers his face into his hands and I notice his shoulders lightly shaking.

I'm sure he's not laughing, unless he's suddenly become delirious, in which case I completely understand. No such luck, though. When he finally looks up, his eyes are watery and bloodshot from crying.

"Andi...the property...the deal with Donovan...it's all...," his voice trails off as he catches his breath and forces the next words, "Its blood money. I benefited at the expense of abused kids, including you."

"No, Mr. Woods. This is exactly why I wanted to talk to both of you before all this comes out in the press. That property belonged to my dad. The deal with Donovan was all business. Neither has anything to do with what Jackson Rhoades did," I explained.

"But I used what happened against you...My God, what have I done?" Sam sounds more distraught as he jumps to his feet and starts pacing. He's rubbing his chest, the left side of his neck and his left jaw. These are not good signs.

"Mr. Woods, take a few deep breaths and sit down. You don't look so well," my words are falling on deaf ears.

Crazy Maybe

"Mr. Woods-if you don't sit down, calm down, and take a few deep breaths, I'm calling an ambulance," I yell at him and get everyone's attention. Sam drops down on the couch without much thought to where.

"What have I done to you, Andi? This is what you meant when you said I didn't know what this could do to me, isn't it?"

"Yes, it is partly what I meant," I confirm. He sounds broken and I know how that feels. Not too long ago, I also felt broken in this very house.

"He wouldn't have wanted those pictures released so now he's concerned about damage control. You, Linda, Luke...everyone...will be part of that damage control in some way. Even if that means he has to ruin you to do it. He may have had me locked up, but he's the crazy one."

Sam and Linda give us a verbatim recount of their visit with Jackson. There's nothing blatantly obvious to me about what Jackson's plans are but there's no doubt he's up to something. I suggested to Luke that we talk to Hugh Donovan to ask if Jackson has visited him, too.

An uncomfortable silence has taken over the room. Sam and Linda are sitting together but neither is looking at anything in particular. Luke is visibly uncomfortable, sitting on the edge of his chair like he's ready to evacuate the premises at any second, and he's staring at the floor. I clear my throat and everyone looks at me.

"So, let's talk about the elephant in the room that no one wants to mention."

Luke snorts and quickly coughs to try to cover it up. I look at him and smile reassuringly. He covers his mouth with his hand, trying to be nonchalant, but it doesn't work. He starts laughing quietly and then he loses control completely as his deep, masculine laugh reverberates off the walls and he leans back in his chair.

"Feel better?" I ask teasingly.

Smiling from ear to ear, he answers, "Yes, actually. Leave it up to you to blurt out what we're all thinking."

I shrug one shoulder to indicate it's no big deal.

"You used to call me 'Dad'," Sam says sadly. The hurt in his voice permeates the room and instantly neither Luke nor I are smiling or laughing.

What am I supposed to say to that?

"Now you call me 'Mr. Woods'. I don't remember you calling me that even when we first met. I could be wrong...but I don't remember it," he continues with a low, sad tone.

"Can you blame her?" Luke demands, in my defense. I appreciate the gesture but I don't want a fight.

"No, son, I don't blame her at all. It's just that," his voice trails off as he looks at me. "I miss it. I miss you calling me Dad."

I wipe away the tears falling down my cheeks as I rise and walk across the room. He stands and I wrap my arms around his neck to hug him. His voice is strained as he chokes out, over and over again, "I'm so sorry, Andi."

"I forgive you, Dad," I reply through my tears and my own strained voice. Suddenly, two more arms have encircled us and I hear Linda softly crying at my shoulder as she strokes my hair, "Baby girl." Then two more strong arms wrap around from the other side and the four of us stand here in a family embrace.

LUKE

Now that Andi and I have made up with my parents, we're enjoying a relaxing evening on the completed patio. At least the big fight with Andi and my parents got me out of most of the damn grunt work. But I would've gladly finished it all myself if I could take back what I did to Andi that night. She has told me several times to let it go, that I'm forgiven, but I just don't get how she can forgive so easily. One more thing that I love about her.

Rhoades coming to my parents' house thoroughly pisses me off. I know it's a posturing move-he wanted to get the inside scoop on my parents, and me, to use against Andi later. I talked to Dad briefly about this when Mom was showing Andi around her newly decorated backyard. He knows that no matter what Rhoades threatens, I will not turn against Andi. Even if that means Dad has to fight for his business again. This time, Dad completely agrees with me.

I know I have to talk to Andi about my revelation earlier about being a psychologist. She had no clue and she must have at least thought, even for a second, that I had something to do with getting those pictures of her. Or even that I could be in league with Rhoades now and will eventually use my training against her.

She's been a little more distant since that talk in the car. I keep trying to tell myself it's because of everything else that's happened tonight-finding Rhoades in my parents' house, just seeing him again, and then making up with my parents. That's enough to drain anyone.

Crazy Maybe

But I know Andi and she's not the same. I apparently don't know how to do relationships very well because I keep screwing up, no matter how unintentional it has been, I know I keep hurting her. Watching her now as she helps bring the food out of the kitchen, I feel so protective of her and I have to fight the urge to just take her away from all this. But she's a fighter, she is stronger than anyone gives her credit for being, and she would never back down from this fight.

"Penny for your thoughts," Andi says as she sits beside me. I lace my fingers with hers, pull her hand to my mouth and gently place a kiss on every knuckle.

"I was just thinking about you, and you're worth way more than a penny."

"So the media keeps telling everyone," she deadpans.

I smile in response to her sarcasm, "That's not what I meant and you know it. I don't care how much money you *have*. You are *worth* far more than that."

She stares into my eyes, searching and questioning, but doesn't let go of my hand. I know she wants to ask me something but she doesn't. She just keeps looking at me like she's trying to figure out a puzzle but there's a piece missing that she can't quite place. I want to ask her what's on her mind but I suddenly feel like that's too much like what a shrink would ask a patient, so I keep my mouth shut.

Mom interrupts Andi's examination of me, "Let's eat before the food gets cold. I'm so glad to have my kids back home!"

With that, Andi releases my hand and begins filling her plate. When she lets go, I suddenly have an odd and ominous feeling, like grains of sand sifting through my fingers and falling away no matter how hard I try to hold onto them. I'm not the damn sensitive type who believes in all that paranormal bullshit. But the feeling is so strong I almost grab her hand back in pure fear of losing her. Giving myself the mental "man-up" pep talk, I shake it off and fill my plate.

We enjoyed our time with my parents but I am so glad when we finally leave so that I can have Andi all to myself. She is unusually quiet on the ride to her house. Her arm is propped on the car door and she is chewing her fingernails. An action I have very, very rarely seen from her. I slowly reach over and take her other hand in mine, rubbing her hand back and forth with my thumb until she looks over at me.

"My turn to offer a penny for your thoughts," I say with a half-smile.

"Why didn't you tell me you were a psychologist before tonight? I thought you were in the same business with your dad."

Her tone isn't accusing, but it's there just under the surface. She has a strong distrust of psychologists and psychiatrists after her yearlong stint in the psychiatric hospital. She's probably feeling very betrayed right now. Like I'm part of those people who turned a blind eye and deaf ear on everything she experienced in foster care.

"I wasn't hiding it from you, if that's what you're thinking. It really isn't part of me, Andi. It's not who I am or what I want. I learned that pretty quickly and I've been trying to break into boxing for quite some time."

She's quiet as she processes this information. I half-expected her next question but that didn't soften the blow any.

"Did you help your dad get those pictures of me?" Her voice is small and sad—like she's afraid of the answer.

"Hell. No. I would never do that to you." I squeeze her hand and tug on it slightly so she will look at me as I say the words to her. She only nods in response.

"He's going to hurt you and your family, Luke. Jackson won't stop until he gets what he wants. I don't know what he wants from me—what he thinks he can gain. But this is all a big chess game to him. He's arranging his pieces so that he has all the advantages. He's going to take out everyone who means anything to me one at a time and make me watch. He won't come after me until he's through with everyone else."

"He's already coming after you, Andi. You still have your name in the damn tabloids every week with some crazy, made up pile of shit. And you're about to lose your contract with your dad's record label over all this negative shit."

"He's orchestrating that, yes. But he hasn't really come after me yet. That's all just mildly annoying compared to what he's planning. I don't know what it is yet but I know it is coming."

"Don't think you're pulling away from me to protect me. I agreed to let you protect me if you let me protect you, too. *Remember?*"

She smiles weakly at me but doesn't respond. I think I know why I felt like I was losing her earlier tonight. She's already pulling away from me in her attempt to protect me from the storm she feels brewing. I feel it, too, but I feel it in her. I feel her angst and her worry but I won't let her do it alone.

"Andi. *I mean it.* Don't. Even. Think. About. Doing. It."

I pull in my spot in her garage and close the door before we exit my truck. Her hand is on the door and she's ready to jump from the vehicle when I place my hand on her shoulder. "I'm not scared of him and I'm not leaving you to face whatever's coming alone."

She squeezes my hand and gets out of the truck. I'm hot on her heels and we can barely walk because my arms are wrapped around her waist from behind, but I'm not letting her go. I need to feel her close and she needs to feel I'm here for her. I feel her tense body suddenly relax as she allows her body to mold with mine as we walk together as one unit.

"See how this works, baby? Together, we are stronger. Together, we can take on anything. Don't pull away from me now. You'll never have to face hard times alone again. I promise."

She turns in my arms to face me and I see love glistening in her eyes. She doesn't speak words, but her kisses and her touch tells me everything I need to know. She loves me and she believes me. She knows I'm here with her no matter what comes. *Bring on your worst, Jackson Rhoades–whatever you have in mind could never be worse than losing this woman in my arms.*

I tell her to wait for me on the couch while I open a bottle of wine and pour a couple of glasses. She's more relaxed now, resting with her back against my chest and I'm just enjoying the feel of her skin, the rise and fall of her breath, and the way she loving strokes my forearm that's wrapped around her.

"Tell me about when you were a psychologist," she requests.

"I didn't feel like I was any good at it. I met with patients, applied my training, tried to get them to come to their own conclusions and give them the tools they needed to work through their issues themselves. But it all came to a head with one patient who was referred to me from the court," with this last statement, I feel her tense in my arms. I hug her tighter and nuzzle her ear and place kisses on her temple until she relaxes again.

"This guy was accused of beating his wife. She wouldn't press charges but the police had been to their house on enough domestic calls that they'd had enough. The judge sent him to me and I saw him several times. His wife even came in a few times—alone—and their stories matched enough that it didn't seem off to me. I cleared him, said they had the normal marital spats but it wasn't abusive and she wasn't in danger.

"A week after his court case, he held her hostage while the SWAT team waited outside. He killed her before killing himself, but he was yelling that he knew she was having an affair with me. The SWAT team said he screamed over and over that was the only way she could've convinced me to testify that he wasn't abusive to her.

"They both fooled me, Andi. It was my job to know they were lying. It was my job to identify the anomalies, the signs, symptoms, and put it all together for the victim's safety. I didn't do that. I fucked up and someone died because of me. I couldn't do it any more after that."

She turned to face me, staying in my arms and lying chest to chest with me. "I understand exactly what you mean. I felt the same way. I should've put it all together. I should've known what he was doing to those little girls. I mean, I took care of them like I was the parent. I should've known, right?"

"No, Andi. People like Jackson Rhoades are devious and have developed ways of manipulating the victims. Making them believe it's their fault, making them feel ashamed and unable to tell anyone what was really going on behind closed doors. If the girls didn't tell you, didn't show you any signs of it, there was nothing you could've done to stop it any sooner."

She pulls back slightly, keeping her eyes trained on mine, and smiles a knowing smile.

"Damn. Did you just use psychology on *me*?" I asked incredulously. I can't believe she just played me like that. Her grin widens into her mega-watt smile and she unsuccessfully holds back a giggle.

"I just helped you come to the conclusion you already knew," she states matter-of-factly.

"You'd make a damn fine lawyer, ya know?"

"And you'd make a damn fine shrink."

CHAPTER TWENTY-SEVEN

ANDI

I have changed my mind about doing a press conference. After Jackson was at the club, then at Luke's parents' house, I don't think it's such a good idea. Plus, I've been invited for an interview by a very popular morning talk show. They say they want my side of the story. I'm seriously considering accepting this invitation, but I'm concerned they will turn on me at the last minute and make me look like the bad guy.

I have one week to decide if I want to do the talk show or not. A lot can happen in one week of my life.

Luke is at the gym training hard this week. He's missed so much time lately because of all my drama that Mack threatened to drop him. I am working at the gym and at the youth center all week, trying to get back into a regular routine and stop letting everything and everyone else run my life. I was almost to the gym when I realized I forgot my gym bag at home and had to turn around to go get it. Now I'm really running behind.

When I walk in the gym, the number of people inside suddenly overwhelms me. Camera flashes are going off everywhere, video cameras and microphones are being shoved in every direction, and people are crowding me all around. Then the questions they're asking finally register in my brain. They're not directed at me. They're not about me. They're not taking pictures of me–they're pushing me out of the way.

They're going after Shane.

What. The. Hell. Is. Happening.

Crazy Maybe

"Shane! Shane! Is it true you've lost eligibility for the title fight because of steroid use?"

"Are the allegations true?"

"Will you submit to more federation testing?"

The questions are being fired at Shane one after another. Even though I'm looking in the same direction as everyone else, I can't find Shane. Or Mack. Or Luke. I start pushing and elbowing my way through the crowd to get to the front. Shane is in the ring with all his gear on, still practicing and sparring like no one else is here. Mack is standing to the side of the ring and sees me approach the ring. He's not happy at all.

Shane finishes his normal workout and exits the ring on the opposite side of the chaos. I turn and start ordering people out of the gym unless they have a paid membership. Will walks up and starts pushing the crowd toward the doors. When I threaten to call the police and have them arrested for trespassing, they begrudgingly leave the building and wait on the outskirts of the parking lot. I make my way in the direction that Shane went to find out what has happened.

Shane is unwrapping his hands when I walk in the room. "Shane—what is going on?"

He doesn't look up when he answers, "The federation said my last drug test came back positive for illegal steroid use. They've blocked me from continuing on my title-fight run until this has been cleared up—one way or another."

Damn you, Jackson Rhoades.

"Shane, this is my fault. I need to leave. I need to get away from you before I completely ruin your career....and Mack's....," I don't even know what else to say. *I'm sorry I ruined your chance at a title fight* just doesn't seem to cover it.

Crazy Maybe

Shane roars as he punches his metal locker with his bare fist. Tears immediately spring to my eyes because I'm the reason he's lost everything he's worked so hard for. His blood, sweat, tears, pain, and exhaustion–everything is in vain now. All this over trumped up charges that Jackson has waved his magical political wand and conjured up from out of nowhere. The same charges he could make disappear if I cave and do whatever it is he wants.

I quietly leave, not knowing what else to say or do, and give Shane some time and space. It's too much to bear watching him lose his dream when I don't even know why Jackson is doing this or what he wants from me.

I've made a couple of decisions in the last thirty seconds. One, I'm going on the talk show next week regardless of what ulterior motives they have for me. Two, I'm going to find out what Jackson Rhoades wants from me so I can put a stop to all this.

Luke is in the ring, sparring with his partner and giving it his best, as I slip out the door unseen. I've interrupted enough lives lately. I can at least let him finish his workout and not keep him from his dreams while I start planning what to do next. I'm not trying to leave him out, though I have a feeling that's exactly what he will think when he realizes I'm not at the gym. I just need to get away by myself for a while.

My Grande caramel macchiato is now in hand and I'm driving back to my house for some peace and quiet to come up with a plan. As soon as I turn on the radio, the local station DJ's are talking about Shane and his "fall of shame." They're going on and on about how he's such a disgrace for our city. I cringe every time I hear them tear him down and I want to call in to give them a piece of my mind. But I know it'll only adding fuel to the fire to have a "crazy lady" taking up for him.

After a frantic drive home, during which I'm sure I cussed out some very nice people in my fits of road rage, I storm in my kitchen and slam my purse down on the counter. I lay my head over and moan loudly in frustration.

"Andi, that's so unladylike of you," a male voice gently chastises behind me. My back snaps up rod-straight and my head whips around to locate the owner of the offensive voice. The voice I recognize immediately.

"What the hell are you doing in my house, Jackson?" I demand.

"Now, is that any way to speak to your father?" He actually has the nerve to smile at me. A sick, sardonic, evil smile.

"No, it's not. But then, *you* are not my father. *You* are a trespasser who is now guilty of breaking and entering. Not very good for your political reputation, is it?" I stand my ground, keeping my back straight and shoulders back. I will not allow him the pleasure of thinking I'm uncomfortable for even one second.

"I'm not worried about anyone taking your word over mine, Andi," he responded slowly, menacing and with that ugly sneer of his. "Or Shane's word."

Although I knew he was behind it, hearing him say the words still nearly takes my breath away. I lean forward, narrow my eyes and hiss my response, "What do you want, Jackson?"

"Ah, you always were one to cut right to the chase," he chided as he puffed out his chest and put on his best stern face. "You shouldn't have let those pictures of you get out, Andi. They've caused too many questions and I can't have that lingering about when I'll be making a run for the Presidency soon."

"I didn't *let* them get out. But if you want to talk about things that never should have happened, we need to back up a lot longer ago than when those pictures were leaked." I puff out my own chest and meet his glare head on.

"Tsk, tsk. That's no way to clear up this nasty mix up at the boxing lab. If they don't discover it soon, Shane's career may never recover," Jackson replies nonchalantly, as if he doesn't have a care in the world.

I know better, though. His bluff doesn't fool me. Yes, he can hurt Shane, Luke, Sam, Linda–everyone who knows me–but there's something he needs from me or his own career will never recover.

"Just spit it out, Jackson. This conversation has already gone on way too long."

"It's only a matter of time before the media discovers I was your foster father when you had that terrible nervous breakdown and had to be institutionalized," he cocks his head to the side and watches for my reaction to his blatant lie about me.

"And?"

"And they will want to know why you so viciously attacked me…without cause or provocation."

I take a deep breath and try to calm my nerves. He's setting the scene, he's giving me the story he wants me to feed to the press.

"And why would they think it was without cause or provocation?"

"Because that's what you need to admit to doing…as part of your continued rehabilitation, you need to take full responsibility for what happened. You want to show that you've learned, grown, and changed from the troubled youth you once were."

"I was troubled," I said each word slowly, disbelievingly, and like I was talking to a complete moron.

"Yes, I know you were, dear. Thankfully, we found a doctor and hospital staff that could help you."

"You're not so delusional that you really believe that line of bullshit you're trying to feed me, are you?"

"You will believe it and you will tell it to every single person who has a camera, microphone, recorder, or even a damn camera phone! You will make them believe it or everyone you know will pay for *your* mistakes." His voice became deeper and gruffer as he moved in closer to me. I know he's close to being desperate—and desperation makes him even more dangerous.

"It's time for you to leave. Get out of my house." I make sure my voice doesn't quiver but inside I am shaking like a leaf. He just smirks, inclines his head and turns toward the front door.

"Don't even think about getting any bright ideas, Andi," he calls over his shoulder just before the door shuts behind him. I rush to the door, lock it and let out a long breath.

I know what I have to do now.

LUKE

Damn, Mack is putting me through the ringer today. I have missed way too much training lately and it definitely shows. I can feel it in my stamina and in my sore muscles. The muscle burn feels good though—I don't know if I'll be able to move tomorrow, but at least I know it is working.

No doubt Mack is taking his frustrations on me over the damn circus in here. All these lies and rumors surrounding Shane have nearly cost him the title fight. Mack kept telling Shane to keep his chin up because he would make sure it all got cleared up, but Shane's not so sure Mack will be able to do it.

Shane finished his workout and went to the locker room to get away from the fucking media swarming around the place. I am impressed with Andi and Will's ability to get them out of the building but they're still outside with their damn intrusive telephoto lenses and video cameras. Shane finished his workout to keep up appearances but I know it is all taking a toll on him.

I watch Andi as she follows Shane toward the locker room. If anyone can get through to him, it's her. They've had a tight relationship for a long time and he listens to her. He's going to need her now, and she will need him because I know she feels responsible for all this.

About two hours later, I'm finishing up a grueling five-mile run when I see Mack and Shane talking. I stroll up to them just in time to hear Mack.

"You can't blame her for this, Shane. You damn well know it." There's no mistaking Mack's harsh tone. Shane quickly shifts his eyes away and immediately looks ashamed. *Was he actually blaming Andi?*

"Can't blame *who*?" I ask, even though I have a good idea of what they're talking about. I am immediately ready to defend Andi to anyone.

Shane won't meet my eyes but Mack has no problem with answering me.

"Shane had a moment of feeling sorry for himself. He's over it now." Shane nods in agreement but still looks away.

"Surely you don't think Andi should be blamed for this. You know her better than that, Shane. Do you know the whole story of what happened to her?" I'm dumbfounded. I can't believe Shane would really think that.

"Yeah, I know, I know, man. It's not her fault and I shouldn't have even thought that for a second. I'm just really fucking mad. If this isn't cleared up soon, and I mean *yesterday* soon, my sponsors will drop me."

"Didn't you talk to her? I saw her follow you toward the locker room," I look around, suddenly realizing that I haven't seen her in a while now.

"Not really. She tried to talk to me but I...she said she should leave because she's hurting my career. I didn't disagree with her," Shane hangs his head and looks at the ground. "I didn't even really say anything to her."

"Where is she? Did she say where she was going?" I'm really looking around the gym now and I don't see her here anywhere. She didn't tell me she was leaving, but I know she wouldn't interrupt my training just to tell me she was leaving the building. Still, it's unusual to not hear from her for so long.

Concern blankets Shane's face as my question registers with him. Shane quickly looks around the gym and back at me.

"I don't know where she is, man. She just left–she didn't say where she was going."

"Don't get your panties in a wad, ladies. You haven't even tried calling her yet," Mack chastises us while shaking his head. "I trained her myself. Give both of us a little credit."

Crazy Maybe

I grab my phone out of my gym bag and call Andi. It rings four times and goes to voicemail. It's not turned off but she's not answering. I'm trying to not freak out and have Mack call me a girl again. Shane looks at me expectantly and I shake my head 'no.'

Mack huffs and says, "One missed call does not an emergency make."

Mack walks off, leaving Shane and me to worry without him. Shane grabs his phone out of his bag and steps away to make a call. He's talking to someone and while I can't help but hope he's talking to Andi, I know it's not by the timbre of his voice. It's much more intimate than the tone he uses with Andi.

A few minutes later, he walks back over to me and tells me no one has heard from her all day. She's not at the youth center and she's not answering either of our calls. I head to the locker room to shower and dress as quickly as I can.

I'm finished in record time and headed toward my truck when my phone starts ringing. Andi's smiling face lights up my phone's display and I'm instantly relieved.

"Andi, where are you?" This is how I answer the phone.

"Well, hello to you, too, my love," she chuckles as she responds to my abrupt greeting.

"Sorry, baby. I just couldn't find you and I was worried. Where are you?"

"I'm at home. Are you finished? Can you come home now?"

"I'm getting in my truck right now. Be there in twenty," I say before we hang up. She sounds fine but I know something is up. I know I haven't had these strange feelings about her for nothing.

She's sitting at the kitchen table, staring at nothing and drumming her fingers, when I walk in the house. I lean against the cabinets and just watch her, taking in her facial expressions, her body language, and the fact that she doesn't even know I'm here yet. That feeling deep in the pit of my chest increases, squeezing my lungs and making my breath catch with its sharpness.

"Baby, what's wrong?" I ask softly, trying to not startle her. She doesn't jump at the sound of my voice. In fact, she doesn't move at all.

"I left the gym early because of what's going on with Shane. It's my fault he's about to lose his shot at the title fight," she responds with no emotion in her voice. I start to object but she continues.

"When I got home, I had a visitor waiting for me inside the house. It was Jackson. I knew he was behind what's happening to Shane, but he admitted it."

I know she was still talking after she said Jackson was in her house, but my brain stopped comprehending the words when I pictured her being here alone with him.

"He basically said I have to publicly take responsibility for everything or he will destroy everyone around me. Shane, you, your parents...He knows his involvement will eventually be found out by the media—because he plans to run for the Presidency."

"*Back. Up.*" It seems I've finally found my damn voice. "I don't think I heard anything after you said Jackson was here." I start pacing now to try to contain the adrenaline that's coursing through my veins.

I just thought I was tired after my workout today. Seems I have plenty of energy left to kick Jackson Rhoades' ass all over Atlanta. I run my hands through my hair and groan in frustration. Just knowing he was here, in her house, waiting for her to get home. He could've done anything to her and I wouldn't have been able to help her at all.

"How the hell did he get in?" I bellow. Not meaning to direct it at her, but my fear for her safety and my anger at Rhoades are getting the best of me.

She calmly responds, "I don't know how he got in. But he walked right out the front door when he left."

"Why are you so nonchalant about this?" I demand, still pacing and now pointing at her. I know I should calm the fuck down.

"He's desperate. He needs me to take the blame and cover for him. He thought he had this all figured out when he sent me to that psychiatric hospital but he didn't. There's something I've missed. Something obvious that I didn't consider. Something big," Andi continues speaking as if she's simply reading off stock market values.

She's talking to me but she's deep in thought, like she's not really here with me. I think she's been reliving everything that happened that night and trying to come up with the missing puzzle piece. I also think that reliving it has taken quite a toll on her.

"I've gone over every detail of that night…and the whole time I lived with them before that night…and every detail of the time in that hospital…and –," she suddenly stopped talking and jumped up from the table.

Her hands flew up in the air over her head as she yelled, "Oh. My. God. I'm such an idiot! *Of course!*"

"I hate to be thick, but what are you talking about?"

"I know exactly why he's so desperate now. He made a comment about how I let the media get those pictures of me. He never considered that I would be all over the news and tabloids after inheriting my father's business. When those pictures hit the news, the story was sensationalized even more. They will keep digging until they find out who the anonymous foster family was that took me in."

"Okay, but I still don't get why he needs you so much. What did you figure out?"

She gives me her mega-watt smile and she honestly looks so happy. Her excitement level just increased a hundred-fold and she's even making me believe there just may yet be hope. She's pacing, her eyebrows are furrowed, but she has a determined glean to her eye. She's not scared or in shock now–she's sure she has figured it out and she's working out a plan now.

"I need to get everyone together, Luke. Shane, Mack, your parents, all our friends–everyone. This will impact them all and I need to make sure you all can handle the fallout until Jackson is taken down for good. I want to explain everything to everyone at once and give everyone a chance to speak before I do anything."

I agree to call an emergency meeting. I feel like a damn idiot even saying that, like I'm some kind of fucking geek government official. But I promise to do it for her anyway. Everyone is coming over to Andi's house within the hour and she's back at the table feverishly making out a list.

Soon everyone is gathered in the den where Andi has put out drinks and snacks. We're all chatting and just generally mingling when Andi comes in the room. My parents are here, along with Brandon, Alicia, Greg, Christina, Tania, Katie, Shane, and Mack.

"Thank you all for coming on such short notice. I had an unwelcome visitor when I got home today. Jackson Rhoades was waiting in my house for me."

After a collective gasp from the ladies and a few comments of rearranging his manhood from the guys, Andi told everyone the same story she had told me. She started with her parents' death, then she described what happened the night she ended up in the psychiatric hospital, and everything else up to this point.

"The reason I've asked you all here is so that you understand what is at risk with my plan. Jackson is a very powerful man with contacts and resources that we can't match. He has threatened every one of you in an attempt to control me. He's banking on me taking full responsibility for everything–for attacking him, but also for convincing the girls that he molested them, that it was all fabricated by me. That's his plan and if I go along with it, he will win. He will always have something to hold over our heads and no one will ever believe the truth if I change my story later.

"My plan is to take the offer to go on the talk show and answer all their questions honestly. Once the truth hits the media, there's a chance that the girls he molested will come forward. Maria would be old enough now to remember what happened and tell the media. There are others, too. But it all depends on if they're willing to speak up or not.

"It's a big gamble to put ourselves on the line like this. It could mean the end of Shane's career. It could mean the end of Mack's business and Sam and Linda's business. And for everyone else, I don't know what he will do, but I know he will find something to hurt you.

"I won't do it if everyone isn't onboard. And I will understand–no hard feelings, no questions, nothing. I just need everyone to consider what this could do to you and make up your own minds."

She sits and waits as everyone contemplates every possible scenario. Most everyone is quiet and it is hard to tell what they are thinking. I speak up first.

"I don't care what he tries to take from me as long as it isn't you, Andi. I'm with you. I will stand beside you regardless of the consequences and regardless if anyone comes forward to confirm what he did."

"But son," my mom's desperate plea is evident, "you don't know what he'll do to you and Andi. Or to us."

"That's true, Linda," Andi responds kindly, "It is crazy, maybe, to take him on like this. But I think of those little girls and what they had to endure, and it doesn't seem so crazy anymore."

Mom is taken aback for a second. She hadn't considered it from that angle and she immediately changes her tune. "I'm with you, too, Andi. You're right—if those little girls could endure that monster, I certainly can, too."

Then Shane speaks, "I'll admit I had a moment of…selfishness…when all of this first hit. But I agree – I will stand with you, Andi. I want to see him brought down for what he's done. I want to make him pay for what he's done to those little girls, to all of us here, but most of all, for what he's done to you. He's tried to turn you into a victim for a long time and it's time we put an end to it."

The others chime in with their agreement. We are now one unified family, standing together to weather the storm that is approaching. The storm we all know could have serious repercussions and implications on our lives and careers. But it's the right thing to do and we're going to stand together and see it done.

CHAPTER TWENTY-EIGHT

ANDI

I'm so nervous right now I'm biting my nails and pacing relentlessly. I know this is the right thing to do but I just don't know what all the consequences will be. I can face the consequences for myself but I feel guilty that everyone else is suffering because of me.

I just confirmed I will do the interview with the talk show host and they'll start running the promo ads soon. The show is taped so it won't actually air until about a week after the interview. The studio audience will also be allowed to ask me questions.

The producer said if there were too many audience questions, they would edit some of it out of the final show. The "editing" process concerns me – especially if they edit some of my answers. I had a condition added to the contract that I have final approval for any editing of the questions and answers to make sure they don't swap any around or cut out important parts of my answer to make it seem like something else.

After everyone left the other night, I tried to convince Luke that this wouldn't work and that it was a bad idea. He saw right through my fear and continued to be my rock, giving me strength at the very times I don't think I can keep this up. I don't want to let him down—his faith in me gives me determination.

Shane hung back and we had a long talk about everything that's going on around him. I wanted to make sure he was good with me answering questions about him. I'm sure they will come up. With all the tabloids and paparazzi running stories, also known as lies, about me since my birthday, they know that Shane and I are close. And he's made it a point to have his picture taken with me on several occasions.

He wants me to tell everything and leave nothing out. He reminded me of something I already knew. If it looks like I'm holding back on one thing, then no one will believe anything I say. It's important that I'm believable so that Jackson's real victims will feel safer in coming forward. Not to save me–but to save others who he may hurt in the future.

Shane offered to come with me on the talk show. While a big part of me would love to have him there, I don't want to make him a bigger target than he already is. So I will answer all the questions about anyone in my life and pray it all turns out well.

I've decided on an awesome song for the competition in two weeks. I've started practicing and gathering my props. It's going to be great and I can't wait. The promos for the talk show will be running by the time I perform again and this time I hope it does bring more people into the club. I *want* this performance to be seen by everyone.

Luke has been staying at my house pretty much all the time now. I think he still feels awkward with it even though I've tried to reassure him in every way I can think of. I'm sitting at the kitchen table enjoying an afternoon caramel macchiato when Luke comes in and surprises me.

"Baby, is the offer to move in here with you still good?" He asks with his best smile but I see the vulnerability underneath the secure façade.

I smile warmly and grab his hand, "Of course it is! Are you really going to give up your bachelor pad now?"

Luke's smile drops, his head tilts to the side, and his eyes narrow in consideration of my question. "*Bachelor pad*? Did you really think that's why I kept my apartment? To use it to run from us?"

It suddenly hits me that his voice has a hurt and offended tone to it. I admit I am totally confused and feel like this is about to turn into an argument.

"Isn't that usually why men hold on to a separate apartment when they're supposedly in a committed relationship?" I ask innocently.

He considers my response and I realize that we both keep answering each other's questions with another question.

"Luke, it's just that we've been together for a while now. You stay here much more than you do at your apartment. But you have never wanted to give it up, no matter how much I want you to be here with me. So, I just naturally thought that you weren't quite ready to make that kind of commitment to me...to us. You haven't been ready to give up your safe house."

I say this to him as non-confrontationally as possible. I'm really not trying to turn this into a big production. I am just really glad that he's asking me about moving in and giving up his apartment. I love him so much and I can't imagine my future without him in it. I don't want to imagine that.

He walks slowly toward me, still thinking and nodding his head as if in a private conversation with himself. I wait and watch him as he processes what I've said and considers his own response.

"So you think I have commitment issues," he finally states. It's not a question.

"I don't know why this conversation is turning to this. I'm really glad you want to be here with me and that's what I want. I just want to know that you're sure about giving up your apartment."

"It's not an unfair assumption. Even though I have had commitment issues in the past, that's not why I've held onto it," he takes a deep breath and turns his back to me as he looks out the back door.

"Andi, I don't feel like I have anything to offer you. You have more money than I could ever dream of making on my own. You have a big, nice home and I have a small apartment. I held onto it because I was afraid you would wake up and decide I'm not enough for you—not good enough, not successful enough—just not *enough* period."

My heart just broke into a million pieces.

I walk up behind him, standing close enough to feel the heat radiate from his body, but I don't touch him. I want him to feel my words right now.

"I was given some great advice when I was young. I was told, *'Once in a lifetime, you may find someone who can give you everything you've ever wanted. A man who can fulfill every desire, grant every wish, provide everything in the world and make every dream come true. Once in a lifetime, that person comes along and when you find him, you'd better hold onto him as tightly as you can.'"*

His shoulders slumped slightly. I continued talking.

"You've given me everything I've ever wanted, Luke. All the ways you love me is more important to me than any amount of money could ever be. You fulfill my every desire and *you* are the world to me. I never even imagined someone as wonderful as you would be in my life. You've more than made my dreams come true and what you provide me can't be bought.

"Don't ever feel like you're not exactly what I want or need. And I don't want to hear you put yourself down like that ever again. I don't care about money or status or material things. That's not what I'm about and you really should already know that. I love *you*, who you are, and how you make me feel."

He turns to face me and his eyes are so full of love, I can feel it reaching out and touching me. He pulls me into his arms and thoroughly kisses me until I feel my legs melting out from underneath me.

"I love you, Andi," he repeats between kisses. "I'm taking you out tonight. Get all dressed up for me." He smiles as he playfully swats me on the butt and walks off toward the bedroom.

I'm so glad that potential argument was avoided I don't even question his demand to get dressed up. I'm just ready to spend some quality alone time with my man tonight! Off to the shower I go.

LUKE

We're back in the same cozy restaurant where we first had dinner as friends. I can't believe how much has happened in our time together. While there are things I wish I could go back and change, I wouldn't trade one day with Andi for anything. I knew she was special the first time I saw her.

I didn't know she would mean more to me than anything I've ever wanted in my life. She's more than my education, more than my boxing career, and more than my family's acceptance. She has shown me what true strength is and what real love is. I can't breathe without her.

"You look so beautiful tonight, you take my breath away. I am the luckiest man ever. I know I don't deserve you, but I should warn you that I will never willingly let you go. I want you with me, Andi. Always."

She leans in and kisses me so gently, so sweetly, but it's still enough to heat me to the core. She runs her soft hand along my jawline and her beautiful smile lights up her face. I hold her hand in mine and just try to take in, once again, that she is real.

The words I've just told her are not just pretty words and they're not spoken lightly. I've never been good at relationships and I've barely managed to hold this one together. But there is one thing I know without a shadow of a doubt. There is nothing that can keep me from her side. I would knock down the gates of hell without a second thought if that was what it took.

I never thought I would even consider marriage. I've never been interested enough in anyone I've dated before to make long term plans. There have been plenty who wanted to talk about taking me home for the holidays while it was still the middle of July. That was enough to make me run for the damn hills. But Andi doesn't make me feel that way at all.

With Andi, if she said she wanted to go to a deserted island with me at the end of next year, I'd make our reservations today and count down the days until I'd have her all to myself. She is everything I never knew I wanted, everything I never knew I needed, and more than I could ever ask for. She gets me, she believes in me and, my god, every way she loves me is unbelievable. Every cell in my body is drawn to her like a magnet is drawn to steel.

The waiter is at our table delivering the bottle of champagne I pre-ordered. I wanted it to be a surprise for Andi and I can tell it definitely is. Her eyes widen as she looks at the champagne flutes being placed before us. She jumps and laughs when the waiter pops the cork and I can't help but laugh with her.

I hand her flute to her and pick mine up. "A toast."

"What are we toasting to?" She asks with a smile.

"To you, Andi. Reclaiming your life, refusing to back down, and taking this stand to help others. You are an inspiration to me and you make me want to be a better man. I love you," I clink my glass to hers.

"I love you, too, Luke," she responds with eyes so watery it's obvious she's fighting back tears from my little speech.

As she places the flute on her lips, I still her hand with mine. "One more thing before we say 'cheers.'"

"Oh—ok—I'm sorry. I thought you were through," she replies and her cheeks blush a beautiful shade of pink.

"I love you, Andi. There isn't a minute of the day that goes by without you on my mind in some way. Even when I'm with you. There is no other woman who can make me feel the way you do. There is no one else who could love me the way you love me. And, in my heart, my mind, and my eyes, no one else even holds a candle to you."

In one swift movement, I slide off of the seat and drop to one knee beside our table. In my outstretched hand, I hold out a black velvet box.

"Andi Morgan, will you do me the endless honor of being my wife? Will you marry me?"

The tears can no longer be contained and are running unchecked down her beautiful face. The light in her eyes is absolutely glowing and she is completely speechless. Her eyes dart quickly between looking at me, on the floor, then back to the still closed black box. Her mouth opens and closes as if she's trying to speak but the words will not form.

Crazy Maybe

I have to admit I'm a little nervous, still here on one bent knee, and everyone around watching in stunned silence. They are also waiting for the answer Andi still hasn't given me. When her eyes dart back to mine, I smile warmly and invitingly as I open the box to reveal its contents.

"I picked this one because I know how much you love vintage stores. I'm not a diamond expert, but it has baguette and princess cut diamonds that wrap around the caviar beaded band, with a round 2-carat center stone."

I take it out of the box and slide it on her finger. The size fits perfectly. She still hasn't made a sound and I'm not certain she's even blinked recently.

"Think I can get an answer now?"

"YES! Yes, yes, yes!" She screams out. She flies into my arms and kisses me as the restaurant patrons erupt in applause. She doesn't stop kissing me or even flinch an acknowledgment when the evening crowd calls out their well wishes for us.

With my free hand, I grab our flutes again and we toast our engagement. We are still in the floor, with me down on one knee and Andi sitting on the other. Several flashes from camera phones go off as people take our picture. Pictures that may end up in the tabloids but I don't even care. At least everyone will know she is mine.

We finish our meal with several people stopping by our table to congratulate us. My pride swells in my chest as I catch her looking at her ring in awe every couple of minutes. Unable to stand it any longer, I break down during dessert and ask her.

"Do you like it? If not, we can go exchange it for something else. You can pick out whatever you want."

261

Crazy Maybe

She jerks her hand away like I'm about to take it back right now. She exclaims, "No! I love it—it's perfect!" Her perfect face transforms into the cutest scowl as she says, "You're not taking it back."

I laugh and reassure her, "Okay, okay. I won't take it back. I'm glad you like it."

"I love it, Luke. Really—it fits me perfectly in every way," she says as she stretches out her arm, fans out her fingers and watches as the candlelight sparkles off the diamonds. It makes me feel like man—and loved, respected, and appreciated—to know that she loves something I've put a lot of thought into getting her. Especially something as significant as this.

The past six months with her have been the best time of my life. As we leave the restaurant, Andi suggests we go for a short walk. The early October air is more crisp than usual and the slight breeze makes it the perfect weather for walking and enjoying time together.

Andi snuggles in close to me as we stroll down the sidewalk. I spot a small deserted park with small white lights strung throughout the trees, several park benches and a few swings for kids. The music from the restaurant nearby filters through the air, and creates a romantic atmosphere. I pull her into my arms for a slow dance in the fall air and enjoy the feel of her body pressed against mine.

I couldn't have written a more perfect ending to this day. The only woman I've ever really loved just agreed to be my wife. She's in my arms, pressed against my body, and looking at me like I hung the moon and stars. Exactly the same way I'm looking at her.

"I'm ready to take you home, Ms. Morgan," I whisper suggestively in her ear.

Crazy Maybe

"I'm ready to be taken home, Mr. Woods," she purrs back to me.

Now *this* is the perfect ending to a perfect evening.

CHAPTER TWENTY-NINE

ANDI

The water jostles over me, sending suds cascading down my arm as I bring the glass of champagne to my lips. Luke is settled in behind me in the oversized claw tub in my bathroom. I'm still in shock over him asking me to marry him tonight. There were no clues, no hints, nothing at all that gave any indication he was even thinking about it.

But I'm so beyond thrilled it's not even funny. I can't wait to start planning our wedding but we probably should set a date first. I'm determined to enjoy our engagement and not rush it no matter what. I hope that we can finally just enjoy our time together without so many surprises and issues cropping up.

Luke's arm wraps around me as he fully pulls me up onto his lap. His hands cup my breasts, the water and bubble bath acting as a lubricant on my skin and allowing his hands to smoothly glide over me. I involuntarily arch my back and push my body into his hands. His mouth finds mine and thoroughly kisses me senseless.

I feel his full, thick erection between my legs and I know he's ready for me. As ready as I am for him and I absolutely cannot wait one more second. I take him in my hand and guide him to my entrance. His hands find my hips and he helps raise me until I'm positioned to take him fully inside me.

I slide down him, feeling him stretch and fill me completely, until he is fully seated inside me. We begin moving in tandem. Our bodies find that perfect rhythm, enticing and seducing us as the pressure builds higher and higher inside. I feel his hips buck beneath me as he pushes more of himself deep inside me.

I snake my hand up and around his head, fisting the hair on the back of his head and crying out in pure pleasure. He turns my face to him and covers my mouth with his. His tongue dives deep inside and he moans into my mouth. His fingers tighten on my hips, pushing me down as his hips push up over and over again. I'm suddenly screaming his name out in ecstasy when I hear the low rumble of his masculine grunt in my ear as he joins me.

After draining the water, Luke lifts me from the tub, dries me off and carries me in his arms to the bed. He lays me down and covers my body with his. Nudging my legs apart with his knee, he settles in between my legs, pelvis to pelvis. He spends several long minutes lovingly kissing me—on my face, my mouth, my neck, and makes his way lower and lower until my whole body has been sufficiently worshipped by his mouth.

Hours and several lovemaking sessions later, we fall asleep in each other arms feeling completely sated. Just before I succumb to sleep, I hear him whisper so softly, "I don't deserve you. But I can never let you go."

I wake up and see that Luke is still sound asleep. The thought that he's no doubt still tired from all his hard work last night brings a huge smile to my face. I stroll into the kitchen, start the coffee brewing, and begin to make our breakfast.

Several minutes later, when everything is almost ready, Luke stumbles in, yawning and running his fingers through his bed hair. Even like this, first thing in the morning and barely awake, he is the most gorgeous man I've ever seen. My heart skips a beat every time I see him walking toward me just from knowing he's mine.

He wraps his arms around me and lowers his head to kiss me. As we end the kiss, I see one hand sneak behind me to grab a piece of bacon. I playfully admonish him for it and he laughs as he gets plates out for us. I realize that I could do this for the rest of my life and be completely happy.

As soon as we finish breakfast, Luke's phone starts ringing and then mine. We each answer and immediately look at each other. It seems our dinner was indeed fodder for the tabloids and our picture has been all over the news this morning. Our friends and family call one after the other to confirm the news is true and to congratulate us. Apparently there was at least one rumor that I am pregnant because Linda demanded to know if we were really having a baby.

"Do I look fat?" I asked, as I turn sideways and examine my stomach in the full-length mirror.

"No, you don't look fat. At all. Why would you even think that?" Luke asks.

"Because they said I'm pregnant! Do I *look* pregnant?" I poke my stomach out and pull my shirt tight against me. "That's it. I'm exercising more."

Luke laughs and tackles me to the couch. "Exercise all you want–you're not fat. You're *fine*, woman!"

Now the world knows we're engaged and they all think I'm fat and pregnant. Nice.

The rest of the week is pretty much the same. More pictures of Luke and me at the restaurant. All different, unflattering angles, and more speculation of why he proposed. So many vicious rumors about us both and most of them are not even based on a sliver of truth. *Bastards.*

Crazy Maybe

The promotional ads for the talk show have started. Thankfully they had already recorded the ads or I'm sure they would be littered with these recent pictures and rumors, too. For now anyway, the ads only show me at my birthday celebration and, of course, the psychiatric hospital pictures. I hope Jackson is shitting his pants right now.

I'm on my way to the broadcasting studio now so I know the ads will change soon. We film today, they quickly edit and then the show airs a week from today. They will redo the ads to include clips from the interview, and, I'm sure, pictures of our dinner where Luke proposed.

I'm in the waiting room and the staff is buzzing around me. One offered me coffee or water. Another is updating my makeup and hair. Yet another adds a little more volume to my hair and makes sure I'm overall acceptable for the cameras. I did notice that no one came right out and asked, but they all looked at my stomach. *They* all think I'm fat and pregnant, too.

Before the studio audience is brought in, the host of the talk show, Lindsey Blair, explains how everything will be handled. She will make the introductions and I will enter from the side of the stage on her cue. She has a list of pre-printed questions that I have about an hour to review.

She will then open up the floor to the audience to ask me questions directly. Only the best questions and answers will be used in the final edited version of the show. I remind her that I have final executive say on the editing of all questions and answers. She doesn't like it but she concedes.

Her assistant just knocked on my door to alert me of the two minutes mark. I wipe my sweaty palms on a towel and walk the long corridor to the backstage area alone. I stop to listen to her introduction of me.

"Joining me today is Andi Morgan, daughter of the late Max and Katie Morgan. Andi officially inherited the lucrative MaxMorgan Music on her recent 25th birthday and reportedly sold it for billions. Andi still maintains her position at the *Tough Enough* gym and also volunteers at a local youth center.

"Andi became instantly famous after the release of *these* pictures of her in a psychiatric hospital at the young age of fifteen and the amazing behind the scenes story of why she was hospitalized. Andi is here to tell us the shocking story in her own words. Please join me in welcoming Andi Morgan to *The Lindsay Blair Show*."

The crowd applauds and I walk across the stage with a smile plastered to my face. I give a small wave to the crowd as I pass by, shake Lindsay's hand and take my seat beside her. Her smile is warm and friendly, but the deep-rooted ambition is evident in her eyes. She wants the story, the scoop, the exclusive— she wants the recognition of being a tough interviewer. I'm about to give her the story of her life.

"Andi, welcome to the show. We had so many people who wanted to be part of the audience today that we couldn't take them all. That has never happened before. Needless to say, there are a lot of people who are interested in your story. So, for the sake of time, let's get started.

"Tell us, Andi. Did you attempt to murder your foster father?"

That question was not on the list she gave me not an hour before. The gleam in her eyes says she knows she's thrown me a curve ball and she's sure I will strike out.

Guess again, girlie.

"Yes. I certainly did," I reply matter-of-factly. Then I smile knowingly at her as her jaw drops open and she stammers for the next question.

"Care to elaborate?"

I was expecting something much more hard hitting from this *Barbara Walters wanna-be*, but this question actually puts me in a much better position to tell the entire story first and then let others ask me specific questions.

So I start from the very beginning of what I consider my story, my parent's death, and walk them through every step of my life until today. I held nothing back. I told them all about my mom's cousin giving me up to the state and how I was bounced to the numerous foster homes.

I explained how and why I ended up in the psychiatric hospital, why I applied for legal emancipation, and how Mack took Shane and me under his wing. I even told them the reason for all my tattoos, the color in my hair, and the youth center.

I ended my story with telling him about Luke proposing to me in *our* restaurant. By the end of my life-story recount, Lindsay had tears in *her* eyes and several people in the audience were audibly crying and sniffling.

Lindsay grabbed and squeezed my hand in a show of support and solidarity. When I realized she was still unable to speak, I continued filling in the silence.

"I'd like to share with you why Shane Fowler has recently become a target of a vicious campaign to ruin his career. Shane has been like a brother to me and has only ever protected me. What he has been accused of is absolutely completely false and has been orchestrated specifically to make me keep my secrets.

Crazy Maybe

"The man I admittedly stabbed is a high-ranking political figure. He was at the time it happened and is even more so now. When I walked in that room and found him raping that little girl," I have to stop and take a steadying breath before I can finish this sentence, "I decided right then that I would never back down from protecting the innocent.

"If I give in to his demands. If I let him get away with this without telling the truth—no matter what it costs me—I will be as much to blame as he is. I will have helped him hurt innocent people and I can't live with that."

Lindsay finally finds her voice. "What do you hope to gain by telling your story today, Andi?"

"My hope is that others will see him for what he really is. I have to believe that as his victims come forward, they will find strength in knowing they're not alone. I want them to see that they can help put an end to the years of terror and pain he's inflicted on them."

The crowd erupts in applause and many people jump to their feet. Lindsay wipes a tear away and rises to take the microphone to the audience for their questions. There are so many questions from the audience that Lindsay and her producers decide to post the complete, unedited version on their website as a marketing test tool. After more than two hours of questions and answers, Lindsay finally wraps up the show.

Many people come forward to share their story of past abuse. They talk to me about what an inspiration I am for standing up to someone who has used his power to do so much evil. I thank them for their kind words and inwardly wonder what kind of evil will now be unleashed on everyone I know.

LUKE

While Andi's at the talk show interview, I make a life changing decision to pursue a change in career. Again. She's too good of a person to hold it against me, but my lack of direction and success is disturbing to me. I don't want to depend on her and her inheritance to live on. I want to be able to provide for my wife and my family. That is, when we decide to have one.

There are things about my past that I have to come to terms with. I have to find a way to move past this and quit mind-fucking myself over it. The truth is I'm afraid I will lose Andi if she realizes out what a screw-up I really am. I want her to be proud of me and proud to be my wife.

Right now, I don't have much going for me in either area. But that is about to change. Her solid belief in me has helped me see that I need to step up my game and be the man she needs. So, I just submitted the application and proof of continuing education credits to have my psychologist license reactivated. After working with Andi at the youth center, I've decided I can put my psychology expertise and the skills with my hands to good use by working with the kids.

The kids there are great too work with and talk to— they absorb everything. Even though I've had previous failures in counseling adults, I'm sure I can make positive changes in the kids. I've seen some evidence of it when I've worked there before. I want to try a mixture of athletic training, neighborhood beautification and positive peer pressure to help change their lives.

Crazy Maybe

Now to get past the hurdle of the parents thinking Andi is crazy and a bad influence on their kids. How ironic will it be when they find out I'm a psychologist? A psychologist engaged to a former mental patient...classic. When this comes out, I hate to think of the repercussions Andi could face.

I really hate the thought of Andi doing this interview alone. I tried to talk her into letting me go with her in case things get out of hand with the questions but she refused. She said she needed to do this on her own. She didn't want the impression that she needed backup or anyone to corroborate her story. The promo ads have been running all week, advertising that Andi will finally tell her story and answer all their damn questions.

I will lose my shit if I stay here any longer and just wait. Useless. So I gear up and head to the gym to work off some frustration. It really doesn't help that there are several reporters with cameras just inside the door as I walk in. I'm tempted to accidentally shove them out of the way when I realize that Shane is standing in front of them—talking.

"I will gladly submit to any type of drug test—urine, blood, hair—you name it. I have nothing to hide and I've done nothing wrong. Every one of you can take it to your own independent lab as long as they conduct the tests live, on camera, and no one interferes. I've been set up and falsely accused. I want it shown to the world now," Shane declares with gritted teeth.

Well, hot damn, I think we have a fighter here.

"I should have offered this the first day this ridiculous accusation was leveled against me, but I couldn't think straight. I wanted to believe that it was a simple mix-up at the lab and would be corrected immediately. It's important that my fans realize that

272

none of this is true," Shane stops and looks directly into the closest camera, "I'm asking you to believe in me."

With that, Mack announces that's the only statement that Shane will make, and unless they're taking samples to the lab, he will answer no further questions. Several reporters jump at the chance to be the ones to either clear him or condemn him.

Shane willingly takes them to the locker room with him and the ringside doctor performs the blood draws himself. Mack's lawyer steps in with paperwork for the reporters to sign and a boxing commission representative arranges for each specimen to have an official escort.

I move to the far corner to work on the speed bag alone and clear my head. Mack raised Shane and Andi–he taught them how to stand up for themselves. Watching Shane actually helped me get past this feeling that Andi needed protecting during her interview. She's strong, she's independent, and she's opinionated–and I wouldn't change a thing about her.

Brandon was right when he said a love like this only comes along once in a lifetime. And I am damn lucky to have found her when I wasn't even looking. Now, there's nothing I wouldn't do for her. If I could get my hands on Rhoades, she would never have to worry about him again. He's a piece of shit who doesn't deserve to live for what he put Andi and those little girls through. His day is coming.

Three hours later, I'm exhausted from my extensive workout, which included sparring in the ring with another boxer for several rounds. When we climb through the ropes, I look up at the clock and realize I haven't heard from Andi all day. Immediately, I feel my heart beat against the inside of my chest at the thought something has happened to her. I reach for my phone inside my gym bag and it starts ringing. Andi's beautiful, smiling faces lights up my screen.

"Hey baby, I was just about to call you," I try to hide the fact that I was worried about her.

She laughs. She knows me too well.

"I'm fine, honey. The talk show recording went way longer than expected and turned out even better than I could hope. I go back tomorrow to view the edited version and make sure I approve of what they cut out," her enthusiasm is contagious as she tells me about her day.

"Good–I'm glad to hear that. Now I don't have to kick Lindsay's ass for being mean to you," I joke with her.

"OH–and let me tell you the best part!" I think she's about to start squealing like a girl now.

"What's the best part?"

"Travis Malone was there! You know, the lead singer of *Sound Bar!* He was there for the taping of a different show but he listened to my whole story. He came forward and told his story of how he was physically abused as a child. He's agreed to do public service announcements with me about abuse. AND– he wants to leave his record label and sign with me!"

Yep, she's a squealing girl now. A squealing girl who sounds like a groupie for the handsome lead singer of one of the hottest bands out right now. Isn't that just fucking perfect?

This is Andi you're talking about. I hear Brandon's voice admonishing me in my head. I may check myself in the damn psychiatric hospital.

"Well, why wouldn't he want to sign with you? You're awesome, babe!" I play off my insecurities well.

Her voice lowers and she suddenly becomes very serious. "You know you have nothing to worry about. Right, Luke?"

"Of course I know that," I lie. Like a damn dog.

"I love you, Luke. I'm marrying you. And there's not another man alive who could take me from you. Ever."

She always knows exactly what to say to make me feel better.

"I love you, too, baby. Meet me at home so I can show you how much."

"That's an offer I can never refuse!"

We say our goodbyes and I start heading to the door. I have to remember to tell her about Shane's interview earlier so no one catches her off guard. Just as I'm about to leave the gym, the new promo for Andi's interview plays. Her beautiful face fills the flat-screen on the wall. She has a serious, determined look on her face and they're playing a small clip of Andi talking about being put in foster care. Lindsay's voice fills the air as she invites viewers to watch her show Friday for the full story, including Andi's claim of political corruption.

Shit is about to hit the fan. I can smell it coming a mile away. All I know is I will protect Andi with my life. Jackson Rhoades is in for one hell of a fight if he thinks he's getting anywhere near Andi. I'm the only one who's getting close to her and I'm almost home now.

And there's my life, waiting for me on the front porch, grinning like a little girl. At first, I think it's because she's happy to see me but she bursts my bubble as soon as I get out of the truck. She rushes to me, hugs me and says, "I can't believe Travis wants to sign with me!" She dances around, doing a victory dance like a school girl whose major crush finally just looked at her, and giggles. I mean, she literally giggles over this guy.

I clear my throat.

She smiles. "Sorry. I just never thought someone already so big would ask to work with me!"

I pull her in my arms and when I feel her body meld with mine, my insecurities are gone. She meant what she said–she is mine and I trust her with my heart and my soul. "I'm proud of you, baby. That is really awesome," I kiss her and wrap both arms firmly around her midsection, pulling her even closer and backing her up against my truck.

"Lucas Woods," she says in the sternest voice she can muster under the circumstances.

"Yes, my love?" I ask, as I lift one of her legs and pull it up to my waist before lifting the other one to my other side.

"We're in the garage," she says as I move my lips and tongue down her neck. Nipping, licking and sucking her soft skin. Her words argue but her head leans to one side, giving me better access to her slender, sensuous neck.

"Yes, we're in the garage," I answer as my hands slowly push her shirt up and over her head.

"And the door is open," she says on an exhale, as my mouth covers her breast. She's still wearing her bra and the damn thing is in the way. My hands rub around her sides, slightly tickling her and giving her goose bumps at the same time, as they find the bra snap on her back. I release her breasts and they bounce in happy response to being freed. I suck one nipple into my mouth and Andi moans in appreciation.

"The door is open, yes," I respond as I slide my tongue from one breast to the other, giving the other nipple adequate attention and hearing a similar moan from Andi. I slide one hand down her torso, lightly rubbing her supple skin along her breast bone, to her navel, and lower still to the wetness waiting for me between her legs. I slip my hand into her skirt and under her panties, hovering just over her nub to tease and build her anticipation.

It works.

"Mmmmm, Luke," she urges me on with the urgency in her voice.

"Yes, baby?"

She pulls my hair and I have to refrain from laughing at her tactics.

"My impatient little vixen," and before she has a chance to respond with another hair pulling taunt, I slide my fingers over the bundle of nerves and into her core. She's already soaked and waiting for me. I slide one finger in and out slowly, tortuously, building her desire more and more.

This earns me a harder hair yanking. "Luke," she warns me and there's no doubt what she means.

I can't hold back my laugh this time. I plunge two fingers deep inside her, quickly withdrawing them and pushing them back in repeatedly. Andi fists my shirt in her hand, scraping her nails against the skin on my back as she does it, as she begins to reach her first orgasm. Just before she screams out, I cover her mouth with mine and her scream drowns in my kiss.

I push her skirt up from the bottom and tear her panties off her body. She looks surprised at the sound of tearing cloth but she's even more turned on than she was a second ago. I free myself from my gym shorts and push myself deep into her. She's leaned up against my truck but she uses the leverage of both my legs and the truck to help push down as I thrust up.

Crazy Maybe

The possibility of being seen doesn't faze me right now. All I can think of is this beautiful, naked woman, who thoroughly loves grinding on me right now. This wonderful creature who will be my wife very soon if I have any say so in it. The mixture of desire, love, and near climax look on her face pushes me to drive into her harder and harder. Her breasts bounce up and down in front of me as she leans her head back against my truck. We come together with her shouting and me grunting loudly.

I don't put her down. Instead, I carry her to the door, up the stairs and to the shower. Where I continue my assault on her body and senses in every conceivable way. Then to the bedroom, still wet from the shower and smelling of her body wash. But we don't make it to the bed. I've awakened a nympho. She stops me and pushes me against the door to take me in her mouth. Her tongue feels so hot, wet, and velvety against my shaft I can hardly contain myself.

I lift her and back her up against the door, parting her legs with mine as I bend my knees. I straighten my legs and thrust up into her over and over again. I pull out and turn her around, taking her from behind and moving in her while I hold her hips. Thirty minutes later, we're both fully sated and completely dehydrated, lying limp and lifeless in the bed.

"When are you marrying me, Andi?" I whisper to her.

She doesn't answer and I look at her, concerned at her quietness, only to realize she's fallen asleep in my arms.

CHAPTER THIRTY

ANDI

The promos running for the past week have really taken a toll on me. It freaks me out when I'm instantly recognized and asked to give them the scoop because they can't wait for the show to air. I have to respectfully decline due to legal issues with appearing on the show, but I can honestly say I'm happy to be bound by the law this time. Most people accept that answer and keep going but there have been a few who have promised to not tell a soul. Yeah, right.

I've received several hang up calls on my home phone and a few unknown callers on my cell that refused to say anything. Luke has called them—or I should say *him*-every name in the book to try to goad him into responding. No luck in that, but the calls keep coming. I know *the bastard* wants me to be afraid but I refuse to give in. I can handle whatever he does to me but when he messes with those I love...that's a different story. But I'm holding strong.

We made our rounds to our friends and family to share the good news about Luke proposing to me in person. I was surprised to find out he had asked Pop for permission when he was at the gym. When Pop said yes, Luke immediately went and bought my ring.

I still can't believe this is really happening. I'm about to start my own family, even if it's a family of two for now. Luke's parents were thrilled. His sister, Alicia, wants to throw my wedding shower and my girlfriends can't wait to throw my bachelorette party.

Crazy Maybe

Brandon was a little more subdued at the news but he said if this is what I want and what will make me happy, he is all for it. Luke had an odd look on his face and I have to admit I felt a little uncomfortable. I love Brandon like a brother and I get the feeling he's trying to protect me from facing the problems Luke and I had before. I certainly can't blame him for that. I don't ever want to go through that again.

Now that I think about it, Luke has been acting strange this week. Like, secretive strange. He's been on the computer with his serious look—brows furrowed, chewing on the end of his pen, and huffing and puffing like he's frustrated. Definitely not the signs of a man who's secretly watching porn. I know he'll tell me what he's up to when he's ready but I still have a hard time shaking my old abandonment issues.

To get my mind on something else, I've spent time prepping for the song I'm singing this weekend. With everything going on, it seems frivolous to still compete in a karaoke contest. I mean, there's really no prize to win other than bragging rights, and I don't believe in bragging. But I'm secretly hoping *the bastard* is there again because this song is for him. Even if he isn't, I have a feeling there will be plenty of people there to record my performance, especially after my interview airs Friday.

I'm actually looking forward to this one.

After all this bad publicity, the CEO of MaxMorgan Music called me and we talked for over an hour about everything that's happened. He was about to terminate my contract work with them but he heard about my conversation with Travis Malone through unofficial channels and quickly reconsidered. I thought that was *so very considerate* of him. I was vague and noncommittal about my intentions in my responses to him, regardless of how many times he tried to pin me down.

"Hey baby, whatcha doing?" I ask Luke as I walk in the den. He shuffles some papers, quickly puts them away and stands to meet me. He draws me into his arms and kisses me senseless.

"Waiting for you, of course," he replies slyly with his sexy grin. "How about I take you out to eat tonight. There's a new Mexican restaurant close to the gym that's really good."

"Hmmm, sounds good. What have you been working on in here?" So the curiosity got the best of me. Sue me.

He pulls back and looks at me for a second and I could tell he was weighing his options. Use my tactic of dodge and deflect? Straight up lie? Cave and tell the truth?

Dodge and deflect, it is.

"Boring stuff. I'll tell you about it later," he replies and cuts his eyes to my left. One sign of lying. But, why would he lie?

I try to keep my emotions neutral and give him the benefit of the doubt. Maybe it's a surprise for me and I'm about to ruin it. So I pull up my big girl panties and deal with it. He wouldn't be here if he wasn't happy with me. I refrain from saying or doing anything stupid and we have a great Mexican dinner.

Somehow we both felt relaxed and happy tonight, even knowing the impending storm that is brewing just outside. But tonight, we're just a happy couple enjoying an evening together.

It's finally Friday morning and I slept absolutely none last night, and it wasn't all Luke's fault this time. It was some of his fault, but mostly it was because I know the interview will air first thing this morning and then all hell will break loose. I got up early to shower and prepare to face the day. Now I'm sitting at my kitchen table and my Keurig just provided my morning cup of heaven.

Luke bought Panera Bread bagels and cream cheese yesterday. Out of sheer anxiety, I slather a cinnamon crunch bagel with honey walnut cream cheese and devour it in record time. No longer able to wait, I turn on the television and watch for the interview. The promos have increased in length to give a little more information to entice the audience to watch.

And, it's time. Luke and I sit glued to the show and neither of us speaks during the whole hour-long interview. Throughout the show, the camera pans to the audience and shows some people crying, some shocked, and of course, some in complete disbelief. At the end of the show, Lindsay added a few minutes to say a few words of her own. She spoke words of support and belief in me, even knowing that there will be severe backlash from certain influential circles.

When the show ends, Luke turns to me and pulls me into his lap. Planting kisses all over my face and neck, he whispers words of love and encouragement to support me. "I'm so proud of you, Andi. You gave a great interview. The audience loved you and even Lindsay Blair was on your side."

I nod and he continues.

"You are the most amazing person I've ever met. You're strong, independent, loving, and giving. You're unbelievably kind and thoughtful of others and everyone you meet loves you. You're extremely sexy and beautiful. I've never wanted anyone like I want you–in every way imaginable. You've consumed me and spoiled me and made it impossible for me to even consider living without you. Whatever happens, I'm with you. I won't leave you."

He knows my weakness. He knows my fear. Even after all these years of making it on my own, the fear of losing those I love is still very real. He knows this even though I've never even said it. Yet, he always reassures me that he will never leave me. Words are not enough to describe how much I love him. Feelings are even grossly inadequate to describe the depth my love. It's all consuming, scary, exhilarating, and comforting all at once. He's become my life and I would do anything for him.

I gently rub the stubble along his jawline and lean in to kiss him. I turn to face him, straddling his lap and wrapping my arms around his neck. I feel his strong arms wrap around me, pulling me tight to him. I feel his erection growing between my legs and I squeeze my legs around him, pulling myself down toward him more. His hands glide up my legs, skimming my hips until his fingers find the hem of my shirt.

Just as he slowly starts to pull it up, the phone rings. We both freeze, still nose to nose but staring intently into the others' eyes. All the hang-ups instantly flash in my mind but somehow I don't think this call will be a hang up. I think this call is the declaration of the coming all-out war. Jackson will make good on his threats to Luke and his family. I know they're in danger now because of me.

Luke's arms wrap back around me and he holds me tightly. "I. Won't. Leave. You. Andi. Even if you *tell* me to go."

I reach over and pick up the receiver.

"Hello?"

"*You. Bitch.*"

Oh great, the evil foster mother.

Crazy Maybe

"Funny. That's the name we've given you," I respond, like a true smartass.

"You will pay for this. You don't know who you're fucking with, little girl," she hisses through the phone. Her voice is lowered to just above a whisper and that makes me wonder why she's not screaming like a banshee. Like she normally did.

A click later, the dead line tells me she hung up on me. I chuckle a little and hang up the receiver while I tell Luke about that abrupt conversation. He looks worried.

"She hasn't been involved until now. I wonder why not," Luke states thoughtfully.

"I'm sure she saw the interview," I say with a single shoulder shrug. "She couldn't *not* say anything after I told everyone she knew what was happening in her house but didn't care—that she actually *encouraged* it."

"Maybe," he says absently, but he's looking away from me. I know he's concerned about my safety.

The national network news broke into the local programming for a special story. Guess who it was about...

"A Georgia woman appeared on a local talk show this morning and claims that she saw Speaker Jackson Rhoades raping a young girl when she was a foster child in his home. These claims are currently unsubstantiated but with a recent amendment to Georgia law to remove the statute of limitations on felony child abuse, Speaker Rhoades could be facing long-term prison time, if convicted.

Again, these are unsubstantiated claims at this time. A Georgia official, speaking anonymously, tells us that these claims are being taken very seriously and will be investigated to the fullest extent. We'll wait to see if the Speaker will schedule a press conference to

Crazy Maybe

publically address these allegations. Stay tuned as we bring you live updates as they happen."

And the three-ring circus begins. My phone starts ringing and this time I check the caller ID before picking it up. Unknown caller is always sent to the answering machine. One news station after the other leaves messages asking for an exclusive interview. Everyone wants to get the scoop first. Some offer money, others offer promises of fame and fortune, while others are just downright rude in demanding I pick up the phone because they know I'm home.

That is just creepy.

"I'm going to take my shower now," I announce, as nonchalantly as possible, as I rise from the couch. He looks at me with his eyebrows raised, eyes wide open and his sexy, half-grin. I know that gesture means he wants an invitation, so I grab his hand and tug on it.

He hops off the couch, throws me over his shoulder and takes the stairs two at a time. "I thought you'd never ask, woman!"

The water is hot but my man is hotter. He undresses me, opens the shower door and slowly backs me under the water while he melts me with his kisses. He pushes me back against the wall then his hand reaches under my leg to pull it up. My other leg joins it and now both are wrapped around his waist. His fingers trace the folds between my legs, and his tongue mimics the movements along my lips, as he teases and tempts me.

Two of his long, thick fingers plunge deep inside me. "Why are you always so wet for me, baby?" The deep, bass timbre of his whisper reverberates through my body and my hips move involuntary, grinding on his fingers.

285

Crazy Maybe

"It's...what you...do...to me," I stammer out during the times I can actually breathe.

I feel the rumble through his chest when he groans in appreciation and desire. He removes his fingers and I feel his thickness rub against me, waiting for its turn. I lean my head back against the wall as his mouth takes my nipple, sucking until my nipple is hard, then he lightly rakes his teeth across it. The pleasure and pain mixture is such a turn on I can't hold in my approval.

"Oh God, Luke," I exclaim. Loudly.

"That's my girl," he says as he lowers my legs until my feet are on the shower floor. I'm so confused until he turns me around, wraps his arm around my waist and pushes me forward to bend me over. Have I mentioned how much I love it when he takes complete control and treats me like his rag doll? Oh yeah, I definitely do.

When my hands touch the floor, he thrusts into me from behind and the sensation of him inside me, stretching me wide open and hitting the top of my cervix makes me scream out his name. "Soak me, that's it, baby," he says as he continues his welcome assault on me. Our combined moans, groans and words of love drown out the sound of the water sloshing between us. Luke increases his tempo, his fingers dig into my hips to hold me in place, as he commands me, "Come for me now, Andi. I want it now."

My response is his name is screamed from the top of my lungs. Which, technically, is at my feet right now. But it's good. So good. I tighten my inner muscles and he moans my name when I feel his release into me, his warmth flooding me and his shaft pulsating inside me.

He melts me to my core.

Crazy Maybe

Luke and I walk down the stairs and the sound of someone suddenly pounding on the front door makes me jump.

LUKE

I really wish I could take Andi away from here for a while. A year or two should do it. But I know there's no way in hell she will walk away now. She never backs down from anything and I can't expect her to start now. Especially not now that she's shared her story and it's gone viral on the national news. She single-handedly made *Andi Morgan* and *Lindsay Blair* household names within the span of a one-hour television show.

While watching the interview with Andi this morning, everything she's been through kept running through my mind. But those thoughts were quickly replaced with what's to come in the next few days. I know it'll be bad—Rhoades will come after her in one way or another. I am waiting and watching for him. He's already shown up at the club at least once and there's no doubt he's stupid enough to do it again.

Andi insists on still competing in the karaoke competition even if it's only to sing a song that'll piss Rhoades off. She said she has the song all planned out and she can't wait to do it. She won't tell me what the song is though. She must think I'll try to talk her out of it and she'd be right. I don't think this guy needs to be antagonized any more than the interview's already

287

done. But I'll be beside her when he decides to make his move.

We're walking down the hall after our long shower together where I thoroughly washed every inch of her body more than once. Just as we leave the last stair, someone starts beating on the front door and Andi jumps. In one fluid movement, I grab her and put her behind me, shielding her from whoever has the balls to pound on our door like that.

"Stay here," I say as I walk to the door to look through the peephole. There's a man on the front porch and he looks angry.

Without opening the door, I add several octaves of bass to my normal speaking voice, "What the hell do you want?"

"I need to speak with Andi Morgan. Right now." Who the hell does this guy think he is?

"Get off our property. Now. I won't give you another warning," I say through the door.

I watch for several seconds and the guy doesn't budge. I jerk open the door and take two intimidating steps toward him with my fists balled up. I wasn't a street fighter for nothing. He senses I meant what I said about no further warnings because he takes off running toward a news van at the curb.

"Damn reporters," I say as I close and lock the door. "It's going to be a long day, baby. They are lined up down the street and they all want to talk to you."

"No more interviews! It was hard enough doing the one I did. We are banking a lot on at least some of his victims coming forward. I don't want to scare them off by creating a three-ring media circus everywhere I go," she takes a breath, narrows her eyes in thought and finishes with, "Except for tomorrow night when I'm singing."

Crazy Maybe

That gleam in her eyes makes me cringe.

She steps outside the front door and calls out to the waiting news crews, who had already started approaching when she stepped onto the porch.

"Everyone, please listen," she yells over the questions being yelled at her, "I will not answer any questions today. Come to The Beta Room tomorrow night and I will answer all your questions. *Except for* anyone I see parked on my street or following me today. I will have you banned from the club. Now leave."

Several walk briskly back to their van and leave while a few waited around in shock for a minute. She stops on the front porch and looks pointedly at the stragglers and they quickly leave. All I could do is smile at her—my girl has style.

"Very nice, my love," I say as I pull her to me, wrapping my arms around her waist as hers go around my neck. I love the feel of her body molded to mine.

She smiles and kisses me, "Thank you."

"Now that you got rid of them, what do you want to do today?"

"I need to go by the club later and practice my song onstage, but I'm *all yours* until then."

Nice try, but I'm not falling for that trick. "You're not going to the club alone, Andi," I reply dryly, "but I'll take you up on that offer to be all mine."

She gives me her pouty look for a second but finally relents. She knows I'm not bending on this. Besides the fact that I'm not leaving her alone with all these damn nutcases everywhere, she doesn't want me to know what song she's singing or what's in her show. That makes me want to go with her even more.

"While I have you," I start tentatively because I'm not sure how to finish this sentence.

289

"Yes?" She draws out as she answers, prompting me to continue.

"We should talk about our wedding date. Have you thought about what kind of wedding you want? And where? And when you'd want it?"

Don't all girls plan this shit in their head from the time they're little? Just tell me where to show up and what to wear. I'll be there. Open bar? Even better.

"Oh. Ummm. I'm not sure, Luke," the hesitancy in her voice is palpable. There's a little bit of nervousness in it, too.

"Have you changed your mind, Andi?" I ask in all seriousness.

"No! No, of course not. I just...I thought we'd have a long engagement and figure that out over time. I'm just not prepared to answer all that right now." She's looking around the room, looking for something to put her focus into and buy herself some time.

"Okay, baby. If that's what you want, I will wait for you however long you need." I mean it from the bottom of my heart. I lost her once and I'll be damned if I'll go through that shit again. She now looks visibly relieved and I can't believe how much that bothers me. I'm legitimately concerned that she doesn't really want to be my wife.

She wraps her arms around me to reassure me. "Stop thinking that, Luke."

"What?" I ask innocently, even though we both know exactly what.

"I love you and I do want to marry you. I just want this behind us before we start planning our life together. I don't want it in the way at all. Okay?"

"Okay, baby."

I fucking love her.

CHAPTER THIRTY-ONE

ANDI

The promo commercials leading up to my interview airing created a lot of media buzz for me and for MaxMorgan Music, some good and some bad, but all of this has really made me think about our life together. I don't want to start it with this black cloud hanging over us–always waiting to rain on our parade. I just want a clean slate when I walk down the aisle and become Mrs. Lucas Woods.

Even though Travis Malone is supporting me, *the bastard* and *the bitch* upped their smear campaign immediately after the first promo aired in their preemptive strike and they have plenty of people to help them. The attacks on my character increased yesterday immediately after the Lindsay Blair show ended. The big national stations began airing several "*biographical exposé*" segments-also known as complete loads of bullshit-that were aired by journalists no one has ever heard of before.

In one form or another, every one of the exposés portrayed me as a complete liar who was constantly seeking attention and love because my parents died at a young age. They also portrayed my foster families as the most wonderful people who just tried to give me a loving home, but in return, I lashed out at them in anger and didn't appreciate their generosity. Most of the stories were just entertaining fiction but some were blatant attempts to sway public opinion against me.

Crazy Maybe

I don't normally care what others think of me, but this particular fight isn't for me.   One story was particularly upsetting because it included a brief interview with the family who gave me all these scars. They talked about how impossible it was to control me and how I lied about everything.   The doctor who treated me also briefly appeared to verify their story. He looked very unhappy with being forced to blatantly lie and say that I lied about my claim of being physically abused.

If I were a vengeful person, I would look into the legal aspects of that doctor breaching the confidentiality laws by talking about my medical information. IF.

Luke and I have talked a lot about what has been reported over the last few days. With each report that came out, I've corrected the "mistakes" the reporter made in the storyline. Local journalists got in on the action and started airing stories about Pop, Shane and, of course, Luke. By the time this is over, it'll take *Lisa Renee Jones* to figure out all the twists and turns.

We also end up having another conversation about who should protect whom and I gave in to him again when he kissed me. With Luke settled on why I want to wait to set a date and with him being the protector, we relax on the couch to watch a little television and just spend some time together doing nothing.

Imagine my surprise, as Luke is flipping through the channels, he stops when he sees a familiar face being interviewed about me. Funny thing is, the story on the national network news isn't slander against me this time. Lindsay Blair is being interviewed on CNN right now. She is explaining why she pursued the interview with me.

"To be honest, at first I wanted to skewer Andi Morgan. I saw a spoiled little rich girl who didn't already have enough fame and attention. I saw a young woman who just inherited her father's kingdom and reportedly sold it for billions of dollars, but that wasn't enough for her. I wanted to be the one to expose her for what she really is.

"What I wasn't prepared for was the complete life story of Andi Morgan. What I didn't consider was how many years she suffered-first at losing her family at such a young age, being turned away by a blood relative, and finally the long line of abuse at the hands of her foster families. But what blew me away was how selflessly she devotes her life to helping others-both the younger girls who lived with the Rhoades and the youth center she funds here in Atlanta.

"She has never publicly announced that and I hope I'm not betraying her confidence by revealing it, but her involvement with the youth center is being unjustly scrutinized. The kids are the ones who will suffer if the parents keep them away from Andi," Lindsay quickly wipes away a tear and takes a breath to give the anchor a chance to ask another question.

"Would you allow her around your children, Lindsay?"

"Absolutely. I would consider it an honor if she spent time with my children."

"Lindsay, as I understand it, the local station is changing their programming lineup for you to do a *live* show today. Tell us a little about that," the anchor prompts.

Lindsay's smile is knowing and confident, "Elle, that is correct. I am doing a live show this evening and I appreciate being able to comment on it. Immediately after my interview with Andi Morgan was taped, I tracked down other children who have been in the Rhoades' foster care over the years. Several of those who are now young adults have agreed to appear on my show to give their account of life in Speaker Rhoades' care. It will air at four o'clock Eastern today."

"Will they corroborate Ms. Morgan's version?" the anchor challenges. She's trying to get the scoop but Lindsay is too shrewd to answer that outright.

"Their revelations will definitely be something you'll want to hear. I will also have a couple of surprise guests," Lindsay answers.

"We will all be waiting with baited breath. Thank you for joining us today, Lindsay," the anchor responds before starting the next story.

I am completely amazed and surprised at this turn of events. "I can't believe she found some of their former foster kids. I wonder who they are."

Part of me worries that it is Maria and that she resents me for not protecting her when she needed me the most. I wonder if she hates me for leaving her when they sent me off to the psychiatric hospital. I'm afraid I'm the last person she would ever want see- besides the Rhoades he-and-she-devils, anyway.

Luke rubs up and down my arm as he continues to stare at the TV without speaking. I've noticed he does this when he's contemplating the best way to protect me. He doesn't think I've noticed this. I love the little acts of love he shows me without saying it. I secretly love how protective he is of me and how he wants to be the king of the jungle. I love my complex, alpha-male/street brawler/counselor/fiancé.

"Luke, you ok?" I ask, smiling and a hint of teasing in my voice.

"Uh, yeah. Lindsay's been busy, hasn't she? You didn't know about any of this?" The concern in his voice is blatant. But the suspicion that I was actually a part of it is a little more disguised.

"No. I didn't know anything about it, Luke." I'm not disguising the pissed-off glint in my tone.

He squeezes my hand in response-his way of apologizing for his minor offenses. He's well aware that he was about to cross the line. No reason for me to bring it up though.

"Are you nervous about seeing it?" Luke asks me, genuinely concerned.

"A little. I really don't know what to expect. But I can't help but think that since Lindsay has been so supportive of me, she's found someone who will speak out against him. That's what I'm hoping for anyway."

The next thing he says completely shocks me but it also makes sense.

"This may not be the best time to talk about this but there's something I want you to know."

"Okay," I respond in a drawn out manner.

"I submitted an application to have my psychologist license reinstated. I think I want to go back into practice, but with the kids at the youth center instead of adults."

My jaw droops and I don't know if I want to scream or hug him, but either way I'm so shocked by his admission that I can't make a sound. I'm beyond stunned at this.

"What about boxing?" I ask, waiting to gauge his reaction. I remember how serious he was about it when he walked in the gym. Watching him in his street match that night was intense. I never told him this, but he really was awesome to see in the ring.

"I love it. I really do. I'm not sure about making it my sole career choice though. I'm not Shane when it comes to the ring."

"Don't doubt yourself, Luke. You're really impressive in the ring. I'm not trying to persuade you one way or another. I will support you in whatever you decide. But you should know that you have real potential."

He inclines his head slightly toward me, his eyes are locked intently on mine and he considers me for a moment before answering. "Thank you, Andi. I'll keep that in mind. Speaking of, it's time for me to get to the gym anyway."

LUKE

Showered, shaved and dressed, I head out to the gym but I can't get that damn interview with Lindsay Blair off my mind. She dug up old skeletons in Rhoades' closet-skeletons he's gone to great lengths to hide. There will be hell for Andi to pay for that, I'm sure. I just don't know yet what he will do or how desperate he will be for Andi to recant her story and take up for him. Does he even think he can convince her of that now?

Mack and Shane are at the gym when I arrive. They've probably already been at it for hours. I planned on getting here much earlier but Andi and I slept late this morning. Then we were busy and I enjoyed that time with her way too much to regret not leaving sooner. Shane's on the punching bag and Will is hitting the weights hard.

"How's Andi taking all this?" Mack asks me.

"Pretty well, actually. She has no idea who Lindsay Blair has found. I'm more concerned about this shit than she is," I answer dryly.

Mack nods his head knowingly, "She always was headstrong. Don't know where she gets it from."

I laugh heartily. "I know exactly where she gets it from."

He beams with fatherly pride. He may not be her biological father, but he is her father nonetheless.

"Y'all set a date yet?" It's a question but he doesn't intend it to be taken that way. It's a command to make the commitment to our marriage and I know it. I know him well enough to understand that.

"Not yet. Andi wants to wait until this is all settled before picking a date."

Mack only grunts in response, but it's not an approving tone. I know how he feels.

I finish my workout and get back home in time to quickly shower off and watch the live feed of *The Lindsay Blair Show* with Andi. I can tell she's a nervous wreck. She keeps wringing her hands and biting her bottom lip. She's being so rough on it that I can't resist leaning in and kissing it softly.

She smiles her sweet smile, "What was that for?"

"I felt sorry for your bottom lip. You're about to bite it off. Thought it needed some tenderness."

She busts out laughing at this, leans in to rest her head on my chest, and wraps her arm around me. "Thank you for that. You can always make me smile and laugh just when I need it the most."

I know exactly what she means. My arm is around her and she adjusts her position to draw her feet up on the couch and put her head in the crook of my shoulder. This is when I'm the most content–just sharing the normal, everyday moments with her. Much like my parents have been my whole life. Nothing like Andi has any real memories of anyone in her life doing.

Crazy Maybe

I'm about to comment on this when the show comes on and Andi sits up, her back straight as a rod and every muscle in her body tensed. This is going to be hard on her and I'm not sure what type of support to give her. So I try to watch her and the television both as much as I can.

"Good afternoon and welcome to *The Lindsay Blair Show*. We're doing a special, live show today after the heart-wrenching interview I did with Andi Morgan. As you know, Andi is the sole beneficiary of the late music mogul, Max Morgan. After Mr. and Mrs. Morgan were killed in a car wreck, Andi was eventually placed in foster care where she claims her former foster father, Speaker Jackson Rhoades, molested and raped young girls in his house. AND, she also claims that Mrs. Rhoades was aware and even *encouraged* Speaker Rhoades to engage in these atrocious acts.

"Our producers received an overwhelming response from the studio audience to validate Ms. Morgan's claims immediately after the show was taped. If Speaker Rhoades is guilty, the audience demands he be held accountable for his actions. If he's innocent, they want Ms. Morgan to be held accountable for *her* actions.

"I immediately set out in search for and found several young ladies who were all former foster children in the Rhoades' household. They have agreed to appear here with me today to share their stories, memories, and take questions from the audience. This show is being aired live for a couple of reasons. One, because this type of issue needs to be brought to light, and two, because neither party will have any claim that this show has been edited to sensationalize it."

So far, so good. Andi's holding up, even though she's now biting on her nails and occasionally her lip. I

298

know she's waiting to see whom the girls are but Lindsay has purposely kept them off camera during her introduction. All the attention is on her right now.

"My first guest is Maria Gonzalez," Andi's sharp intake of breath quickly draws my eyes to her and I notice she doesn't exhale.

Lindsay continues, "Maria is nineteen and student at the University of Georgia in Athens, majoring in veterinary medicine. Ms. Gonzalez was a foster child in the Rhoades' home at the same time Andi Morgan was there. Thank you for coming today, Ms. Gonzalez."

"Is that her, Andi?" I ask softly. Andi's nod is barely perceptible.

"Thank you for inviting me, Lindsay," Maria replies. She's obviously uncomfortable onstage but there's an also air of determination about her.

"Maria, do you remember Andi Morgan?"

"Yes, I remember everything about her," Maria answers with a warm smile. I hear Andi sniffle and look over at her to see her face covered in tears.

"Maria, I'm going to ask the hard questions because that's what the public demands to know. Are the allegations made by Andi Morgan against Speaker Rhoades and his wife true?"

The cameraman zooms in on Maria, capturing her facial expressions, body language, and her overall demeanor very well. The analysts will have a field day with this shot and the cameraman knows it.

"Yes. What Andi said is true. I am the girl he was raping when she stabbed him. She had been taking care of me because I'd been so sick. She came back in to check on me that night and when she saw what he was doing to me, she stabbed him to help me," Maria's voice quivers and tears escape her eyes, but she doesn't back down and she doesn't look away from Lindsay.

The audience gasps loudly. Lindsay smiles at her and holds her hand in solidarity. Letting her know she's not alone and that she understands how hard it must be to declare this on live television to a cynical nation.

"Maria, there's something I want you to see. Something that wasn't aired on the original interview with Ms. Morgan. I don't think she'll mind you seeing it now, though." Maria nods and Lindsay instructs her producers to queue the piece.

The footage is of Andi, telling Lindsay that she's afraid Maria hates her—for not protecting her, for not staying in the room with her that night, and for leaving her alone when she was put in the psychiatric hospital. Andi is crying on the clip, but on the live show, Maria is sobbing. She can barely catch her breath for a second and Andi moves to the floor and puts her hand on the television screen, as if she's giving Maria her strength to continue.

It must work because Maria catches her breath and quickly composes herself. Maria looks directly into the camera, and from Andi's position in the floor, they are now eye to eye as Maria says, "I have never, NEVER, hated Andi. I love her and I miss her to this day. I've never blamed her for anything. She was as much a victim of the Rhoades' as I was."

Andi leaves her hand on Maria's face as her head drops and tears flow freely from her eyes to the floor. I move behind her, wrap my arms around her and hold her as she sobs. I whisper words of comfort and love, restating what Maria said and telling her what an impact she made on that young girl's life.

One by one, Lindsay brings out five more young ladies who were all in the Rhoades' care and every one of them corroborate Andi's story. Everyone young woman gives an account, with specific details only someone in their position could know, and validates what Andi has shared. Her face is filled with relief that they're willing to speak out and amazement at the strength these young ladies show in describing their molestation.

As Lindsay makes her closing remarks, she said there is more evidence against Speaker Rhoades. There are more girls who were unwilling to be interviewed on television but who will testify against him. She said the evidence she has uncovered is irrefutable and she will gladly turn a copy of it over to the FBI.

The show ends and five minutes later, Andi's cell phone rings but the caller ID says "unknown." She gives me a tentative look and takes the call anyway. I can tell immediately that the caller is Maria. For the next thirty minutes, Andi and Maria talk nonstop to catch up on each other's lives. Andi ends the call after giving Maria our address and telling her she wants Maria to come see her and meet me.

"Lindsay gave her my number. I can't wait to see her again and for you to meet her!" Andi is so excited she's nearly skipping through the house toward me. She jumps into my arms, kisses me and tells me she loves me. "Now I have to go get ready for my song tonight!"

She races off toward the bedroom before I can say anything. She hasn't told me what the song is or what she's doing that's she's so excited about. I cringe every time I think of it because I know it'll make her more of a target. All I can do is go with her and never leave her side.

"Andi," I call after her and she surprisingly stops. "You know it's hard to prosecute a sitting congressman, much less the Speaker of the House. Not because he's above the law but because of the ties he has. He plays golf with the President of the United States for crying out loud. Nothing about this will be easy."

"You're right. But more people than not *know* now. They know he did it. They know what kind of man he is now. He won't be able to hurt little girls anymore. That's what matters."

CHAPTER THIRTY-TWO

LUKE

Holy hell. What the hell is she thinking? There's no way in hell I'm letting her do this!

"Andi. Not just no. But *hell* no. *No-fucking-way* no. *I-will-kidnap-you-again* no." And to my intimidating bass voice and unyielding fighting stance, my sexy little vixen just smiles sweetly and walks right around me.

"Mitch! I need the main spotlight moved to center stage. It's a little too far to the left for me," she calls out to the owner of The Beta Room, who is also playing the lighting manager tonight since his original one is out sick.

"How about that, Andi?"

"That's great! Thank you!" She's moving about the stage, getting things set up exactly where she needs them to pull off her song. And they're both completely ignoring me even though I'm following on her heels and breathing heavy down her neck. But not in a good way.

"Andi!"

"Yes, dear?" She says this absently, but she knows damn well what she's doing. She's making me crazy.

"You're killing me, Andi. You know this song will enrage him. You know you're just calling him out for a fight!"

"That's the plan," she responds in her sing-song voice.

"And just how, exactly, do you plan on handling him?"

Crazy Maybe

She has the nerve to turn to me, smile even wider, and say, "That's what I have *you* for, Luke. So I don't have to worry about man-handling him."

So, should I be flattered or offended by that comment?

Is she being for real or is she being sarcastic and playing on my need to protect her?

How in the hell did I get so whipped by this beautiful creature?

Shane is sitting at our usual table in the empty club and he's clearly amused by this whole exchange. When I turn to glare at him for not helping me convince her to change her song, he quickly hides his smile with his hand but his eyes are still all crinkled up. And his fucking shoulders are jumping from trying to hold in his laughter.

"Just let her go, man. You're wasting your breath. She's not going to change her mind. Will's coming in a little while so the three of us will watch her all night. He won't get to her. There's no fucking way he can get past us."

Shane's trying to make me feel better but I just don't have a good feeling about it. I didn't have a good feeling when she first had that gleam in her eye after choosing the song, but refusing to tell me what it was. Now that she's been forced to reveal it to me, it's even worse.

"Shane, man, I don't like it. At all. The only way I found out what the song even was ahead of time is because I demanded to come with her today. She tried to send me to the damn grocery store claiming to need *tampons!* She put on this big elaborate show about not being able to leave the bathroom. She was going to sneak away and just leave me a note that it was a false alarm. I went back in the house to ask her what the

304

name on the box was again and caught her in the kitchen writing the damn note."

Shane doubles over in laughter. I'm sure he's picturing Andi, locked in the bathroom and screaming at me through the door how she needs tampons *right now*. But she can't come out to go get them herself and I have to help her. She *needs* my help. Sneaky little sexy vixen. Shane regains his composure to speak but that shit-eating grin never leaves his face.

"Good thing your memory's shit, huh?"

"Yeah. Funny, man," I say as I take a swig of my longneck bottle. I'll need a couple more of these tonight by the time Andi finishes her song.

Soon the club is packed to the maximum occupancy and Mitch is turning people away at the door. There are so many reporters here tonight but Mitch wouldn't let them bring their huge cameras in with them. So a lot of people are using their camera phones to record pieces for their segments. This should make for an interesting news night.

The DJ just announced that Andi's up next and my senses are on full alert. I scan the room, trying to take everyone in but there are just *so many people* crowded in here to see Andi tonight. The girls are in the back with her, guarding her dressing room door and watching for strangers, while she gets dressed for her show. The lights dim and the DJ announces Andi.

The song she picked for tonight, and especially for Jackson Rhoades, is *Gunpowder and Lead*, by Miranda Lambert. She's singing a song about a woman who plans to shoot the man who's been abusing her. Great. Just fucking great. This will go over well.

She walks out on the stage with the spotlight directly on her and she's wearing a damn straight jacket. Her arms are wrapped around herself in a giant hug and she looks uncomfortable in the white jacket.

She starts singing, the beginning of the song is pretty slow and her eyes are darting around like she's...well, crazy. Her eyes suddenly stop and linger in one area a little too long to be a coincidence. I know she's spotted him in the crowd from the subtle change in her voice and the look in her eyes. Both changes happened when she hit the part about them both going to hell. Yeah, she found him in the crowd all right.

When the tempo picks up on the next line, she bursts out of the jacket and throws it to the opposite side of the stage. As most of the crowd watches the straight jacket fly through the air and land on the stage directly across from her, she moves in the opposite direction and picks up a toy shotgun. She cocks it, walks to the edge of the stage and aims it directly at, none other than, *the bastard.*

While she's doing that, she's singing and telling him that she's ready to fight and he, in fact, has never seen her act crazy before. But she's showing him that he's about to catch a glimpse of that very thing and he should be shaking in his damn boots at the thought of it.

A video of Andi starts playing on the flat screens around the club. It's a montage of all the headlines from the smear campaign that was waged against her, including the pictures of her in the psychiatric hospital. One story after the other is displayed all around the club, every single one a complete lie about Andi. Slamming her for stabbing her poor foster father, berating her for being admitted to the psychiatric ward, and several tabloid stories about how she's really an alien and has a love child with Elvis.

She continues to dance around the stage, singing and pointing the toy shotgun at Rhoades damn near every time the word *'shotgun'* comes up in the song. The crowd is going wild and cheering her on, unaware that Jackson is here, in disguise again.

She changes the lyrics when she gets to the bridge of the song.

He locked me up, but now I'm stronger
He won't hurt them any longer!

The five girls from the live Lindsay Blair show walk up behind Andi onstage, all carrying toy shotguns and all dancing and singing as her backup. The crowd goes crazy with screaming, whistling and cheering. The ladies are all looking at *the bastard* but he doesn't move. He's probably trying to draw as little attention to himself as possible. To others, it may appear to be part of the show. I know it's not.

As the song ends, the video ends with a clip of Lindsay Blair encouraging anyone who's being abused to tell someone. She advises them to tell anyone, just get help and get out of that situation. After Lindsay's clip ends, Andi yells into the microphone, *"Save yourself and help someone else!"*

The six ladies all exit the stage and I watch the bastard slowly lower his glass to the table and stand up. He's looking at the backstage door so I slowly get up and make my way closer to the door. I want to be ready if he heads toward Andi or any of those young ladies who were so brave to come forward.

Rhoades sees me and he stops to stare at me for a minute or two. It's an obvious showdown but there's no way in hell he will beat me. He's fucking lucky to still have his head attached to his body right now. The only reason I haven't jerked him up is because I can't protect Andi from a federal penitentiary. I cross my arms over my chest and grind my teeth from the firm set of my jaw.

Crazy Maybe

He must sense I'm teetering on a thin edge of sanity myself because he averts his eyes from mine and quickly makes his way to the exit. I know the war is far from over but I can't help but feel good at the small battles we've won here tonight. The thought of what those young ladies went through at his hands makes me want to follow him out to the parking lot and drag him behind the building. Someone needs to show him what it's like to feel helpless.

Andi and the others all come filing out from the backstage area. She's walking on cloud nine but I see her eyes dart around the room, looking for him and waiting for him to appear out of nowhere.

"He left," I lean in to tell her just before I kiss her cheek. "You were great, as usual, baby."

She smiles and puts her arms around my waist to hug me. "Thank you. And thank you for waiting here for me," gesturing toward the backstage door.

"Well, he was watching it pretty intently. I wasn't about to let him get through it."

She nods in understanding and looks at the other girls. After a round of introductions, we're all back at our usual table with Shane, Will, Brandon, Christina, Tania and Katie. I look around the table and realize how blessed I am to have such a great group of friends and family.

I take Andi's hand in mine and raise it to my mouth, kissing each of her knuckles softly. She was in midsentence conversation with someone when she looks at me, confusion etched in her beautiful face.

"What was that for?"

"Because I love you, Andi Morgan," I answer.

She doesn't smile in response this time. In fact, she has a very serious look. She suddenly leans toward me and covers my mouth with hers. Her free hand wraps around my neck and pulls me closer to her. Since she started it, I'm more than happy to oblige her, so I wrap my arms around her and hoist her over the chair and into my lap. Once she's reseated, I put my hands on either side of her face as I kiss her back.

"Get a room, already!" Someone from our table shouts. I'm pretty sure it was Brandon. He's still a little jealous that Andi's mine. Andi breaks our kiss and laughs while throwing a wadded up napkin in his general direction.

"Dance with me," I say as I incline my head toward the dance floor. She nods and we push through the throngs of people to the dance floor. It doesn't matter if it's a slow song or a fast song. All I want is to hold Andi in my arms—we move to the beat of our own music.

ANDI

What a great night! Tonight went far better than I thought it could. I have the hottest man on the planet and we're getting married...um, eventually. I've been reacquainted with Maria and she doesn't hate me. Plus, I've met several more courageous young women that I'm proud to call my friends.

Luke is driving us home now and even this feels good. It feels right—holding his hand, seeing him raise my hand to his mouth and gently kiss it before he secures it back in his hand, and knowing that we're going to our *home*. Home is where the heart is, they say. My heart belongs to this wonderful, sexy manly-man beside me. I don't care where we live as long as I'm with him.

Crazy Maybe

Finally home, Luke goes inside first, as always, to make sure it's safe for me to enter. It really is the small things that end up mattering the most. It is the small things that make up everyday life together. Even just the fact that he cares about my safety enough to enter the dark house first, time after time, melts me every time. Everything he does for me is out of love and I can't imagine my life without him now.

I follow him toward the kitchen and we purposely keep the lights low. It's finally just the two of us again and I'm looking forward to it. Luke opens a bottle of wine and pours two glasses. He hands my glass to me and holds his up in a toast.

"To my beautiful fiancé. The man I am today is because of you. Your strength, your gentleness. Your love, your fight. Your thoughtfulness, your boldness. I love every quality you possess, Andi, and you inspire me to be a better person. Every day."

We clink glasses as I wipe a tear away. Having someone to call my own still doesn't feel real sometimes. I've been alone for so long. He starts to take a sip from his glass but I halt him with my hand on his arm.

"Wait," I say. He lowers his hand and keeps his eyes trained on mine. "I have something to say first."

"Okay," I hear the trepidation in his voice.

"To my handsome and sexy fiancé," and his face lights up in that gorgeous, panty-dropping smile that still gives me goose bumps. "You've given me more than I could've ever hoped for. You've been everything I've always needed and never had. You are my rock, my encouragement, and my protector. You've fulfilled dreams that I never let myself even consider. I love you, Luke, more than life itself."

We clink glasses again, drink to each other, and suddenly the wine glasses are crashing to the ground and we are in each other's arms. I'm totally lost in this man's arms, his masculine scent, the hard muscles in his body, until....

"Well, now. Isn't that just. So. Fucking. Sweet," the male voice from the shadows mocks.

Luke and I jerk apart and Luke automatically pushes me behind him, shielding me with his body and readying his for all-out war. I've seen him in this fighting stance before and it's a balls-to-the-wall, take-no-prisoners stance. It would be a huge turn on if Jackson Rhoades weren't hiding in my kitchen right now.

Jackson steps out into the light and lightly chuckles.

"You know, I never knew you had it in you, Andi. To be so passionate. If I'd known, I'd –"

"Rhoades, if you value your fucking tongue, you won't finish that sentence. Or so help me God, you'll choke on it when I rip it out of your mouth and shove it down your fucking throat," Luke growls out as he takes a step closer to Jackson.

Jackson may be an older man but he has been careful with his health and fitness. He obviously still works out and looks much younger than he is. He is still no match for Luke in a fair fight, but I don't expect Jackson to fight fairly. I know Luke's time as a street fighter will help him. I just don't want to take any chances with his life.

"What do you want Jack-," my question is suddenly cut off when Jackson lunges at Luke.

He throws a right jab and connects with Luke's nose. Blood sprays out from the impact then runs down his face. If Jackson thought that would knock Luke off-kilter, he is sadly mistaken. It only serves to make Luke madder and more dangerous. Luke counterpunches with a right hook to Jackson's jaw followed by a left uppercut to the chin. Jackson loses his balance and goes down with Luke quickly jumping on top of him to pound him into the ground.

Jackson gains some leverage underneath Luke and they roll around in the floor, each getting close body shots in on the other. Jackson is the first back to his feet in an attempt to flee but Luke isn't finished with him. He hits Jackson with a right cross, his power punch, on Jackson's left cheek, which spins him around. Just as Luke is about to hit him with a straight right and end the brawl, the sound of a revolver hammer clicking draws our attention.

The *wicked foster-bitch* steps into the room and has her .22 magnum aimed at Luke. "That's enough, Woods. Step away from him." Then she looks at me.

Luke steps away from Jackson and steps over in front of me, using his massive body to shield me from the gun aimed in our direction. His left hand slowly reaches back to secure me behind him while he holds his right palm facing Delia Rhoades.

"I'm really sorry to break up this little party," Delia says mockingly, "but The Speaker and I have previous engagements we simply must attend to. Darling, if you're ready to go?" She speaks as if she's leaving early from the country club instead of the stark reality that she's threatening to shoot us both in my own home.

Jackson straightens his clothes and starts to back away when he says, "I don't think I'm done with Andi yet, darling. It'll be good for Luke to watch."

Delia thought it over for a second before conceding, "You always did have a crush on her. Just this once, then."

I stand gawking at her, completely speechless at her flippant attitude toward what her husband just said.

And her response! Before I can even form an intelligent response, Jackson is striding toward me with an evil gleam in his eye and a wicked smile on his face. I intuitively take a couple of steps backwards.

"Ah, Andi. I've waited for you for a long time now," he drew out each word and each step, increasing the anticipation and anxiety as he approaches me.

"Over my dead body, Rhoades," Luke bellows.

"That can easily be arranged," Delia's reply sounds completely uninterested. She levels her gun at Luke's chest and puts her finger on the trigger.

I knew instantly from the satisfied look in her eye and the triumphant smirk on her face, she is going to kill Luke. My heart is about to pound completely out of my chest—my chest that is in a vice and it's as if the life is being squeezed out of me.

I can't watch him be shot. I can't watch him die!

"Not yet, dear. I want him to see what I do to Andi. I want him to hear her scream over and over when I finally take her." He looks pointedly at me, locking eyes and slightly lowering his head so that he's looking at me through his eyebrows. "You sang to me tonight about '*a real man*.' I'll be more than glad to show you what a real man is."

Luke steps forward and Delia threatens him again, "I don't have to *kill* you yet, Luke. I can merely *wound* you and still let Jackson have his fun. Move again and I'll show you exactly what I mean. Don't try me."

I see the rise and fall of his shoulders, signaling that he's taken a deep breath. Luke doesn't move as Jackson takes another step toward him and intentionally bumps his shoulder as he walks by. It's an act of utter disrespect and it's killing me that Luke has to take it. I know he's trying to figure out a way to fight back without getting shot and leaving me alone with these two lunatics.

Jackson's gaze is intent on me and it's as if there's no one else in the room. He's licking his lips and rakes his eyes from my head to my feet, undressing me as he goes. It's sickening and I would like nothing better than to snatch his eyes out of his head. With his next step, a shot rings out followed by a blood-curdling scream. After a second, I realize I am the one screaming and running toward Luke.

There's blood on his shirt and he's lying on the floor. I drop to his side and start searching for the entrance wound. He grabs my hands as he sits up and I finally hear him speaking to me, "Andi! Andi—stop, baby! I'm okay—it's not my blood. Rhoades knocked me down when he fell into me."

What?

I look up just as Jackson and Delia are leaving through the back door. Jackson is leaning on Delia and blood is gushing out of his arm with every beat of his heart. I cut my eyes back at Luke, still confused, and he's looking at something over my shoulder. He lowers his voice to an easy, soothing tone as he says, "You're okay now. He's gone. You can put the gun down."

What the hell is happening?

I snap my head in the direction Luke's looking and see a young girl, maybe sixteen years old, standing in the doorway. She's still holding the gun and her finger is still on the trigger. Her eyes are wide, her skin is ashen, and she's shaking uncontrollably. The adrenaline dump she just experienced is taking a toll on her body. The fact that she just shot someone is weighing heavily upon her now.

Wait a second.

"Kelly?" I say as I rise from the floor–very, very slowly. "Kelly, sweetheart, is that you?"

She finally moves her eyes and looks at me. At first, it's as if she's looking through me. I'm not sure she's really here with us until her eyes start to focus again.

"Kelly?"

She chokes out, "Andi," before sobbing and her knees fold under her.

I rush to her side and catch her in my arms as we both crumble to the floor. She drops the gun beside us, buries her face in my chest, and clings to me as tightly as she can. I'm in an extremely uncomfortable position, but I don't dare move. I lightly stroke her hair and give her calm, soothing words.

"You know her?" Luke asks.

I nod, "This is Kelly. She was my little sister when I was in the *house of horrors*. She was only about six when they sent me off. She has to be about sixteen now." I'm still holding her, much like I used to when she was younger, and gently rocking her back and forth.

"Andi, he was going to hurt you," Kelly whispers into my neck. "I had to stop him."

"Everything's going to be okay now, sweetheart," I whisper back.

Luke moves a little closer and Kelly jumps, drawing into me as if she's scared to death of him.

"Sweetheart, this is Luke. He's my fiancé and he would never, ever hurt you. You can trust him. No one will ever hurt you again," I vow to her.

"It's okay, Kelly. I will keep my distance if you want. I just want to talk to you. Is that all right?" Luke gently coaxes her.

Kelly looks at me, I nod to let her know that it's okay and she nods.

"Thank you, Kelly. Can you tell us about tonight?" Luke asks. I keep rocking her and gently rubbing her hair.

"He said he was going to hurt Andi. Delia said she would kill her. Jackson wanted to have his way with her. I had to stop him. Had to stop her," Kelly's rambling a little but I get the gist of what she's trying to tell us.

"Kelly, we need to call the police and report all this. But Luke and I will protect you. I won't leave you. Do you understand?" I'm trying to be as reassuring as possible, but I'm highly cognizant of the fact that the door is unlocked and they could come back at any time. Jackson was injured but they're both still alive. I don't want to freak Kelly out by pointing this out to her though.

She nods in understanding. She is completely trusting me to take care of her just like when she was little and first came to the Rhoades' house. Luke steps away to call the police. I vaguely hear him ask them to come without sirens. I'm sure he's thinking of how it would impact Kelly in her current state.

I am trying to come up with a strategy for taking care of Kelly when Luke walks back toward us. She doesn't jump this time but she still keeps a wary eye on him. He squats down so he's not lording over us. "The police are on their way. We have to answer some questions about what happened tonight. We won't leave you, Kelly."

"That's right, baby. We're right here." She nods and I notice her stronghold on me has lessened a little. "You saved us, didn't you?" This earns me a tiny smile. I'll take it, though.

Luke looks at me, "They're sending a female detective in to talk to us." Relief floods through me. I

316

didn't even think of that but I can always count on Luke to take care of me.

Hours later, we've answered Detective Burns' questions over and over again. She asked the same question at different times and in several different ways. I know she's testing our story for inconsistencies and she's finally satisfied that she's gotten the full story out of us. She puts out an APB for Jackson and Delia Rhoades, knowing he will more than likely visit a hospital or clinic somewhere between Atlanta and DC. Once he goes in for treatment, they'll get him.

Since Kelly is a minor and the news of the abuse that happened in that house is national news, Detective Burns didn't take Kelly to the juvenile hall or call the Department of Family and Children Services. Her reasoning was there is no body and no definite proof, yet, that Kelly actually shot him.

She discharged a firearm but until she has a bullet in hand that matches the ballistics from the gun Kelly had, there is no crime. Also, if there was a bullet wound, Delia could have just as easily been the shooter. Detective Burns also stationed a couple of units outside my house and they will make frequent rounds to check the entire perimeter of the house.

I really like Detective Burns.

I convince Kelly to stay with Luke and me for the night, or what's left of it now, and I get her settled into the bed after she had a long, hot shower. By the time I tucked her in, she seemed much calmer than before. She hugged me tightly but it was more of a thankful, reunion hug rather than the end-of-my-life squeeze she gave me earlier. I kissed her forehead and told her to sleep soundly because she's safe now. She was sound asleep within a minute of closing her eyes.

Luke and I sat up until sunrise, talking over all the events of the night and what will happen next. It's concerning that they still haven't found Jackson and Delia. He probably used a private physician to treat his wounds so he wouldn't be reported to the authorities. We can't live the rest of our lives looking over our shoulders. I want this to be over. It's really all so...anti-climactic.

CHAPTER THIRTY-THREE

LUKE

"Luke, Andi, come out back!" My dad yells from the backyard. We make our way through the kitchen and head out the back door to Mom's backyard haven. Everyone is gathered around the fire pit, roasting marshmallows and hot dogs. Mom and Kelly just brought out more food.

As soon as Kelly puts the food on the table, she bounds over to Andi and throws her arms around her neck. Andi laughs and grabs her up. Kelly is very little for a sixteen-year-old and sometimes we all treat her like she's much younger. Sometimes it makes her mad, but usually she eats it up, like she's doing now when Andi is fawning over her.

It's really a great sight. Kelly came to live with my parents soon after she showed up at our house that night. Mom and Dad were thrilled to take her in and she still gets to be Andi's sister. She doesn't spend time alone with Dad yet, but she does talk to him and includes him in things, so I know she's trying. They're preparing to officially adopt her and make her a real Woods.

It's been two weeks since that awful night. The night I thought I would have to watch and listen to Andi being raped by that madman. They planned to torture her and kill her in front of me and then kill me. Kelly overheard all of their sick, sadistic plans of what they would do to Andi. How they would torture her and beg for them to kill her long before they finished with her.

Kelly remembered Andi and how she always took care of the younger kids in the Rhoades' house.

She said she couldn't let anything bad happen to Andi, so she took one of Jackson's guns and followed him tonight. She knew he'd come after Andi at the club, so she waited and followed him when he left the club before we did. She was hiding inside the house when we got home. Kelly said she recognized the look he had when he was moving toward Andi. He was going to hurt her badly before finally killing her, so she shot him. Her only regret is that she didn't kill him–not that we know of, anyway.

I've been asking Andi every day when she's going to marry me. I've tried to talk her into going to Vegas and doing it in one of the drive-through chapels. Or we can go to Gatlinburg and rent a chapel. Or we can go to the Justice of the Peace right here in Atlanta and get married right now. I don't care where or how or who is there.

I just know I almost lost her and I can't stand it. Not that being married would've given us special powers, but there's something about knowing she's completely mine, with my name, for all eternity, that is comforting to me now. It's a totally foreign concept to me–I never thought I'd be this guy. The guy who's completely pus-, uh, whipped– and unable to live *without* the same woman for the rest of my life instead of being forced to live with *just one* woman.

I haven't convinced her to set a date yet. Like *tomorrow's* date. I know she loves me and this whole Rhoades fiasco isn't over yet. They haven't found them and she still feels that black cloud hanging over our head. I've tried to convince her that we're stronger together but she has dug her heels in and refuses to budge. She doesn't want our brand new life tainted by the old life. I can't say this to her, because she may hold me to it, but I will wait for her as long as she needs.

I move behind Andi and guide her to a seat with me in front of the fire. She leans back on my chest and I wrap my arms around her. Her hands are resting on my arms and she's drawing lazy circles with her finger. It's strangely arousing and I'm glad she's sitting in front of me, blocking the view from everyone else.

I note that Kelly is watching us with a mixture of curiosity and maybe a little longing. I thinks she's afraid she'll never have what we have—mutual love, trust, respect, and admiration. I think she's in the perfect family to convince her otherwise. I smile at her and I actually get a full-on smile back this time. She's coming around slowly.

Brandon bursts out of the house, yelling for us to hurry and get inside. Something is on the news that we have to see. Andi and I exchange looks and we immediately know it's about Rhoades. We simultaneously jump up and run into the kitchen and see the breaking news banner across the top of the screen and the rolling text at the bottom.

"*Again, the yacht owned by Speaker and Mrs. Rhoades was found capsized off the coast of Africa. Sources say the yacht was riddled with bullet holes. Speaker Rhoades' body was found still inside the living quarters of the ship. His genitals had been savagely removed and preliminary data indicates he was still alive at the time.*

"*The exact cause of death has not been determined as of yet nor have any suspects been questioned. Officials indicated that pirates are most likely responsible. Mrs. Rhoades has not been found as of yet and is presumed to have been taken. Pirates in the region where the yacht was found are well known for human trafficking.*

"You'll remember that Speaker and Mrs. Rhoades have been embroiled in allegations of years of child abuse and molestation. They both disappeared soon after the Department of Justice handed the case over to the FBI to investigate and possibly prosecute them both for their respective involvement."

My whole family stands silent and immobile, staring at the television long after the news ends and normal programming resumes. Kelly and Andi stay in place after everyone else leaves the kitchen, sensing their need to be alone to process this latest information. Kelly turns around to face Andi, with tears streaming down her face, she grabs Andi around the neck and sobs loudly.

I can't see Andi's face from where I'm standing but I can see the shaking of her shoulders. She's sobbing, too. *Are they crying because they're glad it's over? Are they sad for what could've been but wasn't? Are they happy that both the bastard and the bitch got what they deserved in the end?* I suspect it's a mixture of all three and neither could explain it if asked.

Wiping their eyes, I see Kelly's pretty smile light up her face and I know now that she will be just fine. She is becoming stronger every day. She is learning to trust, to love, and to live a normal life. She's actually learning what normal means–a normal family, a normal father, a normal mother. For some, normal is over-rated. For others, normal is the greatest unknown.

Kelly walks back outside to the fire pit and rejoins *our* family. Alicia sits next to her and wraps her arm around Kelly's shoulder. Kelly leans in to accept her comfort and it occurs to me that I have two little sisters now. It feels good.

Andi still hasn't moved from her original spot. Just as I'm about to call to her, she whirls around to face me. She's wiping her tears away and catching her breath to speak. She takes a deep, calming breath and wills the tears to stop. Her eyes meet mine and I'm searching her–searching her eyes, her face, and her body language. I'm trying to read her mind, prepare myself for what she's about to say, and just be here for her no matter what it is.

"Luke," she says in her watery, shaky voice.

"Yes, baby," I reply softly...tentatively...anxiously.

"Can we have a Christmas wedding?"

I fucking love her.

ANDI

The karaoke competition ends tonight and I've made it to the final round. It's down to two others and me tonight. To be honest, after everything that's happened, I don't really care if I win or not. I just find peace in sharing my thoughts and feelings through songs. The lyrics speak to me and I hope others can feel what I have a hard time putting in words.

The song I've chosen tonight is dedicated to my *family*. That is something I never really thought I'd have outside of Pop and Shane. So many people are part of my life now and there's nothing I wouldn't do for them and their happiness. In light of what all has happened over the course of my life, I think this song is rather fitting.

Travis Malone is here watching me tonight. Over the past couple of weeks, Travis and Luke have become good friends so Luke isn't quite as jealous over him now. I guess it's hard for Luke to not see Travis as a larger-than-life lead singer. But I know he's still dealing with the demons of past abuse, so he doesn't see himself like the rest of the world sees him.

I decided to not stay on with MaxMorgan Music. I want to devote all my time at the youth center–in both running it and working as a juvenile lawyer to help the kids who can't help themselves. Like all these young, courageous women who stuck their necks out on the line for me. Luke is still boxing but he's also waiting for his license reinstatement to arrive in the mail so he can help me at the center.

As we all knew, Shane's drug test came back negative for any type of illegal drug use, including performance-enhancing steroids. The boxing commission made a full, public apology for the "obvious mix-up" in specimens. I can't wait to see Shane's next fight–I know he'll be great.

So tonight, as I walk onstage for one last karaoke competition, my family is in the audience, cheering me on. Luke, Brandon, Alicia, Greg, Kelly, Maria–all my girls, actually–Shane and even Pop–they're all here for me, just like they have since the day I met them. Luke's parents, Sam and Linda, are also here and they've asked me to call them Mom and Dad. It feels strange but it feels really good, too.

If Today Was Your Last Day, by Nickelback, says it all for me. If I knew that today was my last day to live, what would I change? What would I give? Who would I love? Who would I forgive?

With that in mind, I've chosen to live like every day is my last day, because one day, it will be.

The End

ABOUT THE AUTHOR

A.D. Justice is happily married to her husband of 25 years. They have two sons together and enjoy a wide variety of outdoor activities. A.D. has a full-time job by day, with a BS degree in Organizational Management and an MBA in Health Care Administration. Writing gives her the outlet she needs to live in the fantasy world that is a constant in her mind.

Thank you for reading and supporting A.D.'s books! Please take a moment to leave a review of this work.

You can find her online at:
Facebook: *https://www.facebook.com/adjusticeauthor*
Twitter: *https://twitter.com/ADJustice1*
Web: *www.adjusticebooks.com*
Email: *adjustice@outlook.com*

Made in the USA
Charleston, SC
25 March 2015